DUPLICITY

DUPLICITY

THE DANGERS OF DREAMING: BOOK 1

CHLOË L BLYTH

For that little girl who dreamt of becoming an author…

It started with a dream

Does it count as a bad relationship history if all the men disappeared?

Don't worry, this isn't me confessing to murder, I mean they ran away. They blocked me, unfriended me, changed their numbers and fell off the face of the earth.

I tried to find one of them, Sam, to return a book he left behind in his haste, and it was like he had never been born. Nobody would tell me where he was, or even admit that he existed. It was bizarre. What could I have possibly done to warrant that kind of disappearance?

It's been happening for years now, and I still haven't figured out what I'm doing wrong. I'm a big fan of rom coms so I know I'm not making the obvious mistakes as exemplified in 'How To Lose A Guy In 10 Days' – I don't name their penises, I don't fill their bathroom cupboards with tampons and Vagisil, and I'm not clingy or whiney. I'm normal. I play it cool. I'm just the right amount of fun.

But for some reason, just when I think things are going well, that the relationship has potential and maybe he's 'the one', they skedaddle.

I'm starting to think maybe it's my vagina, or that I'm really bad at sex. I mean, if nobody ever told me, how would I know?

Sometimes they leave right after, like they got what they came for and now they're off. Other times they just get a bit weird with me, they give me funny looks and then one day they stop returning my messages and that's that. Game over. He disappears into a cloud of smoke.

And no, I don't date magicians.

I was getting to the point of giving up, accepting my future life as a crazy cat lady with no husband or kids, when everything changed.

Three months ago, I fell asleep on the sofa having polished off a bottle of wine, feeling sorry for myself after yet another vanishing act, and I had the best dream of my life. I starred in my very own rom com opposite a swoon-worthy man, and then the next night, it continued. And the next, and the next, and the next. I've been dreaming of him ever since.

But it's become more than just a dream now, it feels real. I know he's a figment of my imagination – no man could ever be that perfect – but I feel like I'm in an actual relationship with him, and it's one that has lasted a record three months so far.

We do all the usual relationship things, we go on dates to the cinema, bowling, ice skating, we go on holiday, we go out for meals, heck we even do our weekly shop together. It's that serious. And when we have sex, it's like, real sex. I mean, I wake up *glowing*. If it wasn't so completely ridiculous, I'd say I'm in love.

Oh, alright then, I'm in love with the man in my dreams.

If only he was real.

PART 1

ELLA

1.

I park in my usual space in the car park and turn off the engine. Okay, I can do this. It's just like any other 'end of month' meeting with the regional manager, Dull Henry, a grey-haired fifty-something year old whose only interests appear to be toads (catching and looking after them) and watching re-runs of 'Only Fools and Horses.' The only difference is, this time, the directors are sitting in, and the results are really bad. They usually get a copy of my presentation afterwards so the fact that they're coming today must mean that they know we've performed badly and – oh no. Did Daniel remember to get the coffee? I fish out my phone from my bag and dial the office number.

"Dan speaking, how can I help?"

I hold back the urge to remind him that is not how he's supposed to answer the phone. He's supposed to follow the lines we all do, introducing the company before himself.

"It's Ella, did you remember to pick up the special coffee?"

"Special coffee?"

"For the directors. They don't drink the crap we give customers, remember, they drink the fancy one. I told you last week. Did you get it?"

"That'd be a negative." I sigh.

"Okay, I'm going to the shop now. Be right back!"

"Can you get me some Doritos?"

I pretend not to hear as I cut off the phone and reverse back out of my space and into the school rush traffic towards the nearest shop.

Daniel is the latest addition to the office and also the reason I had meant to get to work early today. Sir Stinks-a-lot. Thinks he's God's gift to women, but apparently doesn't own a mirror or a functioning nose.

It's not what you think, it's not B.O. No, that'd be an easy fix. His scent is more of a rotting teeth situation. At least, that's what I think it is. His breath can clear a room in minutes, and his teeth are repulsive. We've tried having office mints. We've got plug in air fresheners pumping on the maximum setting from every available plug socket, but it's just not enough. And don't even get me started on his hair. It's greasy, but it's deliberate grease! He is the self-anointed King of the Wet Look. He applies serum every day like he's preparing his head to fry bacon. I bet come summer it will sizzle in that office without air con.

I finally manage to pull up outside the shop without knocking over any school kids, and rush inside.

Back outside, I cradle the coffee, milk, biscuits and a new reed diffuser, and make my way slowly back towards my car just as a kid on a bike speeds past, clipping my shoulder and causing me to collide with an old lady and drop the coffee.

"I'm so sorry!" I gasp, reaching out with one arm to check she's okay.

She tuts at me as if it was my fault and hobbles off as I look down at the coffee. Luckily, the glass jar hasn't smashed. I begin to awkwardly bend down, hindered by my pencil skirt and heels and trying not to drop anything else, as a hand appears, passing me the coffee. I look up.

"Thank you!"

It's a man wearing dark sunglasses, smiling at me. Thank you indeed. My arm hairs stand on end, and I feel a little flushed as I take in his lips and perfectly curated stubble.

I pull myself away and rush over to my car, dropping my purchases onto the passenger seat. Fortunately, I have a bag in my glovebox that I forgot to bring into the shop with me, so I won't have to balance it all again to carry it up the stairs to the office.

I look back over my shoulder for the man who helped me, but he's already gone. I drive away.

*

As I park back in my spot, I immediately notice the unfamiliar brand-new car parked in the disabled bay closest to the entrance. It just about screams 'director.' Through the glass doors to the showroom, I can see the pair of them with Dull Henry, schmoozing with some of the staff.

Kristina is going to kill me for not being here when they arrived. She hates taking the lead, but she's my number two; she's the only one I trust around here. She's also the only one who knows about my dream man, but that's not important right now. I need to stay focused, present, in control. I take a deep breath in and let it out slowly.

The female director, Claudia, has her long dark hair pulled back in a headache-inducingly tight French plait and is wearing a formal and very expensive-looking jumpsuit with sky high heels. The male director, Jeremy, has tussled

7

sun-bleached hair and is wearing an equally expensive-looking suit, with a blue shirt, no tie. I don't usually go for blondes, but I can't help self-consciously checking my ponytail and wishing I'd put a bit more effort in.

I plant a massive smile on my face and walk over confidently, carrying my shopping. I hope they don't mind my reusable bag; it has colourful cocktails with faces on it, hardly professional. I bet Claudia uses designer shopping bags. Ha, as if she carries shopping! She probably has a guy for that.

"Good morning! I'm Ella, pleased to meet you."

I hold out my right hand and proceed to shake theirs. We've met before, not long after I joined the company, but I don't expect them to remember. I certainly didn't remember how hot Jeremy was. And did he just hold my hand a little longer than necessary? I brush the thought aside. I'm pretty sure he's dating Claudia anyway; they look like a power couple.

Dull Henry gives me a curt nod as if disappointed by my tardiness, so I quickly prompt them for drink orders and hurry upstairs.

I rush around opening the windows, checking the plug-in air fresheners are all on, placing the new reed diffuser on the table, plugging the laptop into the big screen, and then I enter the kitchen.

I open the flap on the kettle. Crap. It's full of limescale. Beyond full. I wouldn't drink from it if you told me it was detoxifying and I'd never get a spot again. I would rather take my chances and risk acne for life.

I give it a good rinse and shake and try to get as many of the loose bits out as possible. Oh, it's gross. I hope none of it floats on top. The filter thingy seems to have gone from the top of the kettle too, so there's nothing to stop that from happening. I'll have to have words with Daniel about this, he should have said something; we could have bought descaling tablets. But it's too late now.

I prepare the drinks as best I can, relieved I got fresh milk as the one in the fridge has lumps in it, and lay out the biscuits on a plate. I can hear them starting to come upstairs now, so I quickly carry it all through, placing the drinks on company branded coasters – tap water for me.

It goes about as badly as anticipated. I speak too quickly as I nervously avoid eye contact with Jeremy, and I lose all ability to form complete sentences when Claudia asks me for my opinion on what has gone wrong around here. Bottom line, they've given us a new target for next month, and if we don't hit it, we'll probably be made redundant as they're considering closing this branch entirely.

Yep.

I might lose my job and I just bought some bloody expensive coffee and biscuits for the pleasure of being told that. Oh, and now I have to tell the others.

But what's more demotivating than hearing that you might lose the job that you hate?

Exactly. So, I'm not going to tell them that. I'm going to tell them that we need to improve our sales before the next meeting if we want to win a staff night out.

I know how to manage my people. I might only have the title of Team Leader, but I know what works around here. And, thanks to today's meeting, I also know what needs to improve. Now. Before a customer chokes on a flake of limescale.

"Daniel?" I stand up to get his attention. "Can I speak to you?" I hesitate, I don't want to shut him in an enclosed space with me, "outside?"

He follows my lead.

2.

He carries me easily from my sun lounger over to our private hot tub and swaps my empty cocktail glass for a flute of prosecco. In the warm bubbles, we watch the sun's slow decline as he massages my back, with more than just his hands.

As the sun starts to hide behind the only cloud in the sky, his hands venture to the front of my body. My erect nipples. My bikini bottoms gape from the pressure of the bubbles and allow his hand to slip in...

"Ella!"

A car's horn and Kristina's shout shake me from my daydream. The temporary three-way lights have finally gone green. I drive, putting my hand up and mouthing the word 'sorry' to the driver behind.

"You were day-dreaming about your dream man again, weren't you?" Asks Kristina from the passenger seat.

"Maybe." I can't help but blush. I'd been reminiscing about last night's dream.

10

"Ooh, was it a sexy dream?" She teases.

"It was romantic, yes." I try to keep a straight face and adjust the windscreen wiper speed.

"Oh come on, you need to give me more than that! You used to tell me everything before you decided to date a figment of your imagination, don't shut me out now. What were you doing?" She zips her phone away in her bag and turns in her seat to face me better.

"It was a holiday scenario. Sunset, prosecco, hot tub…"

"Hot tub sex?" She grins. "Oh man would I love some hot tub sex. The bubbles…"

"Yep, the bubbles," I agree, looking straight ahead and smiling.

"He's really ruining real men for you, you know that, right? In the real world, the guy would probably get water in his eye and lose a contact lens, but in your dreams, you get to have mind-blowing sex, and you don't even have to worry about the hygiene issue because it's a dream. Ugh. I am so jealous." She looks out the window.

"How did your date go last night?"

She gives me a look that means it was another complete disaster.

"So his profile said he plays football, but his photos were all kind of distant," she starts.

"Uh-huh," sketchy.

"But I asked him about it and he said it was only because he was worried about his ex-girlfriend finding him on there."

"More like his current girlfriend, or wife." I butt in.

"Anyway, we'd been messaging and getting on well, so I thought, well, all footballers are athletic, right? So how bad could it be? Worth taking a chance on a date, surely."

"If you say so…" I raise my eyebrows.

"Oi, just because you've given up, some of us are still trying!" She pokes me under my ribs, making me squirm and swerve the car.

"Okay, okay, carry on," I say, checking the rear-view mirror. She sits up taller, preparing to spill.

"So, we arranged to meet at this random pub in the countryside, and it turned out they had a tournament on. I didn't bother to read the sign because I wasn't there for that, but I couldn't see him anywhere and, due to the photo situation, I didn't really know who I was looking for.

"So, I sent him a message and sat down at the bar. There was a lot of cheering going on in a back room, but I just sat there, nursing my drink, thinking I'd been stood up. No such luck." She gives me a grin. Here comes the punch line.

"There was another big applause and then out came this little dude wearing a football kit. Everyone was high fiving him, I figured he must have won the tournament, whatever it was. And then he sat down next to me and introduced himself."

I say nothing.

"Now, you know I'm not against short people, but I think that's something he should have disclosed so that I would be prepared. As you know, I'm kind of a female giant. But his height wasn't the only thing he'd lied about. He isn't a footballer. He's a foosballer. Table Football. That's what he'd just won. And worst of all, he thought it was cool."

I laugh and pull up outside her building.

"So, when are you seeing him again?"

"Ha-ha," she mock-scowls at me and steps into the rain.

"Seriously though, thank you for once again proving that dream men are better than real men," I smile, biting my tongue. She leans her head back inside the car,

"Yeah well, you're never going to get married and have babies if you only date in your sleep, you know. Maybe you should at least try to pay attention to real men when you're awake – you never know, maybe your dream guy is real and you just haven't noticed him yet."

She slams the door and runs towards her building, dodging puddles as she goes. She always counts on me for a lift home when it rains.

Over the years, we've developed a good friendship. We only really see each other at work, but we're closer than other colleagues, and she gets me. She doesn't judge me for living in my head. Much.

The idea that my dream man could be real is one I've considered myself on multiple occasions. What if I saw him one day when I wasn't paying attention, but some part of my brain was, and that part put him into my dreams? He could be out there, waiting for me.

Fingers-crossed.

~

Romeo and Juliet
A Montague and a Capulet
So much simpler, just a name
Why can't my problem be the same?

We would not die, of course not, no
But what would happen, I do not know
I'm told it's wrong, I'm told it's bad
But I can't help it; without her, I'm sad

I long to speak to her, to reach out, touch her hair
To have her smile at me; fall under her stare
We could be so good. I know that, I do
But I always do as I'm supposed to

Therefore, I do nothing. I sit, and I wait
Maybe it will pass, or maybe it's fate.

3.

It's not like I need a man, but I would appreciate the company. I would like to have somebody to text when I'm in situations like this, wedged between people I don't know, eating a meal that isn't that great, whilst the people I'm sat next to angle themselves away from me. On my left the guy has even built a barrier between us by lining up the water jug and salt and pepper shakers.

It's my work's 10th Anniversary celebration, a big do with staff from all the branches.

I hate work dos. It's the way that, on one hand, drinking is encouraged, bosses go out of their way to ensure you always have a drink in your hand, and yet, the moment you drink too much, the moment, for example, you throw up all over the table, they never let you live it down. Every time a new event is planned, you're the 'remember that time' reference. Yes, unfortunately, I am speaking from experience.

But, lesson learnt, tonight I am not drinking. That's the plan anyway, although I suspect that having something other than orange juice and tap water to sip would probably make me care less about how much I've been ignored throughout this meal, so I might have to reconsider.

It's just plain rude, turning their backs to me like this. I know I'm not the most exciting person in the room, but honestly, would it be so hard to just include me? To let me nod along and pretend to be enjoying myself, rather than building pathetic jug boarders and rotating their seats as if my loneliness is contagious?

Eventually the dessert plates are taken away and the volume in the room suggests that the drinks are starting to make themselves known. A group from one of the northern branches moves to the dance floor. I am far too sober to dance.

I stand to go get a drink from the bar and nobody even glances in my direction. I feel like I could leave, but I know I shouldn't. Not after Monday's meeting.

Our team have done better this week, but we still need to keep up appearances by staying here until the end and being on our best behaviour. I wonder where Kristina and the rest of my office were seated; I haven't spotted any of them yet. This 'genius' idea to move the Team Leaders away from their teams did not get my vote.

As I make my way towards the bar, I decide I'll get a lemonade and then try to find them. I don't even care if that means talking to Daniel, anything to prove to myself that I am actually here and this isn't just some horrible nightmare.

It's ironic really, the last time I was in a venue like this was Year 13 prom, and I would have done anything back then to have people ignore my presence. I would have done anything to escape the whispering and accusatory stares. At least half of that room thought I'd done it on purpose; thought I was an attempted murderer, a psychopath. But I loved my sister. I still love my sister. It was a bloody accident. Stuff the lemonade, I need a proper drink.

*

As I stand in the queue for the bar, continually being shoved in the back and pushed aside as people force their way in front of me in the least British way possible, I allow my eyes to float over the room, searching for my team. I hear a laugh that sounds a lot like Kristina, but before I can locate the source, my eyes land on someone very familiar.

But it can't be him, can it?

Over by the fire exit, there's a man leaning against the wall looking drop dead gorgeous like he just walked off the cover of a magazine. He's wearing a half-unbuttoned shirt, slim fit to highlight his toned body, with extremely well-fitted jeans.

But it can't be him, he's not real. I made him up. He's a figment of my imagination. A product of my lonely and rom com obsessed mind. This must be a coincidence, a lookalike. It can't be him.

And yet, his brown hair looks right, his height looks right, his-

Oh shit, he's looking at me! I turn back around and focus on making my way to the front of the queue.

"Can I get you a drink?" A voice asks from behind. I can smell his aftershave before I turn around, I know exactly who it is. Blood rushes to my face and for once there's no wine to blame. I am completely tongue-tied.

"I, uh, um, yes, I um, I was about to get a glass of wine. White." I finally spit out.

Being tall, he gets served quickly and hands me my glass whilst holding his own in his other hand. He's drinking something strong, like whiskey.

"I'm Adam, and you are?"

"Ella."

Adam is his name, and he's real? But he didn't know my name, so this is all a coincidence, right? He just looks the same, it's not him. It can't be. Oh, this is so embarrassing. I wonder if he has that mole on his... too.

"Pleased to meet you. Work do, is it?"

I stare at him blankly, watching his face move, searching for similarities and differences from the face in my dreams. He frowns, waiting for me to reply. I snap back into motion and replay his words in my head.

"Yes, sorry, work do. Our 10th Anniversary! You?"

"Wedding, second cousin or something. I think I met her once before today?" He shrugs.

"Ah nice, I love weddings."

"Well, you're welcome to come have some cake if you want, there's loads." He indicates a door on the left-hand side; my work do is through the door opposite it, on the right.

"Erm, no, I think I'd better stay with my people. I'm desperately trying to keep my job to be honest, can't have them thinking I left early!" My wine-free arm swings at a 90-degree angle like I'm saying a catchphrase as I grin like a maniac.

What is wrong with me? Why can't I just behave like a normal human being? My face is probably still bright red too. I couldn't be more unattractive right now, and he's so *so* hot. Why couldn't he just stay in my dreams? I'm much cooler in my dreams.

His smile falters,

"Oh, okay. Well, maybe I'll see you at the bar again later, if you need a refill? Or, maybe we could go out some time?"

OH MY GOD HE IS ASKING ME OUT. The man from my dreams is asking me out. Breathe Ella, breathe! I take a large sip of wine and blink my eyes.

"Seriously?"

"Yeah, seriously. Why wouldn't I be serious? How about Sunday, late morning, we can go grab a coffee and a cake or something?"

"But why? You don't know me, we just met!"

"Isn't that what happens in the movies?"

"Well yeah, I guess so, but in real life people get raped or murdered for making stupid decisions like that."

"I promise I'm not going to murder you. Or rape you." He smiles. Ah, such a good smile. Nice teeth and everything.

"I suppose I should be safe in a café."

"Exactly. Meet me outside Marks and Spencer's in town at 11am on Sunday?"

"Okay."

"It's a date!" He winks and saunters off.

I turn to head back through the door to our do and collide with Kristina. Wine sloshes onto my hand.

"Who was that fine piece of meat you were talking to?" She asks, raising her carefully plucked and shaded eyebrows at me and twisting her hair around her fingers before turning back around to watch him walk away.

"Uh, my dream man?" I answer quietly, still in shock.

"What? That was him?" She grabs my shoulders. "Seriously?" She looks again towards the path he took. "You should go after him! Don't let him get away!"

"It's fine," I explain. "He asked me on a date."

"Oh my God, Ella! That's incredible. And he's HOT! I mean, I know you said he was perfect, but I thought you were exaggerating! That man is perfection, Ella. Do not let him go! Whatever happens, if it turns out that he farts in bed or picks his nose, I don't care, okay? That is the man of your dreams right there, and you are going to make adorable babies someday."

19

She leads me back towards the bar, nudging my wine glass closer to my mouth.

"Now tell me about this date. Where are you going? What are you going to wear? No pressure Ella, but your entire future relies on this date going well."

She uses her height to not only get another two glasses of wine, but also a bottle, which she hooks under her armpit as she leads us back towards a table in our designated room.

~

"The Devil made me do it"
A likely excuse
But near enough true
I had to.

4.

I arrived about ten minutes early and have been pacing past the storefront slowly and on lookout ever since. What if he doesn't turn up? What if it was a joke and I didn't realise? Maybe that's why he winked at me! He was mocking me for believing that somebody who looked like him, would go out with somebody who looks like me.

No, I'm being too hard on myself. I'm okay looking, nothing special but definitely not 'ugly' either. And I was dressed up that night, it's not like I was unwashed with bed hair and wearing wine-stained pyjamas how I am often found in the evenings. And weekends. Okay, any time I'm not at work. But no, I looked alright. He'll come.

Won't he?

It's five past; he's late. How long should I wait? Where's the cut off between patient and desperate? Ten minutes? I'll give him ten, then I'll go find myself something else to do.

Just as I'm about to give up at almost fifteen minutes past, I see him running around the corner towards me. He's quite out of breath and looks a lot less cool than on Friday night, or in my dreams. He reminds me more of a school kid running to catch the bus than my sexy dream man, and I wonder if it's really the same person. I wave anyway.

"I am so sorry!" He says, panting, hands on his thighs. "I had to wait for my mum's carer to arrive before I could leave, but she got stuck in traffic and then when she got there she just kept talking and talking… I couldn't get past her. I swear, I am normally on time!"

"That's okay, it's a lovely day, perfect for pacing outside M&S!" I joke and lower my voice, "if it'd been raining, I'd be long gone."

"I will make it up to you. I know I said coffee, but how do you feel about hot chocolate?"

"Love it, why?"

"The café I had in mind does the best hot chocolate. It's a family recipe. Do you know Cherry B's down the road behind the cathedral?" He straightens up, back to the height I remember. I feel petite by his side.

"Can't say I do, I don't really go out to cafés much, I tend to just make my drinks at home and save the money."

"Well then, allow me to treat you," he hooks my arm in his and begins leading the way. "Sorry, is it okay to link arms like this? I thought it'd be less awkward."

"Sure." I smile, but it is bloody awkward. We're walking like we're fourteen and he's the first boy I've ever loved but, in reality, he's a stranger. Sure, he looks exactly like the man I've been loving in my dreams for months now, but appearances aren't everything. He's still a stranger. This is our first date, not our one hundredth. I must remember that. I know nothing about the man I've linked arms with. Nothing real, anyway.

He seems very different to how I created him in my dream. It's like it's him, but it's not. He's less cool, but still kind of charming. Like Hugh Grant's character in 'Notting Hill.' I smile thinking about when he wears his prescription scuba goggles to the cinema because he can't find his glasses. That feels like exactly the kind of thing this guy would do.

The café is amazing. It has a very eclectic design but somehow it works. There are mis-matched chairs of different colours and styles, and tables of different heights, so you can just pick whatever feels right for you. It's quiet now but there are plenty of seats for the winter when everybody piles in from the wind and rain. The smell of chocolate and baked goods hits you the moment you open the door and a little bell rings. So far so good. I take a seat as he goes to get our drinks.

I know, I should be up there getting the drinks too, to make sure he isn't drugging me, but really? My dream man wouldn't do that! And it's daylight for crying out loud. What's he going to do, carry me out in front of everyone? Tell them I got drunk on hot chocolate? I don't think so!

Adam seems to know the barista taking his order. She's an older woman, maybe in her sixties, with grey hair tied up in a bun and she's chatting away animatedly and keeps smiling over towards me. I smile back, then look away.

"One salted caramel hot chocolate with cream and marshmallows and a slice of millionaire's shortbread for the lady," says Adam as he places the tray down on the table.

"Thank you. It smells so good in here; do you know the barista?" I ask.

"Oh, that's the owner, Miss Cherry B herself! I used to come in here a lot with my mum when I was younger, after a bad day at school. It was our little treat."

"Oh right, how is your mum? You said she has a carer."

24

"Yeah, not great. I do most of it myself, but we have a carer for when I need some time out. She's dying. Cancer. It's hard." He stirs his drink. "I'm sorry, what a conversation killer for a first date! Tell me about yourself Ella."

"Ooh, you remembered my name!" I joke, trying to lighten the mood. "Well, Adam, there's not much to say about me, I'm pretty boring. I don't do a lot. I work, I watch rom coms, I do a bit of yoga from YouTube when I fancy it, I drink quite a lot of wine, and I... watch more rom coms. My friend says I need to ease off the rom coms if I'm ever going to meet someone in real life. They're spoiling real men." A nervous laugh escapes. "What about you? What do you do apart from caring for your mum?"

"Watch rom coms." He laughs. I love his smile. "Honestly? I do watch rom coms with my mum, but other than that, my life revolves around her medications and treatments, sometimes I forget what life was like before her diagnosis. I do love a good burger though. We can do that for our next date if you want to see me again."

Unwilling to commit to that just yet, I continue to quiz him.

"Do you have any siblings?"

"Nope."

"Do you read?"

"I used to, and I try, but I find it hard to concentrate these days."

"Fair enough. Any pets?"

"Our cat got hit by a car a couple of weeks ago," he replies solemnly.

"That's awful! I would love to have a pet. I live in a flat though, and I'm at work all day, so it wouldn't be fair on them. But one day... I love cats and dogs, I'm not picky. I'd get a rescue though."

His eyes light up,

"I'd love to get a dog. When I was little, we rescued Bruno, a sandy coloured Labrador crossed with something, and he was my best friend at times. Like I mentioned, school wasn't great for me." He looks down and stares into his drink.

"Why not? Were you bullied?"

"Sort of, it's hard to explain. Something happened at this one sleepover and then after that everyone stopped talking to me. I didn't do anything bad, but it was as if they all unanimously decided that it was best not to be my friend anymore. I struggled to even find a partner in PE after that – it didn't matter that I wasn't fat or smelly, I was still the last to be picked." He sticks out his bottom lip.

"Aw, well, I bet you don't have any trouble getting picked nowadays," I flirt. I notice his neck turn pink.

"Thank you for saying that, but you'd be surprised."

I straighten up in my chair, I don't want to get too smitten before I've asked the important questions.

"So, how long have you been single?" I've already checked there's no wedding ring on his well-groomed hands, nor a tan line as if one has been removed. No sharp nails either. But it never hurts to ask.

"As long as I can remember! I've been on a few dates here and there, but nothing that's stuck long term. I guess I just hadn't met the right girl…"

He looks me in the eye with those same chocolatey brown eyes from my dreams. Those eyes I've looked into when I…, when he…, when we… argh, I think of ice to try to fight the blush as blood rushes to my cheeks.

"Let's not get too carried away, you've only just met me, you know nothing about me!" The words come out faster and louder than intended.

"Well, I wouldn't really say that…" he looks sheepish, "I've known of you for a while if I'm honest."

"What do you mean? Have we met before? Before Friday night?" My heart races thinking about our dream relationship. Maybe it was more than just dreams. Maybe this isn't a coincidence at all. Maybe he knows exactly what's making me blush.

"Not met, but seen, yes. I've seen you doing your weekly shop, I've seen you rushing around the small shop before work – actually, I passed you the coffee you dropped on Monday. I'm pretty sure I saw you in the library one time, and I never see anyone I know in there. I'm just not very good at introductions."

"Oh." I slump forward in my chair, my heart visibly sagging. I pick up a napkin and begin folding it in half again and again.

Maybe my subconscious really did just pick him out of my peripheral vision and insert him into my dreams. There's nothing romantic about a stalker. The obsessive creepiness completely overshadows anything slightly romantic about it. This is a big red flag. I should run.

"So, you've been watching me? Stalking me?"

"No! Well, not exactly. I'm not a creep, I was never going to do anything weird. I just liked observing you and I was too nervous to say 'hello'."

"Too nervous? Come on, look at yourself. Think how you were on Friday night! That guy was not Mr Nervous, that guy was Mr Smooth."

"That wasn't me... I'd, uh, been drinking."

"Well, you could've had some Dutch courage before then and introduced yourself, couldn't you? Oh my God, were you even a part of that wedding party or did you just follow me there?"

"Um..." He examines his empty mug.

"Wow."

I stand up abruptly, causing the chair to scrape noisily across the floor like nails down a chalkboard. People turn to look. I lean over the table and quietly explain.

"Look, I'm sorry. You're a really good-looking guy, but I don't date stalkers. Thanks for the hot chocolate, it was delicious. But please, just leave me alone." I walk out.

Half-way down the road he catches up with me and spins me around.

"Wait, Ella, I'm sorry. That came out all wrong. Yes, I am a bit weird, but I only have good intentions. I really want to get to know you, properly. Please give me another chance?"

"No Adam, I can't. Get out of my way, get out of my head, and leave me alone!"

I storm off in the direction of the car park. I can't believe I've been such a fool, dreaming about a stalker! What is wrong with me? Am I really that desperate and lonely that my imagination made up sex dreams about my stalker?

I press my key to unlock my car and then struggle with the door as I pull it too quickly and it won't open. I press the button and pull again and then drop my keys into a puddle before finally getting in and slamming the door a little too hard.

Urgh!

I thought I'd literally found the man of my dreams. Of course, it was too good to be true. When will I learn? Life isn't a bloody rom com!

I drive home via the local shop and pretend not to notice the man from number 5 hovering by the bin store as I rush inside clasping a bottle of wine, tub of ice cream, and 'share-size' bag of Maltesers. Now is not the time to be making small talk with my most undesirable neighbour, no matter what Mum said.

When she helped me move in, she saw him watching and suggested I go out with him. Like I needed her to set me up. Anyway, he has a premature bald patch, and he wears socks with sandals.

White socks.

I couldn't be less interested. Appearances aren't everything, but his is a very bad start.

~

The higher you climb, the further you fall
I was right up there, standing tall
I tripped, I rolled, I tumbled and crashed
Into her world, I gate-crashed.
Never the smooth one, never the hunk
But always the winner of 'Kerplunk!'
But who wants a steady hand?
Instead of footprints in the sand?
Romance always wins
I didn't make her head spin
I lost my chance
No slow dance
No kiss
Just a perfect miss
A splat, a blob, an inky smudge on her memory

It was worth it though, if she remembers me.

5.

The next morning, innocently sipping from a Starbucks cup, Kristina asks how my date went, loudly informing everyone in the room that he was, and I quote, 'well sexy.' Fortunately, she doesn't mention the fact I'd been dreaming about him for months beforehand, but regardless, they all turn to look at me. Even Daniel puts down his can of Coke and stops crunching his 9am Doritos.

I watch my inbox fill with emails, and sigh. I hate talking about this stuff, my own personal embarrassments, for other people's entertainment. But, what the heck, it's Monday morning and it's a story everyone can learn from. I stand up and smooth down my dress.

"Well, everyone, 'sexy' or not, he turned out to be a stalker. He had been watching me. Our meeting wasn't by chance at all, it followed months of him watching me do my shopping and go to the library and all sorts. He's a freak."

"Damn, but he was so hot!" Says Kristina. Hannah giggles, hiding her mouth behind her sleeve.

"No, he was not. That is what's wrong with the world. We judge people on looks and that is why people get killed and raped. You've all seen those documentaries about serial killers and paedophiles where people say 'oh but he/she always seemed so polite, so normal, we couldn't imagine blah blah blah' well we all need to wake up, don't we? Especially women."

The phones are ringing, and nobody is picking up; they're all watching me. I raise my voice.

"Ladies, next time a man asks you out, ask yourself this: do you know this person? Do you value your life? Sure, he looks 'hot,' but do you know if he's given you his real name? Do you know if he has a supply of Rohypnol back at home, or maybe even in his pocket right now? Do you trust him? Because you shouldn't. Not at face value anyway. If you just met that guy, chances are he's a liar. All men lie. They can't help it. Sometimes they're little lies which maybe you like, they tell you that you look good without makeup, that your bum doesn't look big, but sometimes they're big lies. Like when they 'forget' to mention their wife and kid, or that they've been stalking you for months, or that they've got five women buried in their allotment."

Someone clears their throat and I look towards the door and find director Jeremy standing there. His hair still looks sun-kissed and tussled like a surfer's and his blue eyes bore into me as I notice the smirk on his face. I sit down and shrink back in my chair to hide behind the partition. Everyone else rushes to answer as many phonelines as possible.

"Ella, can I have a word?" He asks, peering over and indicating the conference room. Kristina looks over the partition between us, eyes wide.

I nod to Jeremy and bite my lip. Should I write my resignation now, or after? I don't want to keep him waiting, but I pull up a blank Word document and write the shortest resignation I will ever write, just in case. I quickly press print and scribble my signature on it on my way over to the conference room, folding it in half.

He's sat down, attempting to hide a smile behind his hands as I enter. He brushes his hands down his thighs and tries to look serious.

"Ella, your behaviour in there just now was unacceptable. You were distracting the entire office. I am going to have to give you a file note."

I am far too fired up to accept this, my knees bobbing with nervous energy. I move my weight from one leg to the other to try to control them. Somehow standing still is now impossible.

"A file note? Don't do me any favours. I've printed my resignation; it's fine. I was ready for a change anyway, and hey, it's one less person for you to make redundant next month."

"Seriously, Ella, take a seat, let's talk about this. You don't have to leave. We all get carried away sometimes, I'm sure this was just a one off. Please, sit down. I'm sure you'll feel differently once you've calmed down."

"Don't patronise me! Here it is. I'm off."

I hand him the piece of paper and leave him stunned as I grab my bag from under my desk and walk straight out the front door imagining I'm Renée Zellweger as Bridget Jones and playing Aretha Franklin's 'Respect' in my head.

6.

Of course, all freedom comes with a price. In this case, HR called me and begged me to work until the end of the week to give them time to find a temp to replace me. The exhilaration from my dramatic walk out had faded by then and I begrudgingly agreed, mostly so I could say some proper goodbyes but also to secure a reference for my past seven years' work, and, honestly, to rescue the chocolates I'd left behind in my drawer. They were Lindt Lindor and I'd been savouring them; I couldn't leave them to go to waste, or worse, be eaten by my replacement!

I returned after lunch and distracted the team for the rest of the week, during which we discussed my plans for the future (none) and their plans for my leaving do (plenty). I had to scale down their plans as it was starting to sound like a hen do.

Eventually we all agreed on the local pub followed by the nearest club, and I'm about to go in now. I haven't been clubbing since my few remaining school friends went off to university and I moved away and started that job, so this should be an interesting night.

I push open the door of the pub and immediately spot Kristina being served at the bar. I rush over so I can hopefully order next but, as I get closer, I am horrified to see her being handed a tray of shots.

"Ella! Welcome, welcome! Grab yourself a drink and then come meet us in the booth over there, I've got the shots for now and then we'll have some Jägerbombs later before we head to the club."

I look at the group in the booth; this is when the age difference shows. There are only a few years between me and the others, but it's enough. The excitement of clubbing has long passed me by; the memory of puking my guts up and swearing off Vodka every Sunday is too deeply ingrained. But, I am here to celebrate, I suppose. I get a large white wine and head over, pausing to take a big gulp.

"So, now that you're over the 'Dream Man Who Wasn't', what do you think of that director guy... Jeremy, isn't it?" Asks Kristina, sipping her drink. I throw my head back and close my eyes before looking back at her and answering.

"I don't know what you mean."

"Well, he was clearly into you before you walked out, he was practically begging you to stay. We all heard it." A couple of the others nod.

"That's a bit of an overstatement. He was just trying to be reasonable."

Kristina raises her eyebrows and Hannah chips in,

"I heard he's single." Hannah's one of those quiet girls who doesn't say much but always seems to know everything that's going on.

"Sure, and probably with a new woman every night." I reply, rolling my eyes.

"Well, what's to say that can't be you one night? I'm sure he's very good," Kristina teases. I sip my drink. We are not talking about my sex life tonight.

Fortunately, the subject is soon dropped as Kristina's friend Amy decides to join us. Amy is beautiful with silky long blonde hair and is wearing a bodycon dress, fully highlighting her assets.

We decide to play some drinking games and at first I'm relieved when we play 'Never Have I Ever' because I haven't done a lot, so I can stay relatively sober. Then we turn to 'Ring of Fire', and it all goes terribly wrong. My world starts spinning, a lot.

We stumble to the bus stop, and I feel like I'm eighteen again. We laugh until I puke on my shoes and Kristina offers to lend me some of hers because she lives the nearest. We hurry there and swap them over. They don't fit, they're too big, but the straps help them stay on and they aren't covered in vomit, so we rush back to the bus stop and make it just in time.

The others decide to hold onto my purse as I can't walk in a straight line and am liable to throw up on it – what a mess! But heck, I'm having fun; I can't even remember why I'm here!

Shivering shoulder to shoulder in the queue, we wait to get in. 'One in, one out' is a phrase I haven't missed. Amy nudges me and points out a girl ahead of us, squatting behind her friend to take a wee. The bouncer turns a blind eye and still lets her in when it's her turn. We have to step over her puddle on our way inside. I am also bursting, but like hell was I going to risk weeing on Kristina's shoes!

I rush straight to the toilets as soon as we get inside and have to do the old 'one hand on the door, one hand for everything else' manoeuvre I remember well. Why do the locks always break on club toilet doors? Or rather, why are we always so desperate to wee that we can't wait for the one cubicle that has a functioning lock? There's no loo roll either, unsurprisingly.

On the dance floor, the music is louder than I remember but it only takes a shot of Tequila Rose lovingly presented to me by Kristina, to get me feeling drunk again. I sway and shimmy to the music, swinging my hips and singing along.

I'm left to dance on my own at times as my now ex-colleagues appear and disappear for drinks and toilet breaks, but I don't mind, I'm having fun.

As I'm dancing, one guy keeps trying to catch my eye and move closer to me. I look away and try to edge to another space. He appears again. I spot Daniel and try to dance over to him, but he is oblivious and walks away to the bar. I try to ignore the guy, but he starts dancing even closer, sort of grinding up my bum. I try to push him away with my bum, but that seems to egg him on even more.

He grabs my waist and spins me around. He starts trying to shove his tongue down my throat. I try to push him away with all my strength, but he's not budging. He shouts something in my ear about air and pulls me towards a side door.

Please be the smoking area, please be the smoking area.

I look around frantically for one of the others to see where I'm going, but I can't see anyone I recognise. I bump into people as he pulls me and all they do is scowl. He pushes the door open and yanks me outside.

Under the glow of the streetlamp, I notice the skin on my arm has gone pink from his effort. It's cold out here and I'm shivering as my ears ring from the loud music. There's nobody around; this isn't the smoking area like I'd hoped.

"Finally, we're alone," he says, pushing me against the brick wall and planting his face on mine. I try to struggle but it's fruitless; I only hurt myself, scraping the back of my hand on the brickwork.

He starts groping my boobs, feeling his way down my body and then reaching up under my dress. I kick my legs, but he just pushes his body in-between.

"Don't act like you don't want this, I know you do. I saw you dancing. You want this." He tells me. I try to scream but the sound is lost in his mouth as he tongues me again. He rips my tights and tries to pull them and my knickers down, touching me with his cold fingers. He undoes his jeans and I see his erect penis.

I brace and close my eyes.

7.

There's a clang and then he releases me. I open my eyes and find him lying on the floor; it seems somebody hit him around the head with a frying pan. I readjust my clothes and look around.

"Hello?"

Standing back in the shadows is a man wearing trackies and a vest top. He steps forward briefly to retrieve the frying pan. He looks a lot like... well, I hate to say it again, but he looks a lot like my dream man.

"Adam? Is that you?"

The man puts a hand up and says, "be right back," before entering the back gate of a property.

Huh. That was weird.

I start to walk towards where he had been standing, wincing with every step. It feels like the balls of my feet are just one big blister on each foot, with extra blisters on the sides of the toes. And I am so, so, cold.

I should tell somebody where I am, but the others took my purse and the fire exit closed behind us, so I won't be able to get back in without ID! How am I going to get home now? I don't even have my keys! I'll have to try Kristina's I guess, wait for her to get back... Oh but that's going to be a very long walk without money for a taxi. I sigh and start to hobble towards the end of the road to get my bearings.

The back gate re-opens and Adam re-appears in the same clothes but looking slightly fresher.

"Hey, Ella! Wait!" He shouts. I stop. I hadn't got far. "Do you want to come inside for a glass of water or something? I'd love to apologise for the other day."

I look at him and consider. He seems genuine, not like a creepy stalker at all. My feet hurt, and he did save me from being raped...

"Okay, I could use a rest. My feet are killing me."

"Say no more!"

He scoops me up in his arms and carries me through the gate, through a utility room and into a lounge where he carefully lowers me onto a sofa. Hallelujah! Dream man is back! That's more like it! (And I know I'm being a stupid vulnerable girl again, entering a known stalker's house, but do you know what? I am a girl, and I can't help it. Stupid stereotypes).

"Do you think he'll be okay?" I ask, thinking again of my almost-rape.

"Yeah, he'll wander off soon with a bit of a sore head. I didn't hit him that hard, just hard enough. Maybe next time he'll learn to take 'no' for an answer, eh?" His eyes twinkle.

"Thank you. How did you know I was out there? Were you stalking me again?"

"No, I promise. I live here, I just happened to see you out of the upstairs window – I didn't know it was you, I just had to put a stop to it. I hate guys like that."

"Don't we all!" I joke.

"Sorry, I promised you water, did you still want a glass?" He seems so concerned for my wellbeing.

"Yes please."

When he returns, he sits next to me on the sofa. He smells great, which is strange considering his gym attire. I'm sure he looked sweaty when I saw him that first time. Although, it was dark.

He encourages me to take my shoes off and really rest my feet, offering me flip flops to wear home if necessary. He doesn't need to tell me twice! I carefully undo the straps and slowly place my feet on the carpet one at a time. They stay in their moulded heel shape for a while as I try to regain movement in them. It's quiet in the house and I turn to face him.

"Can I have a hug?"

He agrees and gives me a good squeeze. I breathe in his scent.

Is this my dream man?

He feels like I thought he would. It's nice to be held again, for real, after all this time dreaming. I feel a bit emotional, my eyes well up and I have to sniff to hold back the snot.

He pulls back, his face creased with concern like it's his fault.

"Sorry, I didn't mean to get emotional. It's just, nobody's been this kind to me in a long time. Thank you."

"Aw, well, if you keep me around, I'll always be kind. I'm just that kind of guy!" He's so endearing, I can't help but smile.

"Thank you." I sip the water. He's even put ice in it, just how I like it.

"I'm sorry about the other day, I think I owe you an explanation." He faces me but scoots back on the sofa, placing his right foot on his left knee.

"Well, I'm not going to argue with that."

"It's just, my life's a bit complicated. There are things you don't know, that I'm not allowed to tell you, and that's why I didn't introduce myself sooner. Because if I let you into my life, I could put yours in danger."

"Okay…" I wait for him to explain further.

"I really can't say much more. Just that, I couldn't help myself, I had to know you. But I am going to do my utmost to keep you safe. You're a great girl, Ella, and I want to get to know you. But being with me puts you in danger so if you don't want to see me, I'll understand."

"Um, okay. What kind of danger?"

"I really can't say." He dips his head apologetically.

"And you're not crazy? Or winding me up? I know I've had more than a few drinks tonight, but this sounds crazy, even now."

"Honestly, I'm just trying to be straight with you. I'm trying to make you understand that I'm not a psycho stalker, I'm just a guy sitting next to a girl, asking her to trust him. Even though it's wrong. Even though it's dangerous. I'm Romeo, longing for Juliet." He reaches out and takes my hand.

"Wow. One minute I was getting 'Notting Hill' vibes and the next you're referencing Shakespeare. You are intriguing." I bite my lip.

"Ah yes, I confess," he raises his hands then places one on his heart, "I am a Shakespeare nerd." I laugh. "But seriously, what's 'Notting Hill'? Besides an area of London?"

"I thought you said you watch rom coms! It's a classic Hugh Grant movie. You should give it a watch."

"Hmm, maybe we could watch it together sometime." He looks deep into my eyes, and I feel my insides melt as I remember what that look would lead to in my dreams.

"Maybe." I concur.

A bell rings upstairs, breaking the moment. He jumps up.

"Sorry, that's my mum, I'll be right back, don't go anywhere!"

He rushes towards the stairs, knocking over a plant on the sideboard, standing it back up and apologising to it before taking the stairs two at a time.

I take this opportunity to look around the room. It seems pretty ordinary, although there are no photos on display like there normally are in a family home. You can tell his mum lives here by the choice of cushions and general furniture style, it's very 'mature feminine.' It's a far cry from the bachelor pads I have often found myself in, where you're more likely to find crusty noodles on a cushion than embroidery.

In the corner there is a box overflowing with what Adam must call 'flip flops' but I would call 'spa slippers.' The soft white kind that never fit properly. It's weird. When he said I could borrow flip flops, I didn't expect them to have such a vast collection. I wonder if they got them as a job lot or if his mum collected them over the years, always keeping the complimentary slippers provided on a spa day. Maybe he stole them off a van for her. I don't really know him, after all.

He's been up there a while. Maybe I should leave.

But he seemed nicer tonight, I felt that familiar tug towards my dream man. I need to give him another chance. Plus, part of me is intrigued about the danger. And Shakespeare? Who would have thought he'd be into Shakespeare? There's still so much I have yet to learn about him.

Maybe he's a more sensitive but wise version of my dream man, with a mysterious secret... Whatever the case, he deserves a second chance.

I find a little notepad next to a wired phone (as per the olden days) and write my name and number. I look at the spa slippers. No. I can't do it. I'll just have to ruin my feet instead.

I leave via the front door. Now to work out the way to Kristina's!

~

Always him, never me
But maybe this time, it will be
A lucky chance, another go
I will not ruin this one so
Rom-com hero, here I am
Take me, love me, I'm your man
But, where did you go?

8.

I didn't think that the whole way through, did I?

When I finally get to Kristina's, my feet are black and sore, some of the blisters have popped, and my tights are shredded. I have somehow managed to wipe mascara down my nose – was I crying? I can't remember – and I feel like a hungover tramp. I'm about ready to climb into Kristina's recycling bin for warmth when the front door of the building springs open, and she shouts,

"There you are!"

Her eyes scan my appearance.

"Are you okay? What happened?"

Daniel appears behind her in the doorway, tucking his shirt into his jeans.

"I'm fine," I reply, convincing no one.

"Come inside and warm up," says Daniel, approaching me with his arms open to guide me indoors. I can't help but heave and back away.

"No, I'm fine, really. I just need my phone and bag and a taxi home."

"But what happened to you? Where did you go?" Kristina asks.

I don't want to tell them. I don't want to admit I was nearly raped, and I was wrong about Adam. She's going to be ecstatic that I was wrong about Adam. She'll be checking my menstrual cycle and telling me dates to 'do it' to make those adorable future babies she's certain we'll have. Is it so hard to believe that at twenty-five I'd be satisfied with a boyfriend who sticks around? I don't want to have babies; not yet anyway. I sit down on the front steps and feel the cold bite my bum.

"Look, some guy took me outside and tried to rape me, but then Adam – yes, Adam," I eye Kristina, "saved me and I went back to his." Kristina opens her mouth to speak but I don't let her. "Yeah, yeah, I know. Even after what I said. But then I kind of ran away from there too whilst he was upstairs looking after his mum because there were all these spa slippers..." I look at them to gage their reactions.

"Okay. So... was there something scary about these spa slippers?" Asks Kristina, trying to make light of the situation.

"Just the fact there were so many. It was weird. Oh yeah, here are your shoes." I hand over her heels that I've been holding by the ankle straps since I left Adam's. They've indented my fingers.

"Are you sure you're okay, Ella? We can call the police, report the attempted rape?" Asks Daniel, kindly.

"I'm fine, plus, I don't want to get Adam into trouble. He hit the guy over the head with a frying pan."

"Naturally," states Kristina before bursting into laughter. Daniel joins in and before I know it, we're all laughing hysterically and clutching our bellies, unable to stop. A frying pan! First, I meet the man of my dreams, literally, then, I find out he wields a frying pan as a weapon... I am awake, aren't I?

When I can finally breathe again, I thank them both for being excellent colleagues and wish them all the best for the future. We promise to stay in touch, even though we know we won't, and just as I'm about to get into the taxi, Kristina shouts across the road,

"I still don't understand why you didn't shag him though! He saved you, what's a few spa slippers? He's hot!" I laugh and get in, avoiding the eyes of the driver.

It's only a short ride; soon I'm home and soaking in a hot bubble bath.

I'll miss them. It will be strange not working with Kristina anymore. I might even miss Daniel, a little bit. Not his smell, but his heart is in the right place.

A disturbing thought crosses my mind – did they hook up tonight? The others were gone, it was just them... I didn't pay much attention to their appearances, but I suppose they were a bit dishevelled. Did he have his arm around her when they waved me off? I can't recall, but they were standing close. Would Kristina really do that? With him? I swallow the vomit which fills my mouth as I consider the taste of the cause of that smell.

I wonder if Adam will call. I don't know if I've done the right thing by leaving him my number, after all, I did suspect him of being a stalker. And he basically admitted it. But he seemed better tonight, that bit closer to my dream man. When he carried me inside, I got that same feeling as when he appeared in that very first dream, like he had just saved my life.

When you get a feeling like that, you can't just let it go, push it away and forget about it. It means something. Doesn't it?

He didn't move in today; it was fate that brought us together again and allowed him to save me. I need to give him another chance.

In the meantime, I should probably get applying to some jobs otherwise paying my rent is going to get very interesting very quickly. It's a good job I'm bathing by candlelight – saving electricity!

9.

A week later, my phone rings and it's an unknown number. I would normally let it go to voicemail, but my heart leaps at the possibility that it could be Adam. I haven't had a single dream since I met him in person, and I miss him. I answer.

"Hello?"

"Ella?" It's a voice I don't recognise.

"Yes, speaking."

"It's Jeremy, from work. Or rather, your previous place of work."

"Oh right, erm, did you need me to sign something?" Why is the director calling me?

"No, actually, this is a personal call." My stomach flips; was Kristina right?

"Okay, what can I help you with?" Rom com recommendation? The cheapest and tastiest wine available at the local shop? I consider my specialist topics.

"I'm outside. I wondered if you'd like to go on a date with me?"

I rush to the window and peer outside. Sure enough, hovering on the other side of the electric gate is the director with the sun-kissed hair, sat in a shiny grey sportscar, top down. He looks up at me and waves.

"Oh wow, erm…" I look at myself in the mirror.

I've already changed into my pyjamas, my hair looks acceptable, but my eye make-up has been wiped off almost entirely and, of course, I've already had a glass of wine. What? It was a long day! Temp work is hard, they give you all the shit that the regular employees don't want because you're being paid that little bit more per hour, and they've got nothing to lose. Who cares if they stress you out? You're only temporary. Those regular employees bloody loved handing me all their paperwork to file today, I'm sure one of them smiled when she saw me sucking one of the many papercuts I suffered, but she looked away when I caught her watching.

I mull over the offer. He is rather good looking, and he has come all this way. Plus, Adam still hasn't called me and, it's been a week. It's not like we're an official couple or anything. Most of our relationship has occurred in my head. And this kind of thing never happens to me. Another hot man asking me out? I'd be a fool to say no. He might be the one!

"Can you wait ten minutes?" I ask.

"Of course," he says and ends the call.

Wow. I can't believe it. I have to tell Kristina. We don't normally text, but I need to share this with her.

Guess who just asked me out?

I rush to my wardrobe to work out what to wear as my phone pings.

Who?

I smile.

ONLY DIRECTOR JEREMY! You were right! He just turned up at my flat! WTF?

I quickly change into a flattering midi dress and cardigan and then I wipe off what's left of my eye makeup and start to reapply.

Whoa, you go girl! Haha, have fun! Maybe this one won't put you off with spa slippers! XD

I give myself a little spritz of perfume. Okay Ella, this is unexpected but let's just go and see what happens, I tell myself as I head out the door.

Walking down the stairs, the nerves hit me. Am I really doing this? This isn't some guy I know from my dreams this time; this is an eligible bachelor that ex-colleagues swoon over. He's wealthy and experienced. I have no idea what he sees in me. There's no way we would have matched on any credible dating site.

"Hi," I say awkwardly as I reach his car. He jumps out to open the passenger side door for me.

Settling back in on his side, he suggests,

"I thought we could go for dinner and drinks? My cousin owns this great Italian restaurant down on the waterfront."

"Sounds good."

He drives and I twiddle my thumbs nervously as I look out the window. What am I doing? This is crazy! I don't know this man any more than I know Adam, possibly even less since I thought I knew Adam from my dreams. This is dangerous. Nobody knows where I am. He could be a serial killer. One of those bold and confident smarmy types who lure women back to their place and then dispose of their bodies somewhere really clever, so they never get caught (or at least not until they've killed twenty women and have made the kind of impact that requires a TV drama/documentary).

Who would suspect him, the well-paid director? He's too responsible, probably even donates to charity every month rather than just when somebody he knows is running a marathon. I really hope I'm not going to die because I took this chance. Bloody Kristina, encouraging me to pay attention to men in the real world. You can't die in your dreams Kristina!

"I have to say, I'm glad you quit your job," says Jeremy, turning to look at me as we wait at a red light.

"Why? Was I that rubbish?"

"No, because I couldn't have asked you out if you had stayed."

"Oh." We drive on.

"It's deemed 'inappropriate' apparently." He does the quotation marks with his fingers. I don't know what to say so I keep quiet. He continues. "What you did took guts. I find that very attractive in a woman."

I pull a face.

"What I did was stupid, leaving a perfectly decent job without another one lined up."

"Perhaps. But I bet you've found another one already, haven't you?" He's right, but it's only temp work, it's hardly an amazing job. He takes my silence as a yes. "I knew you would. You're the kind of person people want to have around them; I know I do."

Oh God. I cringe internally, this was a bad idea. I can't deal with all this smooth flirting.

"Actually, I-"

"We're here." He interrupts my excuse. Well, that's that then, the date is officially starting.

We walk inside and a waiter immediately acknowledges Jeremy and shows us to a table in a quiet corner. Of course. It's probably his regular table, where he takes all the ladies. He peruses the wine menu like a connoisseur rather than picking the cheapest white or rosé like I normally do.

"White okay?" He asks, before ordering something which definitely isn't House Chardonnay. I silently pray that it's not South African extra dry Sauvignon Blanc. I can't stand it when it's too dry.

The waiter returns much quicker than I'm used to and proceeds to pour me a large glass, and Jeremy a small one, before placing the bottle into a wine cooler.

"Thank you," I say, sipping nervously.

"Have you decided what you'd like to eat?" Asks Jeremy as the waiter hovers beside us.

"I'm not sure, perhaps garlic bread and, um, spaghetti carbonara?"

"Oh no, you can't have that here. Let me pick for you, I promise you won't be disappointed. Is there anything you don't like? Fish? Mushrooms?"

"No fish or mushrooms."

He laughs.

"Okay, how about cheese?"

"Cheese is good."

"Okay, you will love this," he says confidently, pointing to some items on the menu for the waiter. So, I guess he's one of those 'I know best' men; I try not to roll my eyes.

Annoyingly, he's right. The food is delicious, and the wine perfectly matched. Although I doubt anything is bad in this place.

We finish the meal with Italian coffee, which is desperately needed on account of my starting one glass of wine ahead when we got here, and Jeremy only having one small glass from this entire bottle. I'm glad he's being sensible, being the driver, but I do wish I had a little more restraint and had managed not to polish off the rest of the bottle by myself.

Luckily, I'm not one of those crazy drunks, I hide it well.

Until I don't.

But that's my lot for tonight, so there shouldn't be any sudden vomit explosions like the one he may or may not have heard about. Fortunately, that work do was regional only, and the directors didn't attend. I daresay I wouldn't be sat here right now if he had witnessed me in that state. It wasn't my best look.

He suggests we take a walk along the waterfront next, so I excuse myself to the ladies whilst he pays the bill.

Looking in the mirror, I find my face is, as usual, flushed from the wine. But, other than that, I look okay. I hold my wrists under the cold tap in an attempt to cool myself down, but I needn't have bothered. When we step outside, the cool April night air reminds me that it's not summer yet. I regret not wearing something warmer.

The sun is just setting, and Jeremy smoothly slips his arm around me 'to keep me warm.' I would ordinarily bat it away, but I'm cold, so I let him.

We walk along, joined like a couple, and I try not to think about Adam. I wish I was here with him. This feels like one of my dreams again, the only problem being, I'm with the wrong man. I know Jeremy is a very attractive and eligible bachelor, but he just doesn't excite me the same way. In fact, whilst I initially didn't like the 'unsmooth' real world version of Adam, I dislike this 'too smooth' behaviour from Jeremy even more.

It is a very romantic date though, and the wine is still flowing through my veins as I lean into Jeremy's warm body as we walk along. I'm probably giving off the wrong signals.

"I was sorry to hear about your sister," says Jeremy, catching me off guard.

"Oh, I didn't realise you knew about that." I didn't think anybody around here knew about that. It's kind of the whole reason I moved.

He stops and holds my hands.

"If you ever want to talk to anyone about it, I'm here. I think you're a very strong woman, but it's okay to be vulnerable sometimes." He lifts my hand to his face and kisses it. "Your speech the other day was so angry. I want you to know, there are good guys out there too." He looks into my eyes and my heart skips a beat.

He lets go of one hand and tucks some hair behind my ear, gently turning my chin towards him. My heart races.

"I would never hurt you, Ella. You don't know how special you are," he leans towards me and pauses, as if following Will Smith's instructions from 'Hitch', he's waiting for me to close the gap and kiss him. I lean in and close my eyes and just as our lips are about to meet, I see *Him*, in my mind. Adam. I jolt back like somebody just tickled my sides.

"Are you okay?"

"Yes, sorry, I, er, I'm sorry, I don't know what happened there." I say, my face bright red.

The moment is lost, so we walk on a bit further.

"I don't want to come on too strong but, you're shivering so, would you like to come back to my place? I have an apartment just up there, with views over the water." Of course you do.

"Umm…"

"It's okay, I can take you home, maybe this was a bad idea. I thought you were into me too."

"No, no, it's not that, it's just..." I can't finish the sentence.

"I'll take you home."

"No, I'll come inside. We've walked all this way; I might as well see it and warm up before you drive me back." I say, finally making my mind up and trying to shake off the ridiculous notion that Adam is somehow inside my head.

Jeremy seems pleased and happily leads me to his apartment.

It's stylish, more like a hotel than a personal residence. It's been carefully designed and tastefully furnished. There are floor to ceiling windows overlooking the water, and a balcony, for the warmer weather.

"Here," he passes me a thick blanket to put over myself. It's a bit much for April, but I appreciate the gesture. He sits beside me, our legs touching on the small two-seater. I think it's what people call a 'cuddle chair', it's more 1.5 seater than two, and the closeness is quite intimidating.

I sense that he wants to continue from where we got to before I freaked out, and I can't decide if I want him to or not.

He distracts and relaxes me with tales from his childhood. It sounds charmed, as expected. He had a boarding school education and spent holidays skiing in the Alps and sunbathing in the Caribbean. It couldn't have been further from my own experiences: the local comprehensive, camping in Dorset and every weekend spent watching Viva, the miracle child, compete in dance and gymnastics competitions.

Whilst he was sipping fruit juice by an infinity pool, under the shade of a palm tree, I was trying to get my adoptive mum's attention as she clung to the hope that her miracle child was going to be the next big thing. My life was fine until she came along, then I lost my shine – they got what they'd always wanted, and it wasn't me. Is it any surprise I turned out bitter?

And it's no wonder people blame me for what happened; my motives appear transparent, the jealous rage of an underappreciated older sister. But it was an accident. I swear.

Jeremy's hand moves under the blanket, bringing me back to the present moment. He starts to gently caress my leg, through my dress, making my insides squirm. Excitement or nerves I'm not quite sure, but the temperature in the room just quadrupled.

"Ella, you know I could have any woman I want, don't you?"

"So I hear," I reply. Was that supposed to make me feel special?

His fingers trace higher up my thigh, making my nerve endings tingle. He traces even further, leaning his face in towards me once more.

"I want you," he whispers into my ear, before kissing my cheek. Then he hovers, mere centimetres from my lips and I look into his blue eyes.

Oh, what the heck!

I kiss him and his hands begin to roam more freely, more confidently over my body. He positions me so that I'm straddling him as he reaches around and unclips my bra. Our kiss intensifies. I can't help myself. It's been so long since I've felt a man's touch, for real. I've imagined it so many times, but now it's happening. He might not be my dream man, but he is a man, not somebody I made up or exaggerated in my dreams, and not a rapist, but a truly exquisite specimen of a man.

He's a great kisser, and he knows what he's doing. Oh, how he knows what he's doing!

He stands up and carries me to the bedroom, my legs wrapped around him. He lowers me onto the bed and pulls his shirt off in one smooth action. He unbuttons his jeans and then crawls over me in just his boxers. His blonde hair hangs forward over his eyes. He has a great body, sun-kissed to match his hair.

The problem is, he's not Adam. It hits me again.

I can't do this.

I want Adam. I want my dream man. Doing this is going to send me on a path further away from him, it might make irreparable damage to the possibility of getting to know him. I can't do this. I can't.

What if he calls me tomorrow, asking me out?

But then, what if he doesn't call? What if he never calls?

Jeremy kisses my neck and I let out an involuntary moan.

If I do this, I might lose the chance of being with my dream man. On the other hand, he might have already decided it's 'too dangerous' to be with me, and I might never hear from him again. He might disappear like all the others.

But what if he does want to be with me? I can't ruin it by doing this. This is stupid, irresponsible. It won't mean anything to Jeremy tomorrow. He's probably only doing this because he can. Because I looked desperate. Everybody knows I'm single. He probably just had a gap in his diary and thought 'why not?' Maybe he thought I'd make a good challenge after hearing my speech the other day.

No. No. I need to stop. I push my dress back down and push Jeremy away.

"I'm sorry, I can't do this."

"I thought you wanted to?" He says, crawling backwards.

"No, I can't. There's someone else."

"Oh?"

"It's new. I don't know if it's going to go anywhere, but I don't want to ruin it, just in case."

He gets off the bed and begins to pull his clothes back on.

"Well you could have said that earlier, rather than leading me on."

"I didn't mean to, I didn't know how I felt until now," I try to explain.

"Yeah. Right. You can show yourself out." He leaves the room.

I suppose I should have expected that.

10.

I can't get an Uber or a regular taxi for an hour, so I do what I vowed I would never do and haven't done for seven years. I call my mum.

"Mum?" I hear rustling on the line. "Can you hear me? I messed up. I need help."

"Ella?" It's not Mum. It's Viva.

"Oh hey Viva, it's me. Is Mum around?"

"She's busy."

"Oh. Never mind then. I'll sort something out. I always do." My fingers prepare to end the call.

"Wait!" She says, "I've been meaning to call you. I'm sorry. For everything. I'm sorry for what I put you through, I know it wasn't your fault and I'm sorry everyone said it was. I'm sorry I didn't speak up. I'm sorry. I'm sorry I was ever born," her voice chokes and I imagine her tears. "I love you Ella, I'm sorry I ruined your life."

I feel myself start to shake and my face gets warm and then tears begin streaming as I sit down on a bench overlooking the estuary.

"Don't apologise for being born, V."

"But I am sorry, I'm sorry I stole all the attention. I loved it. I should have seen what it was doing to you. If I could do it again, I'd tell Mum that I don't want to do gym and dance, I'd pick one, and then you could do something too. You could follow your passion too."

"I didn't have a passion," I say, wiping my nose.

"Only because you didn't get to try," she sobs into the phone.

"I don't blame you. You have nothing to apologise for. Mum does. We are both suffering because of Mum's mistakes. What happened was an accident and neither one of us are to blame. But our childhood? That was all Mum. You can call me, you know, if you ever need to talk."

The line goes quiet. I never meant to cut Viva out of my life, it was just easier that way. Mum and Dad blamed me for ruining their miracle child's future.

When they adopted me, they didn't think they could have a child naturally, so I was the prize. Then a miracle happened and four years later, Violet "Viva" Louise Thompson was born, and she was destined to be a superstar.

Mum threw her into dance and gymnastics classes as soon as she could walk, paid for extra private classes and entered her into every competition on the South Coast. When I was seventeen and had just passed my driving test, I took my thirteen-year-old sister out on a drive. It was only a short journey to the nearest drive thru for a milkshake. On the way back, a truck swerved into us, causing us to crash into a tree and permanently disable my sister. Her legs were crushed. The dance competitions were over. Dreams shattered in a flash.

Some people said it was my fault, that I should have been paying attention, should have seen it coming. But nobody saw it coming, it was an accident, it wasn't anything to do with me being an inexperienced driver – the truck driver was at fault. The courts decided that.

But to Mum, it was me. The jealous sister, vindictively trying to steal back the limelight.

I moved away as soon as I could, got a job in the next city over and never looked back. Four years later, I started driving again.

"What were you calling for, anyway?" Asks Viva.

"Oh, I need a lift. I had a bit of a bad date…" I answer, glad for the lighter subject.

"Ah, well, that I can help you with!" She sounds pleased.

"Did you learn to drive?" I know they have specially modified cars these days, but I never thought she'd want to.

"Hell no, but I do have a driver. I'll send him, where are you?"

I give her the details and we end the call.

I suppose it just goes to show that sometimes, all you really need to do is clear the air. She doesn't blame me, she blames herself. Perhaps Mum and I will never be on good terms, but Viva and I can be. I won't wait so long next time.

~

Life
And death
The tightrope between
Come on, don't let go
There are doctors to be seen
I know
I know it hurts; I know it's hard
But I'm not ready, okay?
Please
Hold on for me

ADAM

11.

When Mum and I finally get home from the hospital, it's 7pm but it feels much later. I'm exhausted and I have no idea how Mum even has her eyes open. I've lost count of how much coffee I've drunk, my hands are jittery, and we've both got bags that would give Count Dracula a run for his money.

She's had every test imaginable, and a blood transfusion, and I've got a paper bag full of new medication to start giving her at four-hour intervals twenty-four hours a day. It just keeps getting harder.

She looks a bit brighter now though, I guess it's the fresh blood. Ha, another vampire connection. I suppose she is a bit like the 'living dead' these days. Like a vampire, not a zombie. A self-hating vampire who makes herself weak and thirsty because she doesn't want to drink human blood, not the kind who goes around ravaging whole towns and leaving a trail of blood-drained bodies behind her.

"Can we watch a film now?" She asks, sounding more like a five-year-old than a fifty-two-year-old.

"Of course we can, let's just get you comfortable first, in case you fall asleep."

I help her to the armchair, with a cushion behind her back and a footstall in front. Then I carefully lay a blanket over her to keep her warm. It isn't cold, but she always feels cold these days.

I wonder, would vampires have cool skin? I guess so, they're dead after all. So, when they drink blood, it must feel warm, like vampire tea. Hmm, blood tea. Probably better than that herbal crap Mum insists is good for me. It's like drinking a plant. I'm trying to grow muscles, not petals.

Maybe I could write a story called 'My Mum, The Vampire.' It's been a while since I've had the urge to write something substantial, it would be nice to write something other than mopey poetry about Ella; especially now we've met so we can start making proper memories and I can stop moaning like a twelve-year-old girl. Provided she wants to see me again. Maybe I'll dig out a notebook and make some notes later.

"What do you want to watch this time?" I ask. Most of the time she picks films she's seen before, and then it's my job to track them down on a streaming service.

Recently there have been a lot of romantic comedies. I suspect that's because she knows I've been thinking about Ella. I tell her everything, I always have. She knows I like Ella, but she also knows that I won't do anything stupid because I don't want to hurt her. Mum raised me to do the right thing. She wasn't impressed when I introduced myself, but she's come to terms with it. She trusts me.

"'Notting Hill' please."

My eyebrows raise and I turn to look at her curiously. That's what Ella said I should watch. I did hint that we could watch it together, but I can always watch it again. I'd bet she's seen it more than once.

Luckily, it's easy to find, along with 'Four Weddings and a Funeral', '2 Weeks' Notice' and 'Nine Months,' to name but a few. There are a lot of Hugh Grant movies out there for us to work our way through if Mum has her way. I swallow a lump in my throat as I consider that maybe there are too many Hugh Grant movies to get through; we need more time. It isn't fair.

If she was a vampire, she'd have all of eternity to watch rom coms, but I suppose she wouldn't want to then. For now, they offer her comfort and warmth that she can't get from a blanket or throw. They offer her happily ever afters, when she knows she's running out of time and there's nothing 'happy' about that. She'll never see me married; never meet her grandchildren.

I press play and settle down on the sofa with a sandwich as I've barely eaten in days. Mum happily chuckles away occasionally until about forty minutes in when she falls asleep. I decide to leave her there until the film is over as I know she likes to think she saw it all, and maybe her eyes will flutter open at times and she'll see bits of it.

I stand and my back clicks like an old man's as I walk over to the notepad by the phone to make some notes about my vampire story. I can't be bothered to try to find one of my proper writing pads.

On the first page I'm surprised to see a phone number, with the name 'Ella' written underneath. So, she didn't just run off, she left her number! Phew! I was worried I was going to have to accidentally on purpose bump into her and hope it didn't come off creepy. Again.

Why did I have to admit I'd been watching her?

It was such a stupid move. In the moment, I thought she'd find it endearing that I'd been loving her from afar. Thank God she almost got raped behind my house. I know that sounds horrible, but I needed a second chance, and that prick gave me one. Thank you, arsehole! I quickly enter her number into my phone. I suppose I should wait until tomorrow to contact her.

I flip the page over and try to get back into my writing zone. 'My Mum, The Vampire,' I write at the top. It kind of sounds like a kid's book. Do I want to write a kid's book? I could. Maybe that could turn out to be my specialty; I've not had any luck selling my full-length horror novels so far, so maybe that's where I've been going wrong. I don't know. But this feels good. I want to write again, properly.

When all of this is over, I want to be a writer. I've always wanted to be a writer, but I wasn't sure I could be. Not with what I am, or who I am, and who my father is. I'm not exactly destined to have a normal life. But seeing how Mum's life has been cut short, I'm determined to make the most of my own. I will chase my dreams once the dust has settled. Dust. Probably not the best choice of words.

I completed my degree in English Literature at a university only 20 miles away, and then I got a graduate job in Finance. Finance, seriously! I took it because it was the sensible thing to do, I needed an income, and it was the only job I could find that wasn't miles and miles away or paid an absolute pittance. Bizarrely it didn't even require a degree in Mathematics or Economics or anything specific, just any 'good' degree and good A-Levels.

The bank was really understanding about it when I said I needed time off to care for Mum. Initially I was allowed time out to take her to the appointments and chemotherapy without even making the time up, but eventually their patience wore thin. They couldn't afford to keep me on if I was having that much time off, it wasn't worth it for them.

Plus, even when I was there, I was distracted; I started making stupid mistakes and forgetting to do things; I kept disappearing outside to call Mum and check she was okay. So, they gave me a warning, I could either come back to work full time and be dedicated, or I was out.

I didn't want Mum to be at home alone all day, so I quit. I wanted to be with her. She wanted to get a carer so I could keep working, but I wouldn't let her. It would've been a waste of what little money she had left. I could do it. We could live cheaply until she got better.

But of course, she didn't get better. She's not going to.

So now I need a plan, for after. A novel that's really going to sell this time. But I'll start with a short story, just to get the juices flowing.

The words start pouring out on to the page, relieved I've finally taken the lid off that bottle and am setting them free.

12.

I'm preparing to go meet Ella when the doorbell rings. I slowly open and peer round the door; we don't get many unexpected visitors here.

"Is he here?"

I don't respond.

"I said, is he here?" A ginger-haired woman screeches in my face.

"Sorry, is who here?"

"Don't give me that crap! Kyle! Is he here?"

Ah. It clicks. I know who this woman is. I haven't seen her since high school, but it's her. Francesca. Frankie-Lou. Kyle's girlfriend whom he dumped right before prom. She used to be pretty, but this wound-up and unhinged look is certainly not her best.

"No, he doesn't live here anymore." I answer her calmly.

"BULLSHIT! I saw him here just a few weeks ago! Don't you DARE call me crazy! Where is he? Is he hiding?

I need to speak to him, it's important!" Wow, this girl is mad. Like, off her meds mad. Her eyes have a crazy glint to them, and she is literally vibrating. She can't keep still. She's jumping from one foot to the other, looking over my shoulder and then squinting upwards trying to see in the upstairs windows, moving her head faster than a cat watching a laser pointer.

"Well he's not here now."

She huffs at me.

"Well, Adam, will you call me when you see him? Take my number. It's important. I need to speak with him. Okay?" She holds out her phone, displaying her number and waits for me to get my own phone out and copy it. "Now call me, so I have your number too."

"Err..." I'm not sure I particularly want Francesca to have my number.

"DO IT!"

"Okay, okay, I'm doing it." I need to get rid of her so I can go meet Ella. I can't be late again.

Satisfied, she finally takes a step back.

"You will call me, right? The moment you see him, you will let me know? It's important."

"Sure, I'll call you."

"Thanks." She smiles, but it comes off crazy rather than sweet. I watch her take a final look in each window, and behind the shrubs and recycling bin, before she closes our front gate behind her.

I close the door.

I should really be leaving now, but I need to check something, to make sure.

I take the stairs two at a time, briefly pop my head into Mum's room to check she's okay and the carer isn't concerned after that drama, and head to his room. It's usually locked because we don't have any reason to go in there, Mum and I, but I try the handle anyway. It opens.

73

Kyle is sat on his bed. He looks up from his phone, looking sheepish.

"Sorry bro," he smirks, "I seem to have picked up a psycho stalker on my way here."

"What are you doing here Kyle? You said you weren't going to be back for months."

"Nothing. It doesn't matter. I'm just lying low for a few days." I scowl at him. It's alright for some, eh, swanning in and out as he feels like it. I have to stay here and look after Mum.

"What's upset Frankie-Lou then? Why does she 'need' to talk to you? Why are you even still in touch with her?"

"Oh God knows, I can't get rid of her. She always pops up and tries to start things again and then I drive her mad and she leaves me alone for a bit before popping back up again." He lies back on the bed, arms folded behind his head.

"So, you sleep with her, kick her to the kerb, and then hit repeat?"

He wrinkles his nose.

"Well, only when I have to. She's useful. But she's not my preferred sleeping partner. You know that." I know very well what sent Kyle rebounding off towards promiscuity and we don't have time to talk about it now.

"God you're disgusting. Look, whatever you're up to, whatever she's trying to talk to you about, keep us out of it, okay? Mum isn't well and I don't want your drama. We lead a nice quiet life now, and we don't want you destroying it for us."

"Fine."

I close his bedroom door.

This is all I need, my bloody brother turning up to ruin my life.

13.

As I'd originally planned to arrive early, I still manage to get there just in time to beat Ella to our agreed meeting point. I lean against the fence. I hope I don't look like I'm posing, I'm just hoping to come across as relaxed and normal and the complete opposite of a stalker. I deliberately don't watch her park and I feign surprise as she approaches. She looks adorable wearing dark pink walking boots, skinny jeans and a jumper.

"Hi!"

"How are you?"

We speak at the same time and then both laugh nervously.

"I wasn't sure if I was going to hear from you. I'm sorry for disappearing on you that night, I just thought it best I get out of your way so you could help your mum," she explains.

"Oh don't worry about it, I completely understand. I would have called sooner had I seen your note, or had I not had to rush Mum to hospital. It's been quite a week."

I try to play it down. I know it's not 'cool' to be a carer, the nice guy never gets the girl. I need to channel my brother's attitude. He always gets the girl. Francesca is an excellent case in point – he has trampled her heart repeatedly and yet there she was, on our doorstep, looking for him again.

I lead the way down one of the paths I know, and we begin to relax. It's definitely not 'cool', but we end up discussing rom coms and it seems to be working for her. Ella is beaming as I tease her and disagree with her thoughts from 'The Kissing Booth 3' (she is team Marco, I am team Noah) to 'The Notebook' (she feels bad for James Marsden's character) but when we get to 'Sweet Home Alabama' we reach an agreement – Mel should never have left her dog behind when she left her hometown.

"So, if we get a dog and then break up, do you think you're taking him or her with you?" Asks Ella. I shrug,

"I'd settle for joint custody."

As I help her over a stile and into a field with cows in, she gets a crazy look on her face. She looks at me, wind blowing her hair across her face, and shouts,

"Race you to the other side!"

She starts to run and I hesitate to follow, eyeing the overly interested cows. She's sliding in the mud and cow pats with every stride and I attempt to follow with caution. Then, before I can reach her, as if in slow motion, she turns to see where I am and loses her balance. Her hands and knees plunge into the mushy brown substance that coats the ground. I dread to think if it's mud or cow pat.

Before I even know what I'm doing, I lift her up and carry her over the stile on the other side. We made it. And, I saved her. She looks at me like I'm her hero.

"Thank you."

She looks down at her hands and knees and begins to shake. I think she's about to cry when she suddenly bursts into laughter, happy tears running down her face as she attempts to brush her hands together and brown slop splats to the ground and nearby bushes.

Her laugh is contagious, I join in and then I stop and hold her arms still. I lean in, cup her face, gently peel off the hairs stuck to her lip gloss, and kiss her softly on the lips.

"I really like you, Ella."

"I really like you too." She smiles at me.

"We should probably get you home, so you can change. I'll walk you to your car."

"You know, if this was a rom com, you'd probably help me out of my clothes and share a shower with me..." She eyes me suggestively.

I would love to do that, but it's not the plan. It's far too soon to be taking chances like that. If I was to lose control and get carried away, I could terrify her. This has to stay strictly PG-13. For now, anyway.

"Yeah but imagine that stench when you get under the hot water!" I joke.

We walk back towards the car park and agree that we will see each other again, when Mum's carer can be there, or on an evening when the next-door neighbour is happy to sit in. I help her wash her hands with the bottle of water I always keep in the car, and then she hesitates as if waiting for a kiss goodbye.

I go for a loose hug, so as not to transfer any of her mud to me, and leave it at that. I don't want her to expect too much too soon. We need to move slowly. I need to be sure before I take it any further than a kiss. I don't want to scare her.

14.

Dating Ella is the best thing that has ever happened to me. Even earlier, when she made me turn around and go back to her flat so she could get her used 3D glasses instead of letting me buy her a new pair, I couldn't stop smiling. I've never been happier. Every moment with her is a breath of fresh air. She lifts me up from the monotony of being with Mum. I didn't realise how low that had made me feel, being under the shadow of death 24/7.

Taking these breaks with Ella reminds me that I have a future to build, in the light. And hopefully, she will come with me, when the time comes.

We're sat in my favourite burger restaurant now, and Ella is nodding approvingly as her chosen cheese and bacon burger arrives. I've chosen an absolute masterpiece of a burger, I'm starving, and it has everything.

"Looks like you know your burgers," she comments, licking her lips. "Is this a knife and fork kind of place, or can I just dig in?"

"It's an anything goes kind of place," I answer, loving that she's planning to eat with her hands, and wondering if I'll repulse her if I shove this massive burger in my mouth. She goes for it, holding her burger (which is much smaller than mine, but still big for her) in two hands and biting. She pulls back and gracefully attempts to reel in the hanging onion and bacon.

"What?" She doesn't realise she's got something on her chin. "Aren't you going to start?"

"It's just," I lean forward, picking up a napkin. "May I?"

I gently dab her chin, suddenly aware of how intimate this move is. She looks at me, and I think she wants to kiss me. I lean back. Not now.

"Sorry," I mumble.

"No, I'm sorry, for letting the team down," she says, "thank you for not letting me sit here with whatever that was on my face." She grins and picks up her knife and fork. "I think I'll use cutlery for the rest."

I've probably upset her. Was that too much? Wiping her chin like a baby's isn't the most romantic thing I could have done.

We eat the rest of the food relatively quickly with a brief discussion about her new job and some woman called Carol who won't stop talking about her new boyfriend. He has a yacht, don't you know?

I like listening to Ella's little rants, she's so funny. She doesn't realise how much of a good storyteller she is; she'd probably make a good writer. I wonder if she's ever considered it.

We're watching a new 3D action film tonight, Ella surprised me with the idea. I didn't think she'd want to see anything that didn't centre on romance and/or topless men, but she assured me that even action films have topless men, and she wanted to choose something I'd enjoy too. She feels bad about all the rom coms I have to endure now, not only with Mum but with her too. She's thoughtful like that.

She's so much better than I ever realised back when I was watching her. Knowing the person, understanding her and what she's been through, she's beautiful inside and out.

We go to the kiosk to pick up our tickets and buy some 3D glasses for me, and she winds her hands around my arm.

"Shall we get a slushy to share?"

Her eyes do that thing dogs do when they beg for food. I look at the cool icy drinks in their containers. They do look tempting. I smile at her.

"So you didn't want me to waste money on 3D glasses, but you do want me to waste money on a drink which costs about ten times what it's worth? Am I getting that right?" I pull a silly face at her and pull her into me with my arm.

"Yes, that's about right," she smiles cheekily, looking up at me. I buy the drink.

We walk hand in hand into the cinema, and I place the drink in the holder between our seats so we can both reach it. We put our phones on silent and then just as the lights dim further, signalling the start of the proper trailers rather than the rolling adverts for cars and internet providers, I put my arm around her. She snuggles into me. This is nice.

She sips the drink and points the straw towards my mouth to offer it to me. I can feel her eyes on me as I take a sip and then place it back in the holder. She wants to kiss me. I know she wants to kiss me. I want to kiss her too. But kissing leads to other things, other things we cannot do. I have to be careful. I don't want to lead her on too quickly. I'll tell her once I know that she loves me, that she won't run away. Then maybe, we'll find a way. Until then, it's not worth the danger.

I turn my head and whisper softly into her ear,

"I really like you."

It's become our little thing now. We say it because it's too soon to say 'love.' I see her teeth glisten as she turns to whisper back to me,

"I really like you too."

We sit there in that, rather uncomfortable, position for the entire two-and-a-half-hour film. My arm/back/shoulder are all stiff, but it was worth it. To sit so closely in the dark, with our eyes open: no risks.

We will not be having couple's massages any time soon, that's for sure. I can't allow myself to relax that much. It's not worth the risk.

I drop her off at the gate to her building and allow us one brief kiss before she gets out the car. Baby steps, Adam, baby steps.

ELLA

15.

"So, what did you want to be when you were younger?" Asks Adam, holding my hand as we circle one of the more childish exhibitions in the museum.

"A singer."

"Oh, really? I don't think I've ever heard you sing."

"That's because I can't. Not well, anyway. If I belt out a tune, about thirty neighbourhood cats turn up outside my flat." I joke, although it's almost true. Perhaps I would have had singing lessons if Viva had never been born. Instead, Mum used to tell me to stop wailing and get my shoes on – there was always somewhere to take Viva to or pick up from, she never sat still. "What about you?"

"I've always wanted to be a writer, an author actually, like Stephen King. I used to write horror novels, before..." His voice trails away. I know what he means.

"I'd love to read some of your work sometime," I tell him honestly.

"I've never even told anyone that before." He says quietly, frowning.

"Well I bet you're really good. You studied English Lit, didn't you?"

"Yeah, so I'm really good at studying books. It doesn't mean I'm any good at writing them."

"Well, if you ever want me to take a look, just let me know."

I won't push him. I understand him not wanting to show people his work, being scared to let people in and find out if they think he's any good. I once wore a jumper that I knitted myself to work and the moment everyone realised I could knit, it became 'a thing.' Ella, can you knit me a scarf? Can you knit me a jumper like that but with a wider neck? Can you knit me a snood?

I only knitted it to keep myself busy when I was home alone in the evenings. It wasn't some big passion. I wasn't taking orders. I wasn't setting up an Etsy shop. I haven't knitted anything since.

Adam's probably worried that if he tells people he writes then they will pressure him to get published and expect him to be the next Stephen King. Nobody needs that kind of pressure.

We move onto the next exhibit. I'm tired and bored. We've done all the bits I was interested in and it feels like we are now just walking through each room of display cabinets simply because we have to. I am delighted when I see the sign for the café. I know Adam loves cafés. It's not Cherry B's but surely this will do.

"Shall we?" I point to the sign.

"You know it'll be packed." He tilts his head at me.

"That's true. Shall we go somewhere else then?"

He laughs.

"You could have just said if you've had enough. I didn't want to drag you around bored all day."

84

"I'm not bored! I'm just tired and hungry. I enjoyed the first bits, but you know, it's a bit samey after a while; lots of things behind glass with small placards."

"That's generally what museums are like." He replies sarcastically.

"I'm sorry, we can keep looking. What's next?" I walk over to the map on the wall.

"I just want to see the Shakespeare exhibit and then we can go, okay?"

"Deal."

*

As we head down the steps outside the museum, the heavens open and we don't have umbrellas or coats on us.

"What shall we do? Shelter or make a run for it?" He asks me. I look around and spot a kiosk at the bottom of the steps that might sell something useful, although it looks as though it predominantly sells newspapers and soft drinks. But it's worth a try. I'm hungry, I don't want to wait for it to stop raining. I point at it and suggest we try there.

We run down the steps and then stand awkwardly close to the counter in order to shelter under the tiny roof – it's clearly not designed to keep anything other than the shopkeeper and his newspapers dry.

"Do you sell umbrellas?" Adam asks the heavily bearded man behind the till. He's bent down, fiddling with a cardboard box. He lifts a finger up as if to say, 'one minute.' I stick my tongue out at Adam.

The man tears some tape off the box and then lifts it onto the counter. It's a box of compact umbrellas. He smiles proudly.

"How much?" Asks Adam.

The man's smile broadens.

"Twenty pounds."

"You're having a laugh mate, twenty quid for that? It's not even worth a fiver."

The man shrugs.

"You want it, it's twenty pounds. You don't, go get wet. It makes no difference to me."

I study the newspapers on display as Adam hesitates. I don't want to pressure him into buying the umbrella, but I do want him to get it. I would have said get one each if they weren't such a rip off.

Adam sighs.

"Alright, one umbrella please." He fishes out a twenty-pound note from his wallet.

As Adam steps back from the counter and struggles to remove the tag and put the umbrella up, I read the final headline on one of the trashier newspapers. *'RAPED IN MY DREAMS – TRUE STORY.'*

There's a picture of a woman hiding her face and the first lines of the story explain how she claims it's true but has no physical evidence. It sounds more like a nightmare than a dream to me, but who am I to judge? I could have sold my own story if I'd believed my dreams were anything more than a coincidence. My headline could have been, *'I MET THE MAN OF MY DREAMS. LITERALLY.'*

I wonder how much she's been paid for that, maybe I should keep that idea in mind if I ever find myself unemployed again.

Before I can reach forward and turn to page 6 to read the full story, Adam finally gets the umbrella up and we make our way towards the food places on the main high street. I have to do little jumps to keep up as Adam holds the umbrella and I try to stay underneath it. He's walking fast and occasionally I miss-step and the water runs off the umbrella onto me. It's not a fool-proof plan and being such drastically different heights isn't helpful. I'm getting side-spray too. In fact, I'm not sure I'm benefiting from this umbrella much at all. I kind of wish we hadn't bothered, especially when it knocks me on the head as I jump to keep up again.

"Will this do?" Adam stops suddenly and I look up from the puddles to see a place displaying filled baguettes in the window.

"Perfect."

He struggles to put the umbrella down and it goes inside out.

"Stupid thing!"

"Here, give it to me," I offer.

"No, it's a piece of shit." He dumps it in the bin, and we head inside.

He seems to calm down as we sit in the warmth and dry off. We both have soup and a panini, and I feel my mood lift as my hunger is satisfied. The only problem is, it's still raining, and now we don't have an umbrella. It's clear what we have to do.

"Adam," I start.

"What?" He eyes me curiously.

"You know how much you love 'The Notebook'?"

"Yes," he frowns at me. That was an exaggeration, he doesn't love it at all. He thinks the film is too long and they should have cut all the 'present' old couple bits.

"I was thinking, maybe we should kiss in the rain." I grin at him, and he flashes a cheeky smile back. His bad mood from earlier has definitely gone.

"You are impossible!" He stands up and leads me to the door. "Do you want to do it right here, or somewhere more private? Shall I strip a layer off, so I get fully soaked through?"

"It's supposed to be spontaneous!" I giggle.

"Well, okay then," he grins, a mischievous glint in his eye. "Catch me if you can!" He runs down the high street.

I chase after him, carefully, watching my step on the slippery cobblestone. He runs in haphazard lines, weaving in-between shoppers until I run around a bench and surprise him.

"Got you!" I say, laughing.

I place my hands around his wet neck and tiptoe up to kiss him. He puts his arms around me and pulls me in close. The rain runs down my face, forcing me to close my eyes as I lose myself in the moment.

"I really like you," he says.

"I really like you too," I reply.

My hair is stuck to my face, and I dread to think what the mascara situation is looking like, but I'm grinning from ear to ear, and he is too. I kiss him again.

I think I'm falling for him. Really falling for him. The man from my dreams is bloody amazing, and I want him, completely. Everything is easy with Adam. It's not the rom com romance I had in my dreams, but we get on perfectly – it's like we can read each other's minds sometimes – and when we kiss, damn…

I just wish he'd tell me about this this so-called danger and give me that final part of him which I know he's holding back for a reason. Once all his cards are on the table, we can be together, physically. I am dying to be with him like that, and I'm not even worried that he'll do a disappearing act like the others. Because Adam isn't like the others. I know he isn't. He really likes me. He'd never hurt me; he'd never leave me.

But apparently, today's still not the day. He drops me off at home as usual, and I head in alone.

~

I wish we could do it
I want to, too
Don't think that I don't
I love you

It just isn't safe
Or right
I don't want to hurt you
Just hold you tight

Maybe, one day, we'll find a way
But I can't chance it, 'til that day

I hope it's enough
My affection, my care
I hope you will always
Want to be there

16.

We're having a romantic Halloween as we weren't together on Valentine's Day. Adam is going to cook for me at my flat and then after dinner we're going to snuggle up and watch whatever horror/paranormal movie on Netflix takes our fancy. I would have narrowed down the choices already, but I've been a bit preoccupied with cleaning the flat, changing my duvet cover and generally preparing myself.

When I finally collapse onto the sofa for a rest, I get a text from Adam saying that he's just at the shop and he'll be here soon, so I immediately jump back up and check myself in the mirror again.

I'm feeling nervous tonight because I've decided that tonight is the night. I'm going to seduce him and/or convince him to tell me his big secret, in order to finally consummate our relationship. I can't take it anymore. I know it's a risk, both because of his secret as well as my own personal history of what happens after I have sex with someone, but I think we've reached that stage. It's a line that we need to cross.

The doorbell makes me jump and I rush to let him in. He's carrying two full to bursting carrier bags and has a bouquet of flowers squeezed under his armpit. I step aside and let him carry the bags through to the kitchen area. Placing them down, he holds the flowers out to me.

"Happy Halloween my gorgeous! I got orange ones because they're like Halloween pumpkins, but also because I know you like orange."

"Aw, thank you, they're perfect!" I say giving them a sniff. The only problem is I'm not used to being given flowers, and I don't own a vase. "I'll just find something to put them in…"

I look in my cupboard for the biggest/heaviest glass I can find and eventually settle on a pint glass, whilst Adam unpacks his shopping onto the worktop. I chop the ends of the stalks off as per the instructions and pour the plant food into the glass of water before carefully adding the flowers to the glass and balancing it precariously at the back of the worktop furthest away from the oven.

"I think I may have got a bit carried away," says Adam, surveying his purchases. He's not kidding.

I can see he's planning to cook steak with chips and veg, there's a cheesecake for dessert, wine, and then there's the rest: salted popcorn, toffee popcorn, sweets, crisps of multiple varieties, cheese twists, breadsticks, onion and garlic dip, salsa, cucumber, carrot batons, and some special Halloween themed chocolates with mysterious centres.

I wrap my arms around his waist.

"Well, I don't think we'll be going hungry anytime soon!" I joke. "Although, maybe thirsty, only one bottle?"

"Yeah, I won't be drinking, that's just for you. I was going to pick up some soft drinks too, but I forgot. I also forgot the ice cream. I hope that's okay." He looks worried.

I reassure him that he's got more than enough and offer to prepare some of the snacks as an appetiser whilst he works on the main meal, but he tells me to sit down and put my feet up with a glass of wine. Well, I can't say no to that, even if I am disappointed that he won't be drinking with me. I'd been hoping that would help to loosen him up before I pounce.

*

Dinner is delicious, and I wonder how I got so lucky after being so unlucky with men before. The steak is seasoned and cooked to perfection. I feel stuffed when we finally sit down in front of the TV with our insane buffet laid out on my coffee table, with extras on the kitchen work top.

"Shall I turn the light off?" He offers.

"Only if you promise to hold me tight." I snuggle closer to him.

"I think I can handle that," he says, stretching to reach the light switch.

Our chosen film is dark and scary. It's one of those ones that goes quiet, so you lean forwards in your seat, absorbed, until it suddenly goes loud and makes you jump out of your skin. My hairs keep standing on end as I cuddle Adam. I don't normally focus on scary films; I think that's the trick to not getting scared: don't let them absorb you. But I can't help it today, maybe it's the volume or just the situation, I am engrossed and terrified. I cling to Adam as it makes me jump again and I let out a little yelp. He rubs my arm to comfort me.

The credits roll up the screen in silence and the room is almost entirely dark with limited light now coming off the TV. I turn to face Adam, preparing for a sneaky kiss, as the doorbell rings, making me jump. Why is that thing so bloody loud?

Because I live in a flat, I have one of those little screens to show the camera at the front door downstairs. We both go to look, not stopping to put the light on.

There's no one there. The black and white camera shows an empty front porch and nearby bushes blowing in the wind.

"It's probably just kids messing around, it is Halloween after all. Trick or treat!" Says Adam.

"Yeah, I suppose, you're probably right," I say, walking back into the lounge and putting the light on. "But if it was kids, they wouldn't have gone far. Quick, turn the light back off and let's look out the front window!"

I open the blinds. There's no sign of life in the carpark. The lights, which are on sensors, remain unlit. The nearby roads also appear empty. If they're hiding, they're hiding well. But at 1am? Shouldn't they be home by now? I sit back down.

The doorbell rings again and I rush to look, nearly slipping over in my haste.

Again, there's no one there.

"It's probably just kids, ducking out of view after they press it. Do you want me to go check it out?"

"No, that's okay. You're probably right. Will you stay with me until I calm down though? Watch something a bit happier?" He agrees. "How about 'Notting Hill'? Did you ever watch that?"

"I did, but we can still watch it."

"Okay, good." I reach for the remote and try to remember which streaming service it's currently available on.

The doorbell rings, making me jump again.

"Seriously!" I shout. I open the window in the lounge and lean out, peering into the darkness. "Whoever is doing that, stop it! It's not funny! Some of us are trying to go to sleep!" I slam the window shut with a thud. I don't care if I upset the neighbours.

We put the film on and I dig into the snacks again, having a second wind. The wine is long gone, so the snacks help to get my head straight. I love this film.

I notice Adam watching me watch the film as I smile and quote my favourite bits. At the end, I turn and kiss him before he can move away. He kisses me back. I climb on him, the closest we've ever been, and place his hands on my body. He pulls back.

"I'm sorry, we can't."

"Please Adam, I'm ready. Whatever you need to tell me, I'm ready. I'm not going anywhere. Dangerous or not, I'm in. I love you." I use my begging dog eyes.

"Not tonight, okay, but soon. You're right. I think we're ready to take things to the next level, I just need to check some things first."

"Okay," I pull a sad face.

"I love you. I'm sorry. Do you feel safe enough for me to go now?" He pulls me in tight against his body.

"I guess so." He releases me and I walk him to the door. "Text me when you get home, okay?"

"Of course." He kisses me on the cheek.

I lock the door behind him and stand by the lounge window ready to watch him walk away. With the inside lights off again, I look outside. Somebody has graffitied the ground of the car park, it lights up as Adam leaves the building. *DON'T CLOSE YOUR EYES.*

Bloody teenagers.

ADAM

17.

Fireworks Night. Is there anything more romantic than freezing in the cold, holding your loved one to warm up, and edging closer and closer to a blazing bonfire as you look up to the sky and watch fireworks?

Nah, I'm not convinced either. But Ella is really into it, so, here we are, lost in the crowds, watching the sky. There's a funfair here too, but thankfully Ella hasn't said anything about going on the rides. I really don't want to. I think they might trigger me. This is all feeling a lot like that nightmare I had as a kid.

I squeeze her hand and she smiles at me. I suppose it is a bit romantic. She looks cute wearing her bobble hat and her cheeks are warming now that we're closer to the bonfire. I dip my neck and kiss her on the tiny, exposed bit of her forehead.

"What was that for?" She asks.

"Nothing. Just for being you."

She pouts at me.

We watch the rest of the fireworks quietly, hearing the crowd 'ooh' and 'ah' and small children crying.

"So, what now then?" I ask once they're over.

"I don't know, what do you want to do?"

"Erm," I start, but I can't finish. Something has caught my eye. I need to distract myself. Look away Adam, look away. It's not real. Marshmallows. Sparklers. Fibre optic head boppers. Breathe.

"Adam? Are you okay?"

I look at her, her face full of concern.

"Yes, sorry, I'm fine. I'm just feeling a bit sick. I think maybe that hotdog from earlier didn't agree with me. Do you mind if we leave?"

"Sure. We can go back to yours, or you can drop me off?"

"I think it's best I drop you off. I think I'm going to be sick." I need to be alone.

"Okay, I hope you're alright. I'm sorry, I know you didn't even want to come tonight."

"It's not your fault, but I really do need to get going."

We quickly make our way towards the car. It feels like I parked miles away due to the road closures for the parade that happened earlier this evening, but we get there as fast as we can. The further away we get, the better I feel. I just need to keep distracting myself from what I saw. It wasn't real.

I drop Ella off and feel my mask slip. It's easier to act brave when you've got somebody to hide your fear from. Alone in my car, I nearly crumble.

I make it back and hurry inside, looking over my shoulder as I enter the front door, paranoid.

I don't know why it gets me like this, but it's not the first time. I see something and immediately I'm back there, six years old and terrified. The nightmare that changed my social life forever.

How can something from so long ago, still have such a hold over me? It's been over twenty years! But that face, those teeth, a solitary red balloon… It's ironic my literary hero inspired the worst nightmare I ever had. Bloody Stephen King.

Our neighbour, Sue, comes down the stairs.

"I wasn't expecting you back so early," she says.

"I'm not feeling so well, I think I had a dodgy hot dog," I say, the lie falling from my tongue even easier the second time around.

"Are you alright? Do you want me to stay here a while longer?"

"No, that's fine, you go home. I'll be able to do what's needed." I reassure her.

"Okay, but you let me know if you need anything. Remember, I'm only next door." She picks up her jacket, slips on her shoes and leaves.

I sit down on the sofa.

I don't ever want Ella to know how messed up my nightmare was that night twenty-two years ago.

Mum rings her bell, I go upstairs.

She's tucked up in bed, watching her little TV.

"Did everything go okay? I thought I'd be asleep by the time you got back."

"It was fine, Mum. I just needed to come home."

"Why? Weren't you having a good time?"

"We were having a lovely time. But you know how I am. Sometimes, things trigger me."

"Oh." She says, nodding.

"Do you think I'll ever get over it?"

"I think that once you accept that having one awful nightmare does not make you a monster; does not make you anything like your father; I think you'll be okay. It wasn't your fault, Adam. It didn't mean anything. It could have happened to any one of you. People only read into it because of who you are, but you're not like him."

"Thank you."

I leave her to fall asleep watching TV.

18.

It's dark and I'm alone but, I don't feel alone. Somebody is watching me. I look over my shoulder. I can't see anything, only darkness. I start to walk and I realise the ground is wet, it has been raining, my welly-boots splash in the puddles.

"Adam," a voice whispers, sending shivers down my spine. I must never talk to strangers.

"Adam," it calls again. I keep walking in the darkness.

"ADAM!"

I turn to see who or what is calling me. There's a face, low down, as if underground. A clown. He waves at me and chuckles. It's not a friendly chuckle.

"Come here, Adam, I have something to show you." I shake my head. "Don't you want a balloon?" He offers. I back away.

"Adam, don't be a bad boy now, all your friends have come with me. Don't you want to play with them?" This

tempts me, where is everyone else? "Come here, I'll take you to them," he reaches out with a white-gloved hand.

Before I can move, he grabs me, and I'm transported to a fairground. The music is so loud it hurts my ears. The clown looks at me and grins, showing sharp razorblade teeth. I scream.

He jumps acrobatically away from me and towards one of the rides. I recognise some of my friends in the front row, kicking their legs out, excited to ride.

The clown is watching me, watching them.

The ride begins, raising them up and tilting them back in their seats, then forwards as it dips back down. They scream with joy as it speeds up, rotating them back and forth, up and down. I move closer, wanting to join the queue, wanting to have a go.

The music gets louder, and I cover my ears. Their screams turn from excitement to fear as the ride becomes uncontrollably fast – I can't see what they're screaming about, but I can't see the clown either.

I'm standing right below the ride now, as close as I can get behind the barrier. I watch their legs kicking about and hear their screams, and then it starts to rain. But as I look at my yellow raincoat's sleeves I realise, it's not rain, it's blood. My friends are spurting blood as they're being thrown about on the ride and a sickening laughter fills my head. HA HA HA HA HA.

I suddenly realise I'm clasping a red helium balloon on a string. I let it go and it starts to float away just as a leg comes flying at me, somehow separated from its owner. The leg pops the balloon and blood explodes onto me like a burst water balloon. I wipe my face.

The ride stops and the clown pounces behind the seats and walks along a tightrope behind my friends, bopping them on the head,

"Duck, duck, GOOSE!" He grabs a fistful of Susan's hair and pulls it upwards before biting her head off with his teeth. He chews on her ear and then spits it out. It lands inches from my feet.

I start to back away again, but he notices and cartwheels over to me.

"Going so soon Adam? Don't you want to play with us?" He smiles showing his sharp teeth, blood dripping down his chin.

I turn and run, screaming and clenching my fists.

*

I wake up in bed, at home, twenty-two years after I had that nightmare the first time.

It was worse for my friends that night, I only watched their pain, they felt it. That morning in our lounge when I awoke in my sleeping bag, I was surrounded by screaming and sobbing friends. Susan checked her hair in the mirror and caressed her neck and ear, Michael hugged his leg, and they all looked and pointed at me with fear and hatred in their eyes, like it was all my fault.

I supposed it was. I never should have snuck out of bed to watch that film through the banister near the top of the stairs. I should have known anything my dad liked to watch would be traumatising, even if it was about a gang of kids and a clown. I was an idiot. But then, I was only five. *Five and 360 days* I would have said at the time.

My dad must have known I was sat there. I can't have been that quiet; I can't have sat that still. He must have wanted me to see, wanted me to be scared. Maybe he even wanted that to happen. I guess I'll never know. I haven't seen him since he left, and I have no intention of seeking him out. He's a bad man, my father, I am better off without him. Everyone is.

103

ELLA

19.

Christmas shopping with Adam naturally ends with a sit down at Cherry B's; it's where we end up after nearly every outing these days. I can't complain though, it really is good hot chocolate.

I sit by the window surrounded by our purchases as Adam goes to get our drinks. I love people watching, especially at this time of the year. The children look so excited, even more so tonight because rumour has it, it might snow! I see their eager faces checking the sky as they walk between shops, their mittens hanging on strings below their hands as their parents look stressed and exhausted, pulling them along. All the store windows have been decorated, the festive outdoor lights are on, and there's Christmas music blasting from outside the shopping centre.

Adam comes back with our drinks on a tray as usual and places it down softly on the table. As he says,

"Ella, I have something to ask you," my attention is drawn to somebody approaching us on the other side of the glass.

He's the spitting image of Adam and, as he enters the café, I can't help but turn to get a better look as he walks towards us. Two dream men?

"Adam! I didn't know you'd be here. How are you, bro?"

"How am I? How am I? How about, how is Mum?" Snaps Adam, clearly angry. Why didn't he tell me he has a twin? I told him about my love of 'The Parent Trap'!

"I've already been to see Mum, actually," he rolls his eyes, "and you're the one being rude!" He turns and grins at me, holding his hand out. "I'm Kyle, Adam's twin brother, pleased to meet you."

"You're um... wow. Adam never told me he had a twin." I just about get the words out.

"Ah well, you wouldn't tell anyone either if you had a twin who was just like you, but hotter, would you?" He winks. I feel my stomach flutter. Is this my real dream man? Have I been dating an imposter?

"So, what do you do then, Kyle?" I ask.

"This and that, it's a bit top secret, you know 'you never saw me' kind of thing... so, err, I should probably get my order and go... But it was nice to meet you, Ella, isn't it? I hope to see you again soon. No doubt at the wedding if not before!" He laughs and mock whispers, "the way Mum was talking, Adam must like you a lot, and you know she's dying, right?"

"Could you be any more insensitive Kyle? Fuck off!"

We don't speak again until Kyle has left the café with his drink.

"Why didn't you tell me you have a twin brother?" I ask, wondering if this has anything to do with the big secret he's keeping from me.

"We don't talk. He does his thing, I do mine. We don't agree on much, especially about Mum. He'll probably be around for a while and then disappear again as usual. I wouldn't get too attached if I were you."

"What do you mean?"

106

"I know girls fall for his charm all the time, but he's not one to stick around. Love you and leave you without calling, you know?" Oh, I know. He sounds exactly my type. My previous type, I mean. I have Adam now, what am I thinking?

"Well I'm not interested in him anyway, I've got you. I've got the good brother. If only you would just give me that one more thing…" I try to look suggestive.

"I told you, I can't. Not yet. I will explain soon, but for now you just have to trust me. I want to do this right. Anyway, before Kyle turned up, I was about to invite you to Sunday lunch at ours tomorrow, but I'm not sure that's such a good idea now that he's back. What do you think? Can you handle two brothers bantering and sniping at each other over a roast dinner? My mum would really like to meet you. She said to invite you to Christmas too, but I said we'd wait and see how tomorrow goes first. What do you think? Is it too soon?"

I reach across the table and take his hand to stop him fidgeting with his napkin. We've been dating for over seven months now; I was about to go introduce myself if he didn't invite me. I want to meet the woman who raised him and made him the adorable man he is today. The kind-hearted and sexy dream man I have fallen for, despite his mysterious secret.

"Stop worrying, Adam! I would love to come to Sunday lunch and meet your mum. I will put up with Kyle and ignore his charm and, assuming all goes well, I would also love to spend Christmas with you too. To be honest, if I don't, I don't know what I'll do."

Actually, that's a lie. I know exactly what I'd do, the same as I have every year since I moved away from home. I tell my parents that I have to work, and then I sit in my flat watching rom coms and drinking wine, eating a ready meal for Christmas dinner and snacking on mince pies and cheese twists until it's over for another year.

"Okay. I love you, Ella." I still love hearing him say that.

"I love you too." We kiss.

Tearing ourselves away from one another, we put our coats and scarves back on and prepare to head back out in the cold.

"Now that he's back, do you need to buy Kyle a present too?"

Adam laughs like that's the most absurd idea he's heard all day. Apparently, they stopped buying each other presents when they were twelve.

I still send Viva presents, usually vouchers for a book shop. It seems only fair, after everything. Reading is something she got into after the accident, when she was forced to become wheelchair bound. She couldn't bear to watch TV all day, and she detests all the rom coms I watch, so she got into reading. Classics and 'proper' literature, none of the fun stuff I like.

As we walk up to Adam's car, it starts to snow so I stop and face him.

"You know how we ticked off kissing in the rain?"

"Yes…" He knows where I'm going with this but he's going to make me say it.

"Well, kissing in the snow is also romantic and actually, have you seen 'Bridget Jones'?"

"Maybe, they're all starting to blur together."

"Well, near the end Colin Firth as Mark Darcy reads her diary and he storms out in the snow, and she thinks he's left her because of what she wrote about him, so she chases after him in her cardigan and knickers and trainers and then he wraps her up in his coat as they kiss because passers-by are looking and giggling because they could see her bum. Does that ring any bells?"

"My coat isn't the right type, and you're definitely overdressed for that scenario, Ms Jones, but fine," he dramatically drops his shopping bags and dips me like a dancer before kissing me slowly as snow falls on my face.

"Thank you." I squeeze his hand once I'm back upright and then we start loading the boot, ready to go home.

20.

I have never video-called Kristina before, but I need to talk to someone about this. In the few minutes since I arrived home, I have already begun to unravel. I downed one glass of wine and am sat here with my second, pressing call.

"Hey girl!" She answers quickly. "What's up? How's life with your dream man?"

I lift up my glass of wine.

"It's only 4 o'clock! What happened?"

"There's two of them." I state with wide eyes.

"What? What do you mean?" I see her pause whatever she'd been watching on the TV. I now have her undivided attention.

"He has an identical twin."

"Oh my God! And you think maybe it was his brother you were dreaming about?"

"Yes! I love Adam, obviously, I do. But his brother... he just seemed 'right'. You know? Like I remembered him from before. What am I going to do, Kris'? What should I do?"

"Damn. Well, you love Adam so, you could just stay away from this brother, don't even consider him an option, he's not an option – you're taken. So just avoid him and forget about him?" She raises one eyebrow.

"I can't avoid him. I've got to have Sunday lunch with both of them and their dying mum tomorrow!" I drink more wine. "What if I mess everything up? What if I get confused and kiss Kyle? And with their mum watching! Oh my God, Kristina! Help me!"

"Okay, let's just think about this rationally. We figured that you dreamt of Adam because he'd been watching you, right? So, unless both brothers had been watching you, it's impossible that you were dreaming about Kyle – was that his name? I really doubt both of them were sneaking around perving on you. The odds have got to be against that."

I nod and sip more wine.

"I think the best plan is to pay attention to what they're wearing when you arrive, so you don't muddle them up, and maybe avoid spontaneous kisses, just in case. Focus your attention on getting to know their mum and ignore this brother as much as possible. Do they get along?"

"Adam and Kyle? Definitely not. When Kyle turned up, I thought Adam was going to rugby tackle him and smash a hot mug into his head. He was pissed! From what he said after, I think maybe Kyle has a habit of stealing his girlfriends or something. He told me not to get too attached because he's a 'love you and leave you without calling' kind of guy."

"Sounds like your usual type," she says, moving around her room and balancing her phone so she can talk whilst she folds her dry washing.

"Exactly! He sounds exactly like the kind of guy I normally go for! What if I fall for him?" My glass is empty again.

"You won't if you don't pay him any attention. Okay? Just focus on their mum, and Adam. You love Adam, remember?"

"I do…"

"Is there a 'but' coming?"

"Well… No. It doesn't matter. You're right. I love Adam. I can do this. Do you have any advice for talking to a dying woman?" I decide not to tell her about our lack of sex, or Adam's mysterious secret. It doesn't matter, she's right. I love Adam.

"Nope, you're on your own with that one! Good luck!"

"Thanks!"

We end the call, and I place my empty glass on the worktop.

21.

I open the little gate at the end of the front garden and before I can even make my way down to the front door, it opens and out jumps Adam (I assume, anyway).

He envelopes me in a big hug and assures me that Kyle is on his best behaviour and also in charge of the food, and that his mum is going to sit with us but probably won't eat much. As soon as we step inside, the smell of the roast dinner makes my stomach growl.

"Someone's hungry!" Teases Adam.

Kyle leans in the doorway to the kitchen, a tea towel thrown over his shoulder.

"Ella, welcome to our humble abode. Can I get you a drink?"

I try not to look at him directly as I nod and say 'sure.' I must focus on Adam, I don't understand why my stomach butterflies appear to be reacting to Kyle so much. He looks exactly the same for crying out loud, what's wrong with me?

"White wine?" Kyle suggests and I nod again. He knows my drink of choice. But it's just a coincidence… right?

He pours me a large glass and brings it to me. Adam looks furious.

"I could've got her a drink Kyle."

"Yeah, but I was already out there. It's no bother. Stand down!" He jokingly puts his hands up like he's under arrest. "I know she's here with you."

A bell rings upstairs. It must be their mum, ready to come down. I take a big sip of wine and prepare to keep my face neutral. I don't know what to expect.

She looks much older than she probably is, and very frail, but what strikes me most of all is the colour of her skin. It can only be described as: grey. When she gets to the bottom of the stairs, she looks up at me and I see her eyes sparkle as if to say, 'I'm not dead yet.'

"Ella," she smiles. "Adam has told me so much about you. Will you sit with me at the table, whilst we wait for the boys to serve up?"

Adam helps her to her chair, and I sit opposite. Once we are alone, she speaks again.

"I'll say this quickly, before they come back. You seem like a lovely girl, all I could hope for in a daughter in law, but there are things you need to know. They haven't been honest with you about who they are, what they can do. They're not regular people like you or I, they are different. Special. Dangerous, some would say. Ask them to tell you the truth, and if you are not okay with it then run. Run as far as you can and never look back. I wish I had done that when their father told me, but I was a fool; you need not make the same mistake." She takes a sip of water.

"Okay, um, thank you, I guess. But I don't understand, what can they do?"

She looks at the kitchen door to make sure they're not coming back before answering quietly.

"When you met Adam in that bar, was that the first time you'd seen him?" She studies my face. "Exactly."

Kyle and Adam re-open the door and come in carrying our plates of food. Mine is piled high with meat, veg and gravy but their mum's just has a small portion of boiled veg, plain.

My mind is spinning, if Adam and Kyle aren't 'normal' then maybe those dreams weren't so coincidental after all, maybe there really is more to them, one of them may have somehow done it on purpose... but which one?

"You can start," says Adam, nudging me. "We don't say grace here."

"Sorry, I was in my own world then, it smells delicious," I say, picking up my knife and fork.

"It should taste delicious too," says Kyle, "I've always been good at cooking a roast, haven't I Adam?"

"When you're around." He snipes.

"Boys!" Their mum shakes her head and gives me a smile.

It's like sitting around a regular family table, the sons taking it in turns to wind each other up, and Mum, exhausted, trying to keep them in check. But I can't stop thinking about what she just told me, that they are different, special, dangerous. It makes sense. This could be Adam's big secret. But then, what's Kyle's role in this? Why does my body react so strongly to him?

Eventually, I give up eating. I can't clear my plate, there's just too much. I issue my praises of the tasty food and Kyle helps their mum back upstairs, leaving Adam and I alone for the first time today. I sit across his lap on an armchair.

"This secret you're keeping from me, does it have something to do with dreams?" I ask him. His hand which had been caressing my leg, stops moving.

"Why would you ask that?"

115

"It's just something I've been wondering about. I never told you before because I thought you'd think I was weird, but I dreamt about you before we met."

"Oh?" His face goes red, but not with embarrassment, with rage. His fingers curl up into fists.

"Did you… do something?" I ask.

"No, I did not." He replies through gritted teeth.

"But you can do that then? Get into people's dreams?" I ask, standing up.

"Ella, I want to explain but I can't, it's not safe for you to know."

"Tell me, Adam, or I'll walk out that door and you'll never see me again." I start to put my shoes on.

"No. I promise you Ella, I didn't do anything. It's not what you think."

"Then tell me! Fill in the gaps!"

"I can't! Ella, I love you, please don't go." He begs me, eyes threatening to spill.

"Call me when you're ready to tell me the truth."

I pick up my bag and leave.

ADAM

22.

I watch Ella walk down the garden path, and then I confront him.

"Kyle, what did you do?"

"What do you mean?" He asks, coming down the stairs and heading for the kitchen.

"I think you know what I mean."

"No, really, I don't." He's always been good at feigning innocence.

"Ella just told me that she dreamt about me before we met."

"And what makes you think I had anything to do with that? Sounds like destiny to me!" He laughs and proceeds to the sink, turning the hot tap on and squeezing out some washing up liquid. I follow.

"Seriously, Kyle. Just tell me."

"Look, it was nothing, really. Just a little visit to make sure that she was happy and definitely interested when you finally introduced yourself. That's all. I just made your face recognisable." He starts submerging and scrubbing the plates.

"You're sure? You didn't do anything else?"

"Nope. That's it."

"If I find out it was more…"

"What? Just thank me Ad'. The words you are looking for are 'thank you brother'." He smiles smugly. I sigh.

"If anyone finds out…"

"They're not going to."

"But if they do…"

"Then I'll fix it. I always do. Now, grab a tea-towel and help me, I'm not your skivvy."

ELLA

23.

I know I said I wouldn't see him again until he told me the truth, but it's impossible to stay mad at him. Whatever he hasn't told me, I still love him. He's kind and caring, he makes me laugh, he's smart and desirable, and I know he'd never do anything to hurt me. Whatever's happened, it was either unintentional or it wasn't Adam. He told me right from the beginning that he wanted to keep me safe, I have to trust that he was telling the truth. I have no reason not to.

But, if that means I was somehow dreaming with Kyle all those months before I met Adam, well, that's an issue. But it's something we will deal with later. Tonight, we're going on a double date. I've set Kyle up with Amy, Kristina's blonde friend that I met when we went out celebrating, because if anyone's Kyle's type, she is. She's probably every man's type on some level. The boobs, the hair, the bum, the skin, the absolutely perfect makeup…

I'm hoping that with her here to distract Kyle, I'll be able to get some answers from Adam about what's really been going on. I'm certain that if it wasn't him, he'll have confronted Kyle by now, so he must have some answers for me, and when better to ask him than on a double date when he feels obliged to drink and hopefully lets his guard down?

We are greeted by an eccentric curly-haired waiter called Malcolm who leads us to our table and tells us the specials and his personal recommendations in such an enthusiastic manner it's hard not to say 'we'll have that' without even looking at the menu. Luckily Adam and Kyle are less easily swayed and ask for time to decide.

"So, isn't this nice?" Asks Kyle, crossing his arms over the menu.

"Hmm, lovely. A double-date with Adam's secret twin brother, what more could I ask for?" I reply and then mentally slap myself. I must drop the attitude for this to work. I want them chilled out, relaxed. "I mean, yes, it was a lovely idea. Amy, why don't you tell Kyle about yourself?"

Amy twists her blonde hair around her fingers as she begins to tell Kyle about her job as a beauty therapist and flirts with him outrageously. I'm not looking under the table, but I guarantee her legs are no longer on our side.

Unfortunately, Kyle seems unimpressed. He pushes his chair back and mutters something about needing to go to the loo. He's still not back when Malcolm reappears to take our order, so Adam orders for him.

"Is that a twin thing? You know what he wants?" Asks Amy.

"Actually, I ordered what I know he doesn't want, to serve him right for being so rude. I suppose you could call it a brother thing," replies Adam, completely deadpan.

"Oh! Well, I hope he doesn't mind. He can always share some of mine if he doesn't like his," offers Amy.

"I'm sure he'll appreciate that," replies Adam as Kyle finally reappears and sits down.

I'm not so sure he will, distinctly remembering a particular dream in which my dream man quoted Joey from 'Friends' and Joey 'doesn't share food.'

Of course, that's only relevant if I was dreaming with Kyle, which I'm still unclear on. Maybe it doesn't work that way, maybe it's still my imagination, just with their faces... and bodies... What I'd give for some bloody answers!

Kyle whispers something to Adam, which makes him frown. Clearly, they need to talk, but not in front of Amy and me. I stand up dramatically and pull Amy with me to the bar, glaring at them as I leave.

"Kyle is so hot," gushes Amy, "thank you for inviting me. I mean, your man is hot too, obviously, but Kyle... wow. Whatever 'it' is, he has it, right? Just a shame he's in such a mood! What do you think is going on? Is he definitely single? Because I don't normally send guys to the bathroom that quickly on a date, I mean, unless I'm with them! Hahaha!"

"Cheers to that!" I say, raising my freshly filled glass.

It hadn't occurred to me that Kyle might have a girlfriend. Maybe that is his problem, he has a girlfriend, but Adam doesn't know about her, so he has to act like he's single, but he's going to ruin this date on purpose? It seems a bit far-fetched but, at the moment, I'd believe anything.

"But you think I should still keep trying, yeah? I know you wanted me to keep him busy, but, like, I don't know if that's going to work!" She reapplies her lip gloss, looking into her compact mirror and pouting.

"Please try, I need to get Adam to open up, relax a bit, let me in, you know?"

She nods repeatedly,

"Those two need a real good relax, they're so uptight tonight. Nothing a good bit of sex wouldn't cure!"

I laugh along. Ah, sex, I remember when I thought I'd get some with Adam. Nobody knows we're in a sexless relationship, not even Kristina. Although, maybe Kyle knows. I guess he knows what his brother is like. I bet Kyle is a one-night stand king, whereas Adam clearly likes to wait forever.

What if he's a virgin? I've never actually asked, I just assumed you don't get to twenty-eight looking like that and not having had sex. But, maybe that's it, maybe the sex isn't part of the secret at all, maybe he's just scared. Or religious.

We chat at the bar a while longer and then head back to the table. The brothers are at least talking properly to each other now, though they stop abruptly as we approach.

"Talking about us, were you?" I ask into the silence.

"No. Just, er, about Mum," says Adam.

"Oh, is she okay?"

"It won't be long now; she knows it and I can feel her giving up."

"Oh, that's so sad!" Amy grabs Kyle's hand and begins stroking it. I give a knowing smile and shrug to Adam like 'what is she like?' He doesn't react.

"Are you okay?" I mouth to Adam, and he nods.

Our starters arrive at last. Conversation is stilted, we don't seem to have a lot in common across this table, until Amy asks the question I'd been planning to ask Adam later:

"So, where's your dad in all this? Your mum's dying, did they get a divorce? Is he still around?"

Bullseye. Their dad is like them, whatever that means, so finding out more about him will help me unravel this mystery.

"No, he's not around. He left a long time ago," answers Kyle.

126

"Have you not spoken to him since? Do you know much about him?" She continues, I try not to smile. She's doing my work for me, and I didn't even ask her to.

"No," answers Adam, but something tells me he's lying. She's hit a nerve.

Whenever I've asked him about his dad previously, he's only ever answered the question properly once, and I think there's a lot more to the story than that. He told me that his dad was responsible for him breaking his arm on a rope swing – he fell off and onto an abandoned washing machine of all things – and that due to being an irresponsible dad, he left. Just like that, didn't send birthday cards, nothing. Just 'I'm a crap dad so I'm out of here.' As if. That was raising red flags before I heard what their mum had to say.

Amy takes this opportunity to tell us how amazing life was for her having divorced parents, with two Christmases and two birthdays and two Easters and two summer holidays… even I am starting to find her annoying. And Kyle still doesn't seem interested.

After dinner, we move to the bar next door for a few drinks. Amy is quick to latch onto Kyle and drag him over to the dance floor, leaving me to talk to Adam, at last. But I'm not going to get straight back on to the dad subject just yet – that seemed a tough subject to crack. I decide to start with Kyle.

"So, what's his deal then? I thought he was a ladies' man, but he doesn't seem to be interested in Amy at all. Is she not pretty enough for him?"

"No, it's not that. He's –" he pauses in thought, "you know, maybe you should ask him. Maybe he'd open up to you."

"Why on Earth would he open up to me?"

"Because you're a girl. He went through quite a traumatic break up by the sounds of things, but he's not going to admit how he really feels to me, is he? He plays the role of the cool older-by-two-minutes brother with me, he might open up to a girl."

"But I thought you said he was a 'love you and leave you' kind of guy?" I watch Kyle dancing with Amy, careful to keep a little distance between them.

"He is. Was. Whatever. He's in a bit of a self-destructive phase after what happened. I think he's scared of being hurt again." He sips his drink. "Don't let him know I told you that though."

"Aw, so you do love your brother after all!" I tease.

"No, I love you," he smiles, "and he nearly ruined it." He kisses me.

"What do you mean?"

He puts his empty glass down and squeezes my hands.

"Ella, are you sure about us?"

"Yes, you know I am." I squeeze his hands back.

"Even though what I have to tell you will put you in danger?"

"I don't care about the danger! Tell me, Adam, please. I'm not going anywhere."

"It might change your whole life," he threatens.

"Well sign me up! What have I got in my life besides you anyway? A crappy temp job? About one proper friend, and she's really an ex-colleague, so actually no real friends. All I have and want is you Adam, just tell me."

"Not here."

Kyle waves us over to the dance floor, so we join him and Amy. I don't know what to think of Kyle now that he might not be such a bad boy after all – he had his heart broken like the rest of us. I kind of feel sorry for him, unless it turns out he's been manipulating me. I do feel bad for Amy though, she's really going for it, and he's really not interested. It's a little embarrassing. I would tell her to call it off, go talk to someone else, but I don't want to be left with both of them, so I keep quiet.

128

Adam seems to finally let his hair down and on that dance floor, we bond like we never have before. We may have never slept together, but what we do out there is about as close as we've ever been – physically and mentally. I just want to rip his clothes off right now! Okay, maybe not right now, I'm not into public nudity, but that last kiss turned me on so much I am a mess!

As we leave, Amy asks me why Adam isn't coming back to mine, or me back to theirs, and I shrug it off like it's nothing but inside I am screaming with frustration. We share a taxi and as I wave her goodbye, I am once again confronted by my loneliness.

ADAM

24.

We wave goodbye to the girls as they get into a taxi and begin the short walk home.

"Adam, don't look behind but I think someone's following us," says Kyle, increasing his pace.

"Really, why?" I whisper, meeting his speed.

"I've seen a few suspicious people tonight, in the restaurant and the bar, and one of them is now behind us. I think he's been sent by the HJD."

"Kyle…" I use my warning tone.

"It's going to be fine, just, hurry up," he hisses, speeding up to jog. I can't walk any faster.

"This was your idea, Kyle, if anything happens…"

"I'll fix it, just keep walking."

"Ow!" I reach for the back of my head where something hit me. I stop and turn around and am immediately punched in the face. Stumbling backwards, I look around for Kyle as he throws some kind of martial arts drop kick at the man's stomach. I think my nose is bleeding.

"Kyle, I-" I watch him continue to beat this stranger to a pulp. Clearly The Resistance has trained him well. But we can't find out who sent him if he's dead. "Kyle, stop," I whimper. He pays no attention and continues kicking the man on the floor. I struggle to my feet and move towards him, but he elbows me without looking. I retreat holding my neck where he got me. He's fucking lethal.

"KYLE, STOP!" I yell. Finally he looks up at me, the man on the floor clearly going nowhere anytime soon.

"Sure, let's go," he pulls me by my jacket and jogs towards home.

Once inside he asks me if I'm okay, looking at my bloodied and soon to be bruised face and neck.

"Kyle, what was that? Who was that?"

"Like I said, he was following us," he shrugs, going to get a beer from the fridge.

"And that's a reason to beat him to a pulp?"

He glugs the beer, looking up at the ceiling.

"I'd hoped I wouldn't have to tell you this yet, but people have heard about you and Ella. They're coming for us. It's time, Ad'. You need to tell her now."

I pour myself a whiskey.

"You didn't just 'appear' in her dreams, did you Kyle?" I down the whiskey in one, enjoying the burn.

"Adam, I can explain."

PART 2

~

My hands are shaking
Blood rushes to my face
My eyes are hot
I can't breathe in this place

How could he do this to me?
I knew a little
But this
This <u>betrayal</u>?

I can't take it
I can't fucking take it
He's ruined everything
My true love was a lie
Our perfect romance built on a cloud
Nothing but ice crystals
Floating
Ready to shatter and spill to the ground
Washing away my hopes
Her dreams
Oh
Her dreams

ELLA

25.

It's 3am when I check the time, having disconnected the call with Adam. He woke me up, but I'll forgive him. He said they need to talk to me, now. This has to be it, right? The moment I've been waiting for. He's finally going to reveal his big, dangerous secret!

I get dressed quickly and make my way round to their house. The roads are blissfully empty, and I can't stop smiling.

It's still dark as I approach, my footsteps echoing on the path. The fresh air makes my eyes feel wide awake, and I have an absurd urge to skip. I'm excited. Giddy.

Kyle opens the door, but rather than being his usual cheeky and flirty self, he looks so serious I fear I may have got completely the wrong idea. Shit, has their mum died?

I head inside and find Adam sat at the dining table, his face red and blotchy. Oh no.

"Is your mum okay?" I ask, glancing at the stairs.

"Yeah, she's upstairs in bed, this isn't about her." Adam reassures me, though something is clearly wrong. He looks a mess.

Kyle stands up as if preparing to lead an important conference,

"This is going to be a lot to take in, so please just listen and ask questions at the end." I do as I'm told and take my seat. I feel like I'm at school.

"Can I take notes?" I joke.

"No, I'd rather there wasn't a paper trail of this conversation," he replies. So serious! He clears his throat as if signalling the start of his official speech.

"First things first, we are in danger. People are coming for us, because of what we are," he points to himself and Adam, "and what they've seen you two doing," he points accusingly at Adam and me.

"Okay, well we haven't done much-" I start, thinking he means sex.

"Kissing. Remember, questions at the end," Kyle interrupts. "These people that are coming for us will punish Adam, or me, for what is going on here, or what they perceive to be going on. Because you are different to us, and certain people don't agree with the two species frolicking. I'm not keen on it myself, but Adam was besotted with you from the moment he set his eyes on you, and he hasn't had a lot of romance in his life, so I actively encouraged the relationship and for that I will also face charges."

"Actively encouraged," mutters Adam. Kyle continues, ignoring him.

"We have mistreated you, and for that I am sorry, but we have not committed the crime they will charge Adam with, because you fell for him yourself, didn't you? You love Adam, but not because of your dreams, because of your real-life relationship. Correct?"

"Erm, yes…" I didn't realise he knew we were 'in love.' Do brothers talk about that stuff? Even ones that don't get along?

"What dreams Kyle? Expand on those. I'd like to hear more about those dreams," snarls Adam.

"The dreams Ella had before she met you."

"The ones where you promised me, you only showed your face, our face, so she'd recognise me and be happy to see me, right?"

"Like I already told you, I did what I had to do, for you. I knew you were in love with her, she was all you thought and dreamt about, some girl you didn't really know and basically stalked. You hadn't had a relationship for so long because you refuse to date within our kind, so I thought, 'sod it, this guy needs a romance' and I went in to get her for you."

"Brother of the year right there," mocks Adam.

"I didn't mean for it to go on so long before you actually met, but I swear, after the first couple, she was leading the way. I was just playing along. That girl has a lot of romantic scene ideas, I could never have come up with them all by myself. And, anyway, I thought that because she'd dreamt about you, when you finally introduced yourself in real life, she'd extend those feelings into the real world, and you would have a regular romantic relationship. And it worked, didn't it?

"Of course, I didn't realise you'd be so frigid – poor Ella, after our dreams together she was expecting a lot more."

He continues talking as if I'm not sat right here, cheeks blazing, as it sinks in that I was having sexy dreams with my boyfriend's brother before I met my boyfriend.

"How dare you stand there and try to justify yourself! You caused all of this!" Adam stands and launches himself at Kyle and they rugby tackle on the floor.

"I'm not the one that went snogging her in public," says Kyle, holding Adam down. "You couldn't just have a one-night stand and then disappear, could you? You've been spotted all over town."

"And whose fault is that? Who invited us out to that busy bar? For God's sake Kyle, this is all your fault! Why couldn't you just mind your own business?" He shoves Kyle off him.

"I was trying to do something nice for a change; trying to help my brother who spends all his time cooped up looking after our mother; trying to give you something else to live for."

"But you knew this would happen! You literally deal with this stuff all the time, you knew what would happen if I ended up dating her, but you still made it happen – you bloody dream-walked your way into her life – which by the way everyone will assume was me – to ensure that we started a real-life relationship. Anything that happens now, to any of us, is on you."

"Well, that's why I called this meeting: to warn you, and to announce the plan." They brush themselves off and return to their seats at the table.

"I thought it was to tell me what the hell is going on, because I still don't understand. Can we start at the beginning please?" I interrupt.

"Right. Yes. Okay, the beginning. We are Dream-Walkers. That means that when you're asleep, we can get into your dreams and watch, influence or appear in them. There are also some people who are Dream-Watchers, meaning they are able to watch your dreams, but nothing else. A side-effect of being a Dream-Walker is that when we are asleep, we tend to share our dreams with nearby people. It's completely involuntary and is what happened to Adam at a sleepover when we were kids. He scared all his friends with his nightmare that they found themselves

140

starring in, and they were so terrified that they called him a freak ever since. Bit of a loner after that, weren't you, bro?"

He looks at Adam who appears to be concentrating very hard on the wooden eyes in the table, tracing them with his finger. I suppose that explains why Adam has never even slept over, without sex. He has always insisted on going home, even when I fall asleep on his chest watching TV. Kyle continues,

"Dream-Walkers have existed for a very long time, but we've only traced our line as far back as World War One. Our ancestors were used to torture prisoners in their sleep, and also to get false confessions. Think how real some of those dreams we shared felt, Ella. Could you imagine if I'd made you dream that you'd killed somebody? How real it would feel?"

I blush, thinking about the sexual dreams. Yes, they felt real. Adam clears his throat and stands up.

"Ella, can I have a word?"

We go out to the utility room and once again I feel like I'm back in school. I'm nervously waiting to be reprimanded.

"The dreams you had before you met me, were they sexual? Did Kyle do things to you?" Adam narrows his eyes at me. I look around the room, my eyes finally focusing on a pile of laundry, avoiding his gaze.

"Well, kind of, we… yeah, we did stuff. But it was all consensual. And I thought it was you," I look up at him and see the pain written so clearly over his face.

"No, you thought I was him."

"Well yeah, but he was pretending to be you, so technically-"

"No. I'm sorry Kyle brought you into all this, but how can we go on now? Knowing that you wanted him first? You only gave me that second chance because I saved you, and by the way, that wasn't me either – you know how I ran in and came back? That's because it wasn't me, it was Kyle. He ran in, told me to put his clothes on, and said you were outside. So, it's always been Kyle, all along. Sure, he was setting us up, apparently, but it was him you fell for. If it was just me, it would have ended a long time ago. Be honest Ella, you love him, don't you?"

"No! I love you! I have fallen in love with you out here in the real world, not in my dreams. I can't stand how cocky he is. You're genuine, you're nice. I love you, Adam. I do." His mouth moves into a small and slightly pained-looking smile.

"Okay, if you're sure, because otherwise I was going to say that we should just call it quits. You still wouldn't be safe, but at least you wouldn't feel quite so paranoid that we were in your head manipulating you. I would never do that, you know that, right?"

"Of course, but I have so many questions! What happened to your face? And why wouldn't you have sex with me? Is it because of this 'anti-species frolicking' business Kyle mentioned?"

"Oh no, we couldn't have sex because of Transference."

"Which is?"

"Transference is what happens when someone like us has sex with a regular person. I'm told it's very intense, it's at the point of climax, you suddenly see everything I have been keeping a secret. You would know what I am and what I've done and see it all, the good, the bad, the terrifying. I'm told it's literally terrifying, like the dream I scared those kids with. It hurts. You would be scared of me. I don't want that."

"But we can't go on forever never having sex!"

"No, but there are things we can try, to lessen the effect…"

Kyle opens the door slightly and pokes his head through,

"Are you two seriously talking about sex during a time like this?" He straightens up and pushes the door open properly. "Honestly, I think you may as well just do it, take the risk, because they're going to think you have anyway. Do you want me to give you five minutes?"

We glare at him.

"As if you two have been kissing in public and not having sex, and you've been together how long now? I don't think anybody's buying the celibacy card, do you? Now, are you ready for me to continue? I need to tell Ella about who is coming for us."

26.

"They call themselves the Human Justice Department, or HJD for short. Supposedly, they look out for the interests of humans, and they do, but they also encourage the complete opposite for us lot. The Human Justice Department upholds two main laws, both of which they'll be after us for: 1. It is illegal for any living being, human or Dream-Walker, to disclose the existence of, or any of the secrets of, the Dream-Walker society to any human who has not been formally introduced by the Human Justice Department. 2. It is illegal for any Dream-Walker to appear in and/or influence any human's dream, or to deliberately share their own dream with a human, when outside of a Medical Investigation Unit or similarly approved facility. They are particularly harsh on Dream-Walkers who create love through dream-walking."

"Like you did," I mumble.

"Like I said, all your fault Kyle," says Adam.

"Anyway," Kyle continues, "they don't have cameras on us, obviously, so they have found out through other Dream-Walkers reporting us. It's that kind of society. Unfortunately, because of our dad, a lot of people know who and what we are so when we are seen out in public, people tend to talk about it. The stories will have been passed on between the smaller communities as idle gossip, or, as I think in this case, somebody has seen it as a bargaining chip and taken it straight to the top of the ladder to try to free a relative stuck in a MIU. Sorry, 'Medical Investigation Unit.' My contact in the Minister's inner circle overheard they were sending a team to investigate us and gave me the head's up."

"Okay, back up, what exactly is a MIU? Who was your dad? And Minister? Huh? You have contacts?" None of this is making any sense. I'm tired. "Can I have a coffee?"

"I'll put the kettle on," says Adam, excusing himself from the table. Kyle continues,

"Sorry, I was getting carried away. Maybe I should start right at the beginning."

"That's what you said you were doing before!"

"Yeah, but it's hard to know where to start. Let's backtrack. Over the years, Dream-Walkers have been kept like slaves by various discreet justice teams. Have you ever wondered why so many criminals commit suicide in prison? Well, a lot of the time that's thanks to people like us. We can give them nightmares using a piece of evidence or a photo of the victim to link us to the crime. When the criminal falls asleep, we can make them relive the horror if they are repentant or twist it round to make them feel like the victim if they are not. We can create whatever nightmare is appropriate to ensure that they never get a peaceful night's sleep again. After a while, death starts to look pretty appealing, and they will do anything to accomplish it. Who needs shoelaces when you have your bare hands?"

"Okay," I say, accepting the warm mug of coffee from Adam. It's frothy, just how I like it.

"Because it's so successful, the justice teams who favour these techniques have been trying to multiply the number of Dream-Walkers they have by encouraging reproduction amongst our kind, only assuming that it must be genetic, with a slow but fair success rate. When a child born in captivity has not shown any signs of their skill by the age of ten, they are dropped off at a local orphanage to hopefully be adopted and begin their life with a human family. The children that have shown signs, begin their training.

"Other Dream-Walkers are captured. For example, when the teams hear rumours of weird behaviour during the night in public hospitals, like whole wards of patients having nightmares at the same time, Seekers are sent to bring people to their site under false pretences to test them and see if they are undiagnosed Dream-Walkers. If they are, they don't get to leave.

"Some justice teams go a step further. They instruct some of their well-trained and trusted Dream-Walkers give the family of a newly diagnosed Dream-Walker false dreams which seem so realistic, they don't even file a missing person's report. They believe they've died or moved away; they have no idea their loved one is now living in a cage."

I understand why their mum called them dangerous now, there's a lot of potential misuse that could be done with a skill like that. A lot more than sexy dreams.

"Our dad was born in one of these so-called cages, at Herthmoor. There's a big one there, with a keen focus on reproduction. He told us that all the sleeping and resting rooms there had very thick concrete walls under the assumption that this might prevent Dream-Walkers from manipulating their guard's dreams. They didn't really know if it worked, some guards still went mad, but they didn't know what else to do – they didn't and still don't fully understand what they are dealing with. There was apparently a while when the most paranoid guards even wore metal ear covers! The guards are generally safe though because most Dream-Walkers that live there are born there so they don't know any different, they don't have any desire to escape or to hurt those who are using them.

"Our dad was a little different from the others there, he was stronger. He was aware of his abilities from a very young age and would have great fun manipulating people's dreams. The Department were very impressed with him and even started using him on the nearby prisoners before he was thirteen, the generally accepted age. He told us that he used to sit behind a special glass wall which allowed him to see inside the cell, but didn't allow the prisoner to see out, and he'd have to wait for them to fall asleep and then give them whatever nightmare he'd been instructed to provide. He wasn't meant to insert himself into any of the dreams, but he did sometimes on the child killers; he said he got a bit of a sick enjoyment out of acting out his vengeance on them in a dream state."

Kyle pauses to sip some of his own drink. He seems kind of proud. I can't believe he expects me to believe all this.

"Our dad soon realised that he didn't need people to be asleep for him to get into their heads. All he needed was a millisecond of a daydream or the blink of an eye for him to be in their head carrying out their torture. He could make it so that the prisoners couldn't get a second of peace the whole time he was watching them, any time they got tired and started to doze off or stare into the brickwork, he was in their head showing them pain and sadness.

"For a while this made him feel powerful, and kind of evil. Then came Albert, or Al' as he liked to be called. Al' was brought in by a team of Seekers after an eventful Halloween party at a hall of residence at a nearby university; he had given the students all such nightmares that it was doubtful they'd ever sleep with the lights off again. He'd thought that he was special, that he was the only one who could sit back and watch what went on in other people's heads when they went to sleep; the only one who could share his dreams with others without their permission; the only one who could tune in and walk into someone else's dream. When he got to Herthmoor, he was unimpressed to find he was in fact, just the same as many others. Nothing special at all.

"Nobody was interested in him, except Dad. He thought Al' looked cool and he wanted desperately to know more about the outside world. And, due to his above average abilities and evil tendencies, Dad's questions didn't sound like the annoying queries of a younger sibling to Al' and it wasn't long before they became best friends.

"Once Al' had fully convinced Dad that outside was better than inside, they started planning their escape. They decided to use Dad's secret ability to influence whenever the eyes are unfocused (not just when sleeping) to their advantage – they just needed something which would make the guard's eyes sting so much that they had to close them, then Dad would be able to make them think they saw them go one way, when in fact they went another. As it happened, it couldn't have been easier. Al' found some pepper spray in one of the evidence rooms he was allowed to go into for one of his jobs and snuck it out in his pants. The next day, they were out."

"Okay, so are people still after him?" I ask, just about following.

"I'll get to that. So, out in the real world, I'm not entirely sure on the specifics, but they got along somehow and somewhere along the lines, they came across a group of like-minded individuals who had also escaped cages and together they called themselves 'The Resistance.'"

"Can I go to the toilet?" I interrupt, anticipating another long monologue about whatever 'the resistance' is.

I am excused and take my time, giving myself a good stare in the mirror before I return. Are you taking this all in, Ella? Are you believing this? With all this talk of dreams, I'm struggling to believe I'm even awake.

I splash my face and find I'm still here, so I must be awake, and then return to my seat. Kyle doesn't hesitate for a second before launching back in.

"The Resistance are still very much around. I'm a member. The organisation is much bigger now than it was when Dad joined a bunch of scrawny late teenagers planning to take on the world and get justice for Dream-Walkers everywhere. The Resistance now stands solely against the Human Justice Department, fighting for the wellbeing and freedom of Dream-Walkers, and protecting against unlawful testing and imprisonment.

"So," he claps his hands together, "I think that brings us back full circle. The Human Justice Department is led by a Minister, currently Dr Francis Krunk. He is a scientist and so prioritises 'working us out.' The Medical Investigation Units or MIUs are where his staff carry out various tests on Dream-Walkers in hope of discovering our full capabilities as well as our weaknesses. Because of his love of testing, he is very keen to protect the two main laws, because if somebody breaks them, he gets to punish them with sentences like life in a MIU as a test subject."

"So, what you're saying is, the people who are after us want to make one or both of you a test subject – like animal testing, but on 'Dream-Walkers'?" I ask.

"Well, yes and no, they'll put us on trial first, but we won't really be able to prove our innocence. The key is to avoid being caught and avoid going on trial," explains Kyle.

"Okay, and what about your dad? Is he still in The Resistance?"

"Possibly somewhere, we haven't spoken to him since he left our mum, but I like to think he's still fighting the good fight." Kyle answers, proudly.

"Okay," I say, unconvinced. For somebody who seems so proud of his dad, who joined the movement his dad helped to create, it's unbelievable that he wouldn't know where he is. He just doesn't want to admit it. But why?

I'm too tired to ask more questions. I look at Adam and, even though this wasn't new information for him, he looks tired too. And in pain. I still don't know what happened to his face. Kyle, however, seems keen to continue.

"Shall I move on to our escape plan then?" He offers.

"Can you tell me after I've had some sleep?" I ask.

"So long as they don't catch us first. This isn't a joke, Ella; I know it's overwhelming, but I'm serious. I didn't tell you what they do with humans who find out about Dream-Walkers, but they won't let you go out in the world telling everyone about them. You'll never be the same again."

"Oh, well thank you for telling me then!" I wiggle my head sarcastically. "Supposing we're all alive and in our homes later on, you can call me and tell me the plan."

"And if we're not all alive and in our homes, you must run. Okay?"

I laugh. Both Adam and Kyle look at me solemnly and say in unison,

"This isn't a joke."

But how can it be anything else?

I walk to my car as dawn is breaking. It's peaceful, just me and the birds.

27.

I wake feeling refreshed after only a few hours' sleep, I suppose thanks to the adrenaline caused by finally finding out what the big secret was: Utter bullshit. They're clearly insane. Con men. They want to make me disappear. I should have known as soon as Adam admitted to stalking me all those months ago.

And yet, part of me wants to believe them. Part of me wants to believe that there is a whole other side of this world that I know nothing about, a world where people can walk into other people's dreams, to cause pain or evoke love, a world which is both magical and terrifying.

I reach for my phone and am surprised to see five missed calls and three voicemails. I'd put it on silent when I went to bed in case Adam tried calling me to explain himself and emphasise 'the danger.' I look at the call log, all Adam except the last one which is unknown – Kyle, perhaps?

Of course, I can't just listen to the latest voicemail, so I go to the toilet whilst it plays the first two messages from Adam, "Ella, I'm sorry I didn't tell you sooner," "Ella, you're in danger," "Ella, please be careful," blah blah blah, flush.

Now for the mystery caller.

"This is a message for Miss Ella-Rose Thompson. I am detective Sean Banham and I need to speak to you regarding a case I am working on. Please could you return my call at your earliest convenience so that this can be arranged. It is of the utmost importance. Thank you for your help."

I stare at the screen. Is somebody else in on the scheme, or does that mean it's real?

My phone rings again and I practically jump out of my skin. I send it to voicemail and then listen.

"Ella, it's Kyle. Listen, we need to get out of here as soon as possible. They're here. They're looking for you. You're not safe and neither are we. Do not open the door to anyone. If you must go out, stay in busy places and be ready to shout. Do not trust anyone. Also, our mum died this morning so Adam is really struggling; can you please call him back? I need him to pull himself together before he gets us all caught."

Wow, could he be any more unsympathetic? Their mum has just died, and he mentions it as an afterthought. What a dick. I bet Adam is devastated. She was his world; he did everything for her and now his brother is trying to make him run away before her funeral. He won't agree to that, he's too good. He wouldn't do that to her. He'd rather be caught and suffer for all of eternity than not honour his mother's death properly.

I want to run to him, to hold him as he cries and try to console him, but I can't. I need to stay away. Maybe if I just keep my distance, all this nonsense will go away.

As I'm already late, I call in sick to my temp job, blaming a stomach bug and get back into bed.

I want to call Kristina, to update her on the madness, but I stop myself. What if it's true? I could call her and tell her everything and we could joke about how ridiculous it is, but if it's real then I would be putting her in danger too; she'd have weird fake detectives calling her, and crazy scientists ready and waiting to mess with her brain too.

I can't tell anyone. Just in case.

So, am I accepting it then? 'Just in case'? Should I pack my bags and run?

I open my bedroom blinds and look out at the now faded and dirt-ridden graffiti on the carpark, 'DON'T CLOSE YOUR EYES.'

Was somebody trying to warn me back then? Does somebody around here know about Adam?

I grab my rucksack and start packing.

~

Mum
I need you
You're gone and I don't know what to do
My world is falling apart
I've a shattered heart
Like a porcelain vase
Too many pieces to glue
She isn't safe
You were right
I don't know what to do

28.

I should have brought more food. When I packed my life into my rucksack, tampons and all, and headed for the library, I stupidly thought a packet of Jammie Dodgers would keep me going. It will not. And I don't have much change for the vending machine either, so I'll have to save that for when I'm desperate.

I pick up a book and start reading so as not to arouse suspicion. I also get out a notepad so I can look like I'm taking notes, anything to differentiate myself from the other homeless people also seeking warmth and carrying their entire lives on their backs. Hopefully, I look like a student. I'm a young-looking twenty-five, so I reckon I can pull that off.

Inside, I'm anything but focused. I keep wondering whether my feelings for Adam can possibly be real when they were, at least in part, caused by Kyle's dream-walking. There's a reason that's a crime in their society. Sure, he claims a lot of the romantic ideas came from me, but even

155

so, how can I ever be sure what feelings I would have had for Adam if Kyle had never entered my dreams? I can't. I'll never know if it was really meant to be, or if I've just been manipulated over and over again. Adam said it himself, if not for Kyle, we wouldn't be together. Not only because of the dream-walking but because he saved me from being raped too – I had no intention of giving Adam a second chance until that night, and it wasn't even him. I've been falling for the wrong brother this entire time.

Falling? Fallen. I fell for Kyle in my dreams and then bit by bit I fell for Adam in the real world. He spent time getting to know me, learning everything about me and my history and he didn't judge me for anything. He understands me. He loves me, just the way I am.

Ha! It's like I'm Bridget Jones and Adam is Mark Darcy. Kyle is Daniel Cleaver, and he might be great at seduction, but he's not trustworthy and definitely not worth my time. He'd leave me to be arrested for drug smuggling in Bangkok, that's the type of guy he is. But Adam, he's the one I should be with. We might not have experienced the hot passionate side of the relationship yet, but I know it would be there, and it could be there soon now that I know…

I hope he's okay. I wonder how soon the funeral will be. Surely Kyle will try to hurry it along if Adam is insisting they have one, because they will be sitting ducks going to that when people are looking for them; anyone looking for them will just wait and go there. The sooner they can leave town, the better.

But what about me?

I could look for funeral announcements online, but would they really risk advertising it like that, when people are coming for them? Would they really make it that easy? I don't think so.

As I take a wander over to the Romance section, I see an unfamiliar but very serious face standing at the front desk asking questions and looking around. I step back behind a bookcase. Is that one of them? Are they here for me? Is nowhere safe? The man leaves, taking one final look over his shoulder before he pushes the doors open and returns to the bustling street outside.

Maybe I should try Kristina's flat. It's a private residence so they can't just wander in there, and I have no 'proper' connection to her, so they shouldn't even think to look for me there. I don't want to stay here anymore, clearly this was an obvious place for them to look.

I gather my stuff, put my Pippi Longstocking ginger wig on, and head outside. I try to look as casual as I can as I walk purposely in the direction of Kristina's flat, dodging slow walkers carrying bulky shopping bags.

Just as I'm walking behind a bus stop, somebody grabs me and pulls me into the hedge behind it. I scream, scrambling around to see who it is.

"Shh! It's me." Kyle.

"Great," I say, brushing some leaves off and attempting to stand up.

"We need to talk." I roll my eyes and sit back down. It's easier than carrying this heavy rucksack anyway. "Did you get our messages?"

"Yes. I'm in danger, they're coming; your mum's dead. Oh, and some detective called me too, so yeah, they really are trying to get hold of me. Well done, I'm now carrying my life on my back, and I don't know what to do!" I smile, but I'm unable to hide the tears that threaten to spill as I state my precarious situation.

"Look, I've pulled some strings and we're having the funeral today. Not a proper funeral, the body won't be there, but it's the best we can do within the timeframe. Adam's planned it, he's doing a speech, he's bought flowers and all that. But my mate who sent that initial warning said that they're coming for us. A whole team of them. Today. It's really not safe, so I wanted to make sure you got the message."

"Loud and clear; not even the bloody library is safe. I saw some man come in and look around and then leave."

"Shit. Well, you need to stay out of sight, but don't go home. They'll look there."

"Yeah, I've got one friend I'm going to try, but after that I don't know. I left my phone at home in case they can track it."

"Good idea. Look, we're their main focus so I think so long as you don't go home and they don't see you, you should be fine. I'd recommend moving though, when you can. Fresh start and you'll be fine. Unless you still want to see Adam? He thinks it's safer not to, but maybe?"

After all his efforts to supposedly get us together, you'd think he'd be a bit more encouraging.

"I love him." I state plainly.

"Okay, tell me your friend's address. When we leave the funeral, if all goes to plan and our escape begins, we'll grab you from there on our way out of town. Okay?"

"Okay." I give him the details, which are more like vague directions because it's not like I've ever written her a postcard. I know where it is, I just don't know 'where' it is. He seems to understand.

"But now seriously, go hide out." He stands.

"How's Adam?"

"He's a complete mess as you can imagine. You can kiss him better later. See ya!" He brushes off some leaves and climbs over the wall behind the hedge. A moment later, his head reappears. "Oh, one more thing."

"Yeah?"

"Your wig's wonky." He smiles and disappears.

Twit.

I adjust my wig and continue on towards Kristina's flat but before I even turn down the road, I can tell something isn't right. They have one of those secure entry systems on her building, but the door is wide open and it's not like somebody is moving in or out of the building: there is nobody around except a black BMW saloon parked jauntily across the road. I watch from the corner as I see movement through the windows on the stairwell, someone's coming. I creep behind a wheely bin for a better view.

It's Kristina. Whoever these people are, they have handcuffed her and are pushing her into the BMW. Wow. These people are serious. This is not just some petty dreamworld society, these people are like police or something. Shit. How am I supposed to lie low when I have nowhere to go? Where's left now? McDonald's?

No, I have a better idea. I'm going to the funeral.

I'm pretty sure which crematorium the service will be at, I think Adam mentioned it before. It's not far from here, and it's bound to start in the next couple of hours. Kyle probably pulled those strings of his to get a lunchtime service squeezed in. There's no way they could have done it at such short notice otherwise. The funeral celebrant is going to be going hungry today!

*

I approach cautiously, watching everyone else arriving. There aren't that many people. I suppose due to the lack of notice. Perhaps she was a private person; kept herself to herself, with her boys. It must have been hard raising them after their dad left. I wonder what the society made of it, her being a regular human raising Dream-Walkers.

I check the sign at the door to make sure this is the right place. It is. With my wig and bobble hat I feel unrecognisable. I dump my rucksack so it's hidden as best

159

it can be in a thick bush and make my way inside. I sit near the back hoping to go unnoticed.

Adam and Kyle are sat in the front row wearing matching suits. From behind, it's impossible to tell them apart.

It's a beautiful service, and I can tell Adam has thought carefully about each choice he's made.

When it comes to the speech Adam had apparently prepared, both brothers stand up. They glare at each other, and I imagine Adam is glaring to tell Kyle to sit down, but Kyle is glaring back to say that it's safer if they both stand. Kyle is probably thinking that if they do the speech together then if anybody is here to take them, they won't know which of them is Adam.

I do though, Adam is the one whose face is mysteriously bruised. Members of the congregation whisper to each other about the obvious discordance as they continue their stare down. Eventually, Kyle sits down. Adam takes a sip of water and begins,

"My mum, Dorothy Elizabeth Clarke, was a great woman. She was caring and protective and always, always, fought for what she believed in. She was accepting of others' differences, forgiving, and yet strong. She didn't take shit from anybody." He pauses for the muffled laughter in the room.

"When God decided to challenge her with cancer, she fought back, and she won those first few rounds. But the battle was too long, and she didn't have the strength to keep up the fight. I saw the light in her eyes fade away, but I will not remember her in that way. I will remember her how she was when I was seven and she used to take me to Cherry B's for a lemon iced bun after school when I was upset. I will remember her smile, and her ability to cheer me up. She brought sunshine to my rainy days." He pauses to wipe his eyes and blow his nose. "My brother will now join me to read the poem we have selected, 'She is Gone' by David Harkins."

Kyle stands, and together they begin reading. Adam's voice is shaking.

"You can shed tears that she is gone…"

As I listen to them read, tears stream involuntarily down my face and my nose goes snotty. A woman passes a tissue along to me. I can't help thinking how sad it is that I don't have that good, strong relationship with my mum, that we never made up. And here I am, about to run away again. I might never see her again and we've spent so many years silently blaming each other for things which weren't either of our fault. Of course she celebrated when she had Viva, she didn't think she could have a child of her own. I shouldn't blame her for favouring and spoiling her, it was only natural: she was her flesh and blood. And she shouldn't blame me for that accident, because it was an accident. It still would have happened had she been the one behind the wheel. She must see that by now.

Maybe I should try to call her again, it went well with Viva, we could clear the air, before it's too late.

What would happen to her if she needed the same care Dorothy did, if Dad wasn't around? Viva couldn't help, I know she'd do her best, but her ability to help is limited by her wheelchair. She wouldn't be able to help Mum up or down the stairs, into bed… One day they might need me, but will they call? Or is it already too late? Have we 'made our beds' now?

I hope not.

I realise everyone is making their way outside, so I follow with my head down over to the bush which holds my rucksack. I'm relieved it's still there and that I packed my tissues. I'm just zipping it back up, holding a fistful of tissues, as a loud bang startles me.

161

I look up and realise it was the door at the back of a Transit van slamming shut. The driver jumps in and speeds off, wheels spinning on the wet road, breaks squeaking as it takes a sharp left.

Was that them? Was that their escape plan? Have they just left me here? Or were they just taken? I curse my emotions for distracting me.

I look around at the remaining mourners. Nobody looks suspicious or bothered by the van, but I don't know any of them so, for all I know, they could all be Dream-Walkers or members of the HJD masquerading as mourners. I put my hand through the strap and swing the rucksack onto my back, the familiar weight now feeling comfortable and grounding. Everything I have left is in this bag. If I never return home, this is all I will have to remind me of this first chunk of my life. It contains one photo of Mum, Dad, Viva and me, amongst the knickers, socks, t-shirts and tampons.

I start to back away from the group as my eyes lock on a familiar face. The man from the library. Surely no coincidence there.

I run.

29.

I'm sweating under all my layers as I join the queue in the centre of McDonald's and yank my wig and bobble hat off. I begin rummaging in my rucksack for a different hat, shuffling forwards as the queue progresses. When I stand back up, I have removed my coat and am wearing a red jumper and a blue hat. It's not a massive difference, but maybe it'll help to prevent me being spotted from a distance.

I carry my tray of food over to what I hope is a discreet chair by the toilet. It's not close to the window so I shouldn't be spotted from outside. Plus, I can always hide in the loo if need be. (Not that I'd be able to escape from there though, my upper body strength isn't quite up to pulling myself out of small, high up windows like they would in a film).

My Quarter Pounder with Cheese is delicious. I hadn't realised how hungry I was.

I paid with my only ten-pound note in case these people are high tech enough to be looking at my card transactions. Paranoid? Yes. With reason? Yes. I hope Kristina's okay. I hope Adam and Kyle are okay.

Shit! If that was their escape plan, they'll have expected to grab me from Kristina's, but I wasn't there! I was at the funeral, hiding behind the other mourners! What if the people who took Kristina were waiting for them there? What should I do now? I have no way to contact them, and I know Kristina's flat isn't safe, so there's no point in heading there now... is there? If there was no one there, would they have waited for me? What would they think had happened to me? Would they have instantly set off to wherever they think I would have been taken?

I don't know what to do, I don't know what to do, I don't know what to do. I suck on my straw a little too strongly and ice-cold strawberry milkshake shoots up, giving me brain freeze.

I open my eyes and lower my hand from my head as a large and stereotypically sweaty man walks in and pulls out the chair opposite me.

"Can I help you?" I ask.

"You Ella?" He grunts, sitting down.

"Depends who's asking."

"I've got two lads in me van, gave me a photo of you, said if you see this girl, get her to come with you." He shows me the photo. It's a print-out of one Adam took when we were out walking and watching the sunset one evening.

"Those 'lads' in your van by choice?" I ask, sceptically.

"Yeah, they hired me to drive 'em to London. Said we needed to get you first though."

"Okay, can I see them first, or do you expect me to just get in your van and take your word for it?"

"Come outside and you'll see them as you're gettin' in. Okay?"

I study the man carefully. He seems like an average overweight guy with a van, probably doing this for some extra cash. He doesn't look like that other man from the library – he was much smarter dressed, and much more physically fit. I don't think he's lying, but I also don't like the idea of getting shoved into a van.

"Are you going to get a burger whilst you're in here? Maybe something for the 'lads' too?"

There's a moment of hesitation and I fear he's going to tell me he's on a diet, then he answers.

"Suppose I might; why?" I shrug.

"Just need a wee, you go order, and I'll come with you once you've got your food. Okay?"

Relieved the man isn't going to turn down the opportunity to grab a burger, I stand up and head towards the toilets as he turns around and goes to join the queue.

Just as I'm heading into the ladies', a woman comes out of the disabled/baby change loo with a baby in a pram. I walk alongside her back through the restaurant and out of the exit. Fat Man doesn't see.

Out in the car park I spot the white van from earlier. Are Adam and Kyle really in there? Are they there by choice? Should I run or find out?

I decide to walk past and say 'Adam' and 'Kyle' and listen for any movement.

I can't hear anything.

It must be a trick. I turn and see the man heading back outside with his brown bags of food, he must have realised I've gone. I hide behind the hedge and watch. If they're in there, he'll tell them what happened.

He opens the back door, throws in a bag of food, closes it, and goes to sit in the driver's seat. He starts eating a

165

burger held in one hand, as he opens a box of Chicken Selects with the other.

Well, what does that mean?

It means they're in there, or somebody is, and he's feeding them, but are they there by choice or not? How can I possibly find out without putting myself in danger?

Why am I so indecisive?

Assuming it is them, as that photo probably came from Adam's wallet because I don't think we put it online anywhere, I'm going to have to take a chance, aren't I? If it's them and they're stuck, then we'll be stuck together. If it's them and they're escaping, we can escape together. Surely either option is better than not knowing what to do on my own out here. Unless it's not them. But then, even then, at least it'd take some of the decision-making out of my hands. Okay, I'm going in!

I walk up to the van window and the man looks at me in surprise.

"Thought you'd done a runner," he says, wiping a greasy hand on his jeans and rolling the window down further.

"Nearly. But I've decided to trust you. So, let me in!"

"Alright." He wipes his face with the back of his chicken hand, takes a gulp of his drink and opens the door, leading me around to the back of the van. My heart is racing. He opens the door.

"Ella?"

"Adam?"

It's so bright outside that my eyes struggle to adjust to the darkness inside the van. I peer in, squinting, as he suddenly comes into focus, pulling me into a hug.

"I thought I'd never see you again! I thought you'd left me!" I kiss him repeatedly. Kyle looks away.

"All good in here?" Asks the fat man.

"Yeah, thanks Nige'," says Adam. Nige' waits for us to sit down and then closes the door. Adam grabs hold of my hands.

"I'm so sorry, Ella. I had no idea they would actually come looking for you. The HJD rarely bothers to investigate cases like this properly. I thought they'd just grab us two and punish us, using their own witnesses to corroborate their story. I can't believe they went to Kristina's flat too. Are you okay? I'm so sorry."

"Do you know if Kristina's okay? Do you know where they took her? I saw them take her away," I ask.

"No, but they won't hurt her. She doesn't know anything. They'll probably tell her some big lie about how they need to speak to you about something else, and once they accept that she doesn't know anything about us or where you are, they'll let her go." When I don't respond, Adam continues, "she doesn't know anything, right?"

"Well," I look at Kyle then back to Adam. "She doesn't know the latest, but she does know I dreamt about you before I met you." I bite my cheek. "I didn't know that was a secret back then!"

"It's fine. The main thing is, she doesn't know what we are. She'll be safe, even if she incriminates us." Says Kyle, giving Adam a serious look.

I survey the back of the van with the help of a children's Halloween lantern. It's littered with pillows, blankets and sweet wrappers like a children's sleepover.

"So, this is it? The big escape plan? Who is that guy by the way? Can you trust him? How much does he know?" I ask Kyle.

"Nige' is a friend of a friend. Completely trustworthy, I've been in that head of his so many times I can assure you all he dreams about is having enough money to get his daughter back off his ex and starting afresh somewhere new. He had some issues in his past which his ex used against him, but he's a solid guy. And he doesn't know anything about what we are, just that we need to get away without anyone seeing us."

"Okay, sounds good, and he said we're going to London?"

"He shouldn't have said that out there, anyone could've heard. But yes, that's part of the plan."

"Any reason?"

"It's a good place to lose yourself. So many people… I thought we could go to Hyde Park, Winter Wonderland. Make our escape fun, at least."

That sounds good to me, I settle down next to Adam and try to get comfy.

30.

Okay so maybe I should've actually gone to the toilet when I said I was back at McDonald's instead of sneaking out like some super-spy. I am bursting. That large strawberry milkshake doesn't feel so good now. You know those times when you're so desperate for the loo that you feel like you can see it? Your stomach feels like it is filled with wee, like instead of a pregnancy bump, you have a wee bump, and if somebody should press it, you will pee yourself? That's me.

Right now, I am glad there are no seatbelts in the back. It may be dangerous, but at least I don't have a seatbelt digging into my bladder to add to my discomfort. I'm not sure how much longer I can wait.

It has been hours, and so far, the boys haven't really said much at all. Adam's initial pleasure at seeing me has been replaced with a feeling of betrayal. But it's not my fault Kyle tricked me, and as I keep explaining, I still thought it was him.

I understand him blaming Kyle though, obviously. It is all his fault. And I have yet to uncover his ulterior motive.

The van stops and Nige' shouts through,

"You wanna piss break or you gonna wait?"

"Toilet please!" I shout. The boys look at me. "What? I can't hold it as long as you."

He drives on a bit further and then stops again. He opens the back door.

"I don't think anyone has been following us, but you should still make it quick. I'm gonna go grab a sandwich and then I'll be back." I bite my tongue to stop myself from asking how he's hungry again after all that food, and put my wig on.

"You coming?" I ask in the general direction of Adam and Kyle.

"Could do with stretching our legs bro, come on," replies Kyle, nudging Adam to move. I leave them to it and head in search of the toilets, doing that funny walk one does when one cannot stand up straight because one's bladder is that full.

I'm surprised to find the toilets are unisex, but also very well maintained – or perhaps they haven't had much use since the last cleaner was in. I've lost all track of time without my phone. It's dark, but that doesn't mean anything when it's pretty much dark at 4pm these days.

I sit, no 'hover', over my chosen toilet and empty my bladder thoroughly. (It may look clean, but I don't ever sit on public toilets). Ah. Such a long wee! Much better.

As I wash my hands I stare into the mirror and zone out a bit, suddenly feeling exhausted. I jump as a figure appears behind me; I didn't hear him come in. Kyle.

"Fancy seeing you here," he jokes, washing his hands. We dry our hands side by side at the dryers. "I was hoping to get a chance to talk to you."

"Okay," I reply, hesitant to know where this is going. I feel like I've just had a caffeine shot, I'm jittery and alert. I can't help that my body is attracted to him, even though I know he's not right for me. Even though Adam is my man. Why can't Kyle just leave me alone? Hasn't he done enough?

"I wanted to give you this," he pulls out what looks like folded paper, and places it in my hand, closing my fingers around it before I can get a proper look. His hands are warm and comforting. He looks into my eyes. "It's how I was able to get into your dreams, even when I was far away. I want you to have it back, so you feel like you can trust us, we're not in your head. All those dreaming days are over now, unfortunately." He winks.

"For fuck's sake, Kyle!" says Adam, entering the toilets. "If you wanted her, why didn't you just go meet her yourself?" He storms back out, and Kyle turns to follow, but hesitates.

"To be continued," he whispers into my ear before releasing my hand and walking away.

I open my fingers.

Folded up neatly in my palm is a piece of lined paper. A shopping list. My shopping list. He 'connected' to me through my lost shopping list. What the hell?

Back in the van, my head is still reeling.

"So, Adam, Kyle was telling me that he managed to get into my head by using an old shopping list of mine. Presumably he got it from you, as you were the one that fancied me from afar, so would you care to explain how and why you had my shopping list? Did you go through my bin?"

He's sat with his arms crossed and doesn't appear to want to talk. After a good few minutes of silence, he finally answers.

"You dropped it. I picked it up. I thought it might be poetry."

"Oh. Well, sorry to disappoint!"

"Adam's always liked poetry, haven't you Ad'?" Says Kyle.

"So?"

"Just making conversation. Maybe Ella would like to read some of your work someday."

"I bet she wouldn't."

"Oh, I bet she would," he teases.

"Oh just leave him alone! If he doesn't want to show me, he doesn't want to show me," I butt in.

Adam looks at me, eyebrows raised. What, did he want me to fight to read his poetry? His secret poetry? He told me about his horror novels, but he didn't say anything about poetry. It's probably very personal. Or creepy. Maybe he wrote poems when he was stalking me. They might put me off him; no, I definitely don't need to read his poetry.

We continue the journey in silence. I start to nod off and then remember who I'm with and do anything not to fall asleep. Kyle may have returned my list, but we're in the same van, I'm not foolish enough to think it's safe to fall asleep this close.

A phone rings in the driver's compartment and we hear Nige' answer.

"'ello? Ah shit man, really? Now? Ugh. Alright. Yeah, I'll be there. Just give me an hour." He throws his phone back onto the passenger seat and shouts back to us,

"I've got to do something; you alright if I drop you off somewhere else tonight and then take you to Hyde Park tomorrow?"

"Where are you going to drop us?" Asks Kyle.

"You know that hut I said about? I thought there."

"Yeah, alright, go for it," confirms Kyle. Adam and I look at him curiously. "It's a shepherd's hut in the middle of nowhere. We'll be safe there for the night."

31.

"You have got to be kidding me," says Adam. "Will we even fit in there?"

We all stare at the shepherd's hut in front of us. It's the only thing around, besides the gnats. Even the fields are empty of cattle at this time of night. Honestly, I think it's cute, but Adam does have a point, it is rather small.

"There's a king size bed, we'll be fine. Two in the bed, one on watch. We'll rotate." Answers Kyle.

"Err…" I start but can't seem to form words. All I can think is that sharing a bed with them, either one of them, but especially if they're rotating and confusing me, seems like a very bad idea. I'm not sure I trust myself, or them. Or my dreams.

"And it has heating, so don't worry, we don't need to snuggle," he adds, and Adam gives him a look.

"I'll go survey the perimeter whilst you two make yourselves comfortable," says Adam. I can feel the hurt in his words. He still thinks he walked in on us having a special moment in the loos.

I want to comfort him and reassure him that nothing is going on between Kyle and I, but he's not interested. He's gone cold. I know he's hurting, and this couldn't have happened at a worse time, but I just want him to listen and trust me.

"Shall we head in then?" Asks Kyle, unlocking and opening the door. It's surprisingly warm inside, he wasn't wrong about not needing to snuggle. I take my jumper off.

The bed takes up most of the space, then there's a tiny dining table set up with two chairs, a sink, kettle, minifridge, wood burner, and through another door is a shower and toilet. There aren't any toiletries or towels though. I turn back around to find Kyle lying on the bed leaning back against the cushions.

"I'm not going to do anything, you can sit next to me," he says.

"What more could you do anyway?" I reply suspiciously. I don't see how this situation could get any worse.

"Shh, you'll make Adam jealous again," he winks, clearly not on the same wavelength at all. How can I share a bed with him, after everything that has happened?

I stand, looking out into the darkness. It starts to rain.

"We can't just leave him out there," I say.

Kyle slides off the bed and begins massaging my shoulders, standing close behind me. Annoyingly, my body relaxes on autopilot, like in my dreams. My body trusts him, I can't help it.

"Why did you do this? Really? Right from the beginning, did you honestly just want to set me up with Adam?"

He sighs, continuing to work on my shoulders. I look down and he moves his hands to the base of my neck.

"It's complicated," he answers at last.

I turn to face him, inadvertently stroking his hands as I push them down to his sides. There is no space between us, our feet are touching in this narrow gap between the bed and the window.

"You made me fall in love with you; you know that don't you? No matter what I say, how much I deny it, I fell in love with you in my sleep."

I watch as he struggles to find the right words to say, and then his expression changes. He breaks eye contact and says,

"I did what I had to do. For Adam."

"Oh sure! So, none of that meant anything to you? Our dates, our sex…"

He continues to avoid eye contact.

"No. I did it so you would love Adam. I didn't plan on you ever finding out I even existed."

"Oh, come on! Don't you think you took it a bit far? We dream-dated for months! We had dream sex! Do you normally sleep with people you set up with your brother?"

"Well, I -"

"Sorry, by 'sleep' I mean have sex, in case that wasn't clear." I interrupt him to add. "Although, maybe I mean sleep too! Have you done this before? Dream-walked into his crush's dreams?"

"Look, I didn't plan to have sex with you, that just sort of happened. And once we had, well, the harm was done, wasn't it? Adam was taking ages to work up the courage to speak to you. I had to carry on dream-dating you until he was ready to introduce himself. I tried to get him to speak to you loads of times, but he kept wimping out, so I carried on. I didn't want you to lose interest."

"And you didn't feel anything for me? You were just doing it for Adam?"

He doesn't answer.

176

"Did you not at least feel guilty for what you were doing? I mean, no wonder your society has rules about this stuff. You manipulated the shit out of me. And Adam, technically. You deserve to rot in jail!"

He sits down at the end of the bed and takes hold of my hands.

"I wish I could tell you what you want to hear, but for now: you love Adam, okay?"

"I do love Adam. He didn't try to manipulate me," I say, looking back out the window at him as he wanders back and forth with a torch. "I'm going to go see if he wants a drink."

"Of what? Water? There's nothing here."

"Yes, I'll see if he wants a hot water, to hold if nothing else." I reply, stubbornly. I put my jumper and hat back on and open the door. I'm pleased to find the rain has reduced to just a light mist.

"I know what else you could do to warm up," jokes Kyle, reverting back to his usual annoying self.

"Oh shut up!" I say, taking a step out the door.

"I'm just saying, we used to get so sweaty…"

"Urgh!" I screech and slam the shepherd's hut door behind me. How dare he put that image in my mind after being so horrible and heartless. Now I can't stop picturing our naked bodies entwined and glistening with sweat as we catch our breath with smiles of euphoria plastered across our faces. Damn, those were some hot dreams. But I mustn't think about that, I must focus on making things right with Adam.

"Adam! Wait! Stop moving!" I make my way across the uneven grass towards him, trying not to twist my ankle down a rabbit hole. He stops, shining the torch on the grass to help me find my way.

"I thought you liked having alone time with Kyle, cosy chats by the fire, I bet it's really romantic in there, isn't it? Like your dreams together." He says bitterly.

"No, it's not like that. What you saw in the service station toilets wasn't us sneaking around behind your back. He just wanted to give me that shopping list back. That's all."

"It's never that simple with Kyle. Trust me, Ella. I saw how he was looking at you."

"Adam, please. I love you."

"But you loved him first."

"No! How many times do I have to tell you? I love you. What Kyle and I had wasn't real. Adam, please, come inside, switch places with him. We need to have a proper talk about this."

"I don't want to talk Ella. My mum just died, or did you forget that already? The world doesn't revolve around you. I just organised and hosted a funeral on the same day my mum died, after finding out that my brother had dream-sex with my girlfriend before we ever even spoke, and I might have to spend the rest of my life in a Medical Investigation Unit because of it. I don't even want to look at you right now. Just leave me alone."

"Adam, please," I try to hug him, but he pushes my arms away.

"Ella, I love you, but I can't be with you right now. All I see when I look at you, is you and Kyle. It's making me sick. Go back inside and just let me think."

"Adam," I whine.

"Go back inside."

*

Kyle puts his arms around me when he sees me enter in tears.

"He'll come around," he says, giving me a squeeze.

"I hope so."

We lie down and I suddenly remember what Adam said about Kyle having a nasty break-up. Maybe this is our chance to talk, for him to open up to me about what's really going on with him.

"Kyle," I say, looking out the window and watching as Adam's torch makes loops around the hut. He doesn't answer so I roll over to face him. "Kyle," I gently push his back. His breathing changes and a snore escapes. He's asleep already, I'm too late.

I roll back over and wait for sleep to take me too.

It's dark and bitterly cold, rain seeps through my clothes and runs down my face, into my eyes. I see a figure up ahead, marching up the hill in a soldier's uniform. He's carrying a gun.

I follow.

I can hear shouting on the other side. It sounds like a festival. There's a brass band, lots of voices. I think I can smell smoke from a bonfire. I hear someone else coming from behind and hide. He's short and stocky with tight brown curls. He passes and hurries to catch up with the figure ahead. They talk. I crawl closer in the wet grass to hear.

"You can't do this Kyle, it's not right. Let him go."

"No, he deserves this. He has to die."

"Don't you think he has suffered enough?"

"Does he look like he's suffering?" Kyle pulls the man by his shirt and points to someone over the hill. "Does that look like a man who is upset about what he did?"

"People mourn in different ways."

"That isn't mourning, that's celebrating. He's happy! He's having a party!"

"Don't do this Kyle."

179

"You can't stop me." He shoves the man to the ground and continues marching. At the top I see him crouch; the other guy continues to watch from his own place on the ground.

As Kyle aims and is about to pull the trigger, fifty arrows come shooting towards us from nowhere. One stabs me in my leg.

I wake up suddenly, grabbing my calf muscle as it cramps.

"Ow, ow, ow, ow!" I grimace, trying to be brave.

I look up and see that Adam has joined us inside, sat at the tiny dining table.

"Sleep well?" He asks. Kyle snores beside me. "You were in his dream. He shared it with you by accident. You weren't meant to see that, I'm sure. But then, neither was I."

"Do you think that was a memory? Has he killed people?"

"He works for The Resistance; I don't know what he's done; asleep or awake. He told me that he'd been in your dreams just so that you'd find me familiar when we met, and you know the truth about that. He's a backstabber, a liar, and I get to call him my twin brother. Lucky me."

"Do you want me to wake him up?"

"No, leave him, maybe he'll die in the next bit."

KYLE

32.

I toss and turn on the bed, sweaty and aggravated, until I kick the wall and wake myself up. Fuck. I'm relieved to find the other two have gone outside, that could have been awkward if Ella was still on the bed. I might have hurt her.

I need a shower but there are no towels or wash products; I wonder how long I have until they come back inside. I could risk a drip dry…

Fuck it. They've both seen me naked anyway; it'll do me good.

I stand under the shower head and try not to think about Isabelle and our times in the shower. She was wild. If I could just let her go then none of this would be necessary, but I can't. She was the love of my life. Philip was a psychopath. I should have seen it coming. I should never have left her alone. He was obsessed with her, and, after I proposed, it only got worse. If only I'd turned down that assignment; if I'd been there, if I'd been anywhere closer than fucking Iceland, I could have saved her.

He set fire to her apartment, and then tormented her in her dreams. I assume, anyway. The autopsy suggested that she died of smoke inhalation in her sleep. She didn't even try to escape. Izzy would never have slept through her apartment building burning down, she couldn't even sleep through a thunderstorm. He murdered her, out of jealousy. Because she chose me.

My dad's going to help me get revenge. He's the best man for the job, the way I see it. The most powerful Dream-Walker I know. I just have to get him out, which should be easy once I go down in Adam's place.

I turn the water off and try to brush the water off myself a bit, off my legs especially, then I shake myself like a dog and go and lie naked on the bed. It's not like we're going to be staying here another night, so it hardly matters if I get the covers all wet.

I must have nodded off again as I wake up to a small scream as Ella re-enters the hut.

"Oh shit, sorry!" I cover myself with the duvet. Adam isn't far behind her, I'm just standing up and wrapping the duvet round me a bit better, like a skirt, as he steps inside. He gives me a typical Adam glare. "I didn't mean to fall asleep naked," I explain.

"Of course you didn't. Like you didn't mean to date my girlfriend in her dreams. You're pathetic, Kyle." Says Adam, sending a globule of spit towards me.

He's always so fucking high and mighty. Obviously, I didn't fall asleep naked on purpose. I'm not trying to seduce his girlfriend, even if it is insanely tempting because of those super-hot dreams we shared and the way she is currently staring at my chest. She wants me. And I know we'd be good together, because we were good together, in her dreams.

184

But that's not the point, and it's not the plan. Adam and Ella need to stay together so that I can be the self-sacrificing twin who goes down for Adam so that they can be together. It has to feel that way to him, otherwise he'll doubt my motives.

For my plan to work, he needs to be feeling loved up again, which is the real reason I'm taking them to Winter Wonderland – he's sure to lose his mood under all those Christmas lights; there's no more romantic time of the year, is there?

*

Nigel doesn't turn up until it's dark again. I don't know where he's been, but I'm paying him enough, you'd think he'd bloody get a move on. We're all sick of each other, Adam still hasn't softened and Ella's moping around like a lost puppy.

Luckily, Nige' agrees to stop off for food almost instantaneously, so at least that rids us of hanger. I notice Ella cautiously sipping her drink; I bet she's anxious to avoid another toilet situation. Talk about blowing it out of proportion, you'd think Adam had caught us at it the way he's behaving.

When we finally pull up near Hyde Park, we can hear the crowds. Nige' lets us out and I hand him the rest of his payment, in cash, like some dodgy drug deal. I put my arms around Adam and Ella and guide them towards the noise.

"It's nearly closing time for the night, but I reckon you can get one go on the observation wheel; what do you think? Maybe re-ignite some of that romance in your lives?" I suggest. Adam pulls away.

"You two go on, I'll be in the German beer thing over there when you're ready to leave," he says grouchily.

"No, Adam, if you don't want to, we'll stay with you. Beers all round!"

Bless Ella, she's really trying. She hates beer. Ella's a wine girl, through and through. I would know, I endured months of the stuff.

"No Ella, I don't want to see either of you right now. Go off and have fun, I'll be there when we need to go." He pushes her away and wanders off.

"Okay…" Her voice trails. She looks hurt.

I lead the way through the crowds towards the observation wheel; I have to hold her hand not to lose her. That's my reason and I'm sticking to it.

I was right, the man in charge of the queue stops letting people join after us, we made it just in time. As we wait for our turn, Ella looks around in awe of the lights. I think she likes it here.

We sit down and begin our slow orbit, looking out over glittering London. She snuggles into me instinctively and I place an arm around her, to keep her warm. There's nothing wrong with keeping her warm.

"Ella, I'm sorry I got you caught up in all this. If I'd known he'd be this ungrateful, I wouldn't have bothered." I tell her.

"Really?" She raises her eyebrows at me.

Damn. It's like she knows what I'm thinking. If I'd known he'd be this ungrateful, I would've changed the plan – kept her for myself.

"Anyway, I should be the one saying sorry, for all the romantic stuff I made you do, you must have felt so awkward when you were only doing it for Adam."

Is she testing me? Daring me to contradict her? Is she into me too?

"Well, it takes two to tango!" I laugh. "I'll admit, I did feel bad for doing it, but at the same time, damn you made me horny! That hot tub idea…" I pull at my collar as if to cool down. She giggles. "I was so jealous of all the good times I thought Adam was going to have with you once you met. But then, well, I'd forgotten he was so rigid with the rules."

"Yeah. We never had sex." She confides.

She looks into my eyes, and I feel magnetised towards her lips. I try to resist.

"So, in some ways, you could say we were more intimate?"

"I suppose." She blushes.

"I can't betray my brother, again, but I can't deny that he was right about you. If ever there was somebody worth risking everything for, it's you."

Our faces are even closer now, as if the invisible magnets have upped their power. I know it's wrong, but I wish it wasn't. I wish I'd seen her first. Maybe then I wouldn't be obsessing over this revenge plot; maybe I'd have got over Izzy and fallen for Ella. Maybe we would have had a real fairy tale romance. Would one kiss hurt?

Our chair docks at the end of the ride and the bar rises. We stand up and are surprised to find Adam waiting for us. Ella's cheeks burn scarlet and I avoid Adam's eyes.

"Nothing happened!" Blurts Ella.

Adam doesn't say anything, just turns and walks away.

"Fuck!" I shout.

Then I do what I've been dying to do ever since I met her in real life. I pull her into me and kiss her soft and gentle lips. I dare to introduce a little tongue, how we used to. I start cautious and then I forget myself because it just feels so right. My trousers tighten. I pull away.

"At least now we have something to apologise for."

33.

Hyde Park is massive. Especially when you're wandering around in the dark looking for your stroppy brother who most likely doesn't even want to be found. Ella's shivering, but she refuses to give up. Eventually we find him sat at the foot of a tree.

I approach him first.

"Alright Ad'? Your bum okay? Not frost-bitten yet? You know I've arranged somewhere for us to stay, right? It has central heating and everything." The trick is to make him laugh, that way he can't be angry.

"How can I trust anything you say Kyle? If I go where you tell me to, you'll probably disappear in the night with Ella and leave me there to be caught by someone you've tipped off. Maybe that was always the plan, eh? Get me taken so you can have her all to yourself? Just leave me alone."

"Adam? Please, come with us," says Ella, stepping closer.

"Go away, Ella. It's not your fault, but what we had wasn't real. We're both puppets in Kyle's game."

"No! It was real, Adam, much more than some stupid dreams! Come with us, we'll handle this together!" Ella begs.

"No. I've had those dreams; I know what it's like. Dream-Walkers aren't meant to do that to each other, but they did it to me. Kyle did it to me. I've been in your shoes Ella; I know it felt real. It's okay, it's not your fault. Be with Kyle or don't be with either of us. But don't tell me that what you did with him wasn't real." Ouch.

Ella looks at me. It was just typical brother stuff. Humans play tricks on each other too, right? So we have an extra skill, of course I used it on him, like any older (by two minutes) brother would. It's no different to giving him a wedgie. Well, okay, maybe it's a bit worse. But really, it's not as bad as he's saying. I didn't fucking traumatise him like he'd have everyone believe.

"Go! Leave me alone!" He shouts, before storming off into the darkness.

"What should we do?" Asks Ella.

"Leave him to it, I guess. Come back tomorrow and see if he's softened up."

"We can't leave him! He'll freeze out here!"

"He'll be okay," I reassure her, putting my arm around her to warm her up. "Come on, let's go to where we're meant to be staying tonight."

*

Frankie is looking good tonight, she's definitely made an effort considering it's now 2am. She answers the door of her townhouse quickly and leads us, sashaying down the hallway, to the room we'll be staying in. There are three camp beds prepared.

189

"It's not The Ritz, but you'll be safe here," she says, smiling at me.

"Thank you," says Ella. I'm a little distracted by Frankie's low-cut top. Her boobs are almost falling out as she drapes herself across the doorway, her long red hair casually framing them.

"Where's your brother?" She asks.

"Not coming."

"Oh, but I always loved seeing the two of you together." She smiles. "The three of us go way back," she winks at Ella.

"Sorry, I didn't catch your name?" Asks Ella, clearly uncomfortable. And with good reason. This woman is unstable, but she loves me, so she's easy to manipulate. A place to stay in London? Bingo. Just don't let your guard down.

"Call me Donna. It's not my real name though, I don't want to get pulled into your mess!" She laughs. "These boys should come with a warning, am I right? Oh, we used to have such adventures." She strokes the front of my top, feeling my pecs.

"Did you grow up together?" Asks Ella.

"Oh, we did more than that, didn't we Kyle?" She winks at me. I wish she'd cool it off a bit. I'm hoping to get through this visit without sleeping with her.

"Actually 'Donna', we're really tired. We'd like to rest now, we've got another busy day tomorrow, you know…"

"Certainly. Well, if you find it too cramped in here, or she snores, you know where I am, Kyle. Otherwise, rest up, your secret is safe with me!"

Finally, she closes the door.

"Wow… Is she your ex?" Asks Ella, sitting down on one of the camp beds and starting to take her shoes off.

"Uh, sort of. We dated in high school but then I went away to join The Resistance. Technically, we never broke up."

"Well, clearly she still has feelings for you." Do I catch a hint of jealousy?

"Yeah, I didn't expect her to be quite so friendly." Especially after last time. "But I suppose, a lover is best in this situation. Rather that than have her resent me and tip off the HJD." I follow suit and take my own shoes off. My socks are damp.

"Hmm, so she's one of you then?"

"Yeah, I don't date regular humans, generally. It's just easier that way. Apart from in dreams, of course."

"Okay… So that kiss?" She blushes. I know she enjoyed that too. But I need her back with Adam.

"Just a one-off. I'm sorry. I couldn't help myself, and Adam was pissed off anyway, so I thought, why not?"

She shuffles down into her sleeping bag. I think I've hurt her feelings.

"Are you ever going to admit what we're really doing here? What the greater purpose is? Because I still don't believe this was all an accident caused by you wanting Adam to get a girlfriend." She looks at me like she's trying to read my mind. Thank God she can't.

"Nope. But I'll admit, there is more to it. You're a clever one, I can see why Adam likes you." I climb into my own sleeping bag, having removed a few more layers than Ella did. What? She's seen it all before, remember.

"Oh, so now you don't like me?"

"It's complicated."

She sighs and rolls over to face away from me. Then she rolls back, the sleeping bag rustling, and props herself up with her elbow.

"You're not going to invade my dreams again, or watch them, are you?"

"No, I meant what I said. I want you to feel safe."

"Okay. And that 'Donna', she's not going to either?"

"I wouldn't think so. If anyone is at risk of her entering their dreams, it's probably me."

"Okay." She turns back over.

It really is a risk; I've got to make sure I stay awake. I know what she's like.

When Ella's breathing finally changes to signify that she's asleep, and I'm sure Frankie is asleep too (probably waiting for me there), I sneak outside. On to the next stage of my plan.

ELLA

34.

I wake up, slightly flushed and smiling from a sexy dream about Adam and me finally getting it on, to the sound of knocking on the door. I scan the room; Kyle is no longer here. It could be him on the other side, or that Donna woman, or somebody coming to get me.

"Come in," I say, sitting up.

"My my my! I knew I could smell a love triangle when you turned up!" Donna sits down on Kyle's camp bed. Her hair still looks smooth and glossy, and she's already applied her day's makeup. I'm sure she's done it on purpose, to make me feel inferior. I'm probably rocking bed hair with pillow-imprinted face right now.

"What do you mean?" I ask, blushing. Did she watch my dream with Adam?

"Well, I was hoping to get up to some good old dream-world hanky-panky with the resident sex god last night, so imagine my surprise when I get into his dream to find he's dreaming about you! His brother's girlfriend! And he seemed to know you very well, if you catch my drift," she raises her eyebrows. She must be lying; Kyle wouldn't be dreaming about me. She's calling my bluff, and it's working. I stumble over my words.

"I, er, we, er, we've never done anything."

"Maybe not when you were awake, but in your dreams?" My face warms. "You should be careful you know, they're dangerous. We're all dangerous and you have no defence. Upset one of us and we could make you lose your mind, just like that," she clicks her fingers.

"There's nothing going on between me and Kyle, you can have him!"

"Oh, I know that," she smiles, "I can have him anytime I want. He knows not to upset me. And yet... last night... I can't imagine he did that on purpose knowing I might see... and yet, now he's left you here, with me." She laughs like a movie villain.

"What do you mean, he's left me here?"

"Well, can you see him? He's gone! Scarpered. Left you at my mercy."

"Did he say where he was going?"

She laughs again. "Oh, you sweet thing! Do you think I would tell you if he had? Me? The psycho ex-girlfriend he always relies on and then kicks to the kerb once again? Not anymore. This time, he's going to pay for using me." She comes to stand right in front of me, uncomfortably close. She looks down at me.

"Get dressed! We have somewhere to be!"

I do as I'm told. When I'm ready, I meet her downstairs at the breakfast bar. She offers me cereal and coffee which I accept gratefully with a helping of scepticism. I reason that she's probably not going to poison me because she could have killed me in my sleep already – both physically and mentally – and besides, I need the energy. It's a risk worth taking.

"We are going on a road trip," Donna announces, "I think you can guess where we're headed?"

"Wherever those people were going to take me, for Adam's trial?"

"Exactly. And did the boys tell you what the HJD does to humans who know and are no longer of use?"

"Not really, no."

"I didn't think so, otherwise you probably wouldn't have gone along with their plan quite so willingly, love struck or not. I tell you what, when we're in the car I'll tell you all about the last girl they tried to do this with."

"Excuse me?"

"Oh, did you think you were special? No. Sorry. This is something Kyle has been trying to get to work for ages. Stroke of genius using his brother this time though. The twin thing? Brilliant. Come on, let's get in the car, I'm parked up the road around the corner. It's a bloody nightmare getting a space around here."

With no better options, I follow. At least if she's taking me to the HJD I should see Adam or Kyle again; surely that's where they've both gone, for one reason or another.

The car is iced up, so she makes me scrape it off whilst she stands on the pavement texting and tapping her foot impatiently.

Once we're sat inside with the hot air blasting us, Donna begins.

"I suppose you've heard about their dad, right?"

"The basics. He was a Dream-Walker, he was better than people expected, he escaped with someone, and they later formed The Resistance."

"Their dad is the most prolific and dangerous Dream-Walker of our time. He did help to create The Resistance, but ultimately even they turned against him because even they were afraid of his power. He has been locked up in the basement of a MIU for the past decade. They don't even do tests on him for fear of him escaping. Every precaution is taken for dealing with him. The human scientists are fascinated and terrified by him. He's a monster. Imagine it's the turn of the twentieth century and they've got King Kong locked down there, it's like that." We pull up to a level crossing and wait for the gates. "But to Kyle, he's just his dad. He's an aspiration. He doesn't care how many lines his dad has crossed, he just wants him back in his life, a free man."

"Did you ever meet him?"

"Once. I think it was their tenth birthday party so it can't have been long before he left. It was the creepiest party I've ever attended. The clown was clearly terrified, their mum was super skittish, and after the cake, we all lay down for a nap. At nine or ten years old, we were a bit too old for afternoon naps, and Adam had already got his reputation from the sleepover, but nobody said 'no' to their dad. We were a mix of humans and Dream-Walkers in attendance, though most of us Dream-Walkers had yet to really discover or understand our skills. At that age they were mostly bedtime stories we were told by our parents. So, we lay down on the carpet, regressing to our five-year-old selves, and I can remember in my head I heard that song, 'in the jungle the mighty jungle the lion sleeps tonight...' as I drifted off to sleep."

We drive on in silence as she loses herself in her memories.

"You know the game, 'Musical Chairs'?"

"Yeah."

She takes a deep breath.

"I don't know if I can say it. I haven't thought about that night for so long. I had to get sleeping pills prescribed because I couldn't sleep afterwards and woke up screaming if I did."

She misses the exit she wants on a roundabout and takes us around again before exiting.

"He... he violated me. He violated all of us. Rather than one chair being taken away, or as well as, I guess, he became the final chair. The chair that you didn't want to land on. The chair that you physically pushed anyone out of your way not to land on. Fuck. Sorry, I'm going to have to pull over."

We pull into a layby. Her hands are shaking as she wipes her eyes and rummages around in the glove compartment for a packet of tissues.

"If you landed on that chair, he penetrated you, male or female, and then he slit your throat. There was so much blood, so much screaming, so many tears. I remember I woke up still seeing blood everywhere and I felt so sore, down there. I told my mum what happened, but she didn't believe me. None of the parents did. I didn't see Adam or Kyle in that dream, so I don't think they know what a sick man their father really is, but he is scum. He deserves to be locked up. I cannot let Kyle set him free."

"I'm so sorry, I had no idea."

"Yeah." She pauses before continuing. "I know I seem like a slut; like I'm obsessed with Kyle. But honestly, I'm more obsessed with keeping track of him and ruining his plans. I'm not taking you there to hurt you, I'm taking you there to stop his dad hurting anyone else."

"I understand." I try to smile encouragingly. "It's okay. I want to make this all right. Kyle used Adam and I want him to pay for that. He needs to go down."

"Mmm yeah, that might be where we disagree. Kyle can't go down. If he goes down, he'll be closer to his dad and more likely to initiate an escape plan. Adam will have to go down in his place. It's the only way to keep us all safe."

"Shit." I say, and silently mull this over as Donna drives us back onto the dual carriageway.

35.

We stop for coffee, and I remember Donna still hasn't told me what happened to the last person Kyle tried this plan on, so I probe.

"So, what did happen to the last girl?"

She pours some sugar into her cup and stirs.

"She's still there. I imagine you might get to meet her actually. You've heard how the MIUs test Dream-Walkers, well, sometimes they need a human to test their skills on too; to rate the skills of their 'participants.' Torturous skills, I'd imagine. I don't think she gets to sit there and dream of making love like you did."

"And how did Kyle arrange it that time? If he didn't use Adam, he can't have starred in her dreams?"

"He convinced his friend, or acquaintance, this guy called Mark, to dream-walk into her dreams and then start a relationship. He planned to get Mark to do all his dirty work for him, including being sent to a MIU and releasing his dad. But it didn't quite go to plan."

"Oh?"

"Mark wasn't cut out for life in a MIU, he was scared. He killed himself before the trial. But, of course, justice had to be served and they couldn't have a human wandering around knowing all our secrets, so the girl got her sentence in a MIU instead. Don't worry though, so long as Adam or Kyle or both of them go down this time, they'll probably just mess with your head a bit and then send you on your way."

"Will they make me forget?"

"Yeah, forget, go insane, I suppose it depends how much the judge likes you."

I sip my coffee.

"Is it much further?"

"About an hour or so, but we're not going straight to the trial, it doesn't just happen when you turn up you know, things have to be scheduled. We'll wait nearby until I hear it's time. Maybe we can find out what Adam and Kyle are up to whilst we wait."

"Mm," I agree. I suspect Adam has turned himself in, he's probably trying to make a deal so that I'm okay. But Kyle? I have no idea. If Donna's right, maybe Adam's in danger. Maybe Kyle is going to restrain him somewhere so that he can impersonate him and take his place in a MIU. Or, maybe they've both been captured and are currently arguing over who is who for the same reason.

I'm glad I'm not a twin.

I don't even look like my so-called family. That's one benefit of being adopted, I guess.

"Do you have any family?" Asks Donna, looking up from her phone.

"Not really, not that I talk to anyway, if that's what you're worried about."

"Adopted as a baby, then they managed to have their own child. Ouch, that must have been tough."

202

"Excuse me?"

"Oh, it's all over our Dreamer Chat, people are talking about who you are and how much of a risk you pose. The really interesting question is who your real parents are. I take it, you've never tracked them down?" She places her phone on the table.

"No, they abandoned me, why bother?"

"Curiosity I suppose, I don't think I could handle not knowing something so integral to my being. What if they're murderers? You might inherit it! Have you ever killed anyone, Ella?"

"I'm a strong believer in 'nurture' over 'nature' and no, I haven't."

"Makes sense I suppose. And you'd hope the same for Adam, what with his dad being like that... But you did get pretty close to killing someone, didn't you, your sister?"

"Oh for God's sake, why are we even talking if you already know everything?" I unfold my legs in frustration.

"Just checking my facts," she smirks. "Come on, let's get going!"

*

We eventually arrive at another regular looking house which is no doubt filled with Dream-Walkers. I was kind of hoping Adam might try to contact me in my sleep, to give me a message about what he's up to, but he'd be a fool to try that whilst I'm here. We couldn't have a bigger audience. The place is buzzing with chatter as we enter which rapidly stops when they see me. I automatically reach up to smooth down my no doubt frizzy hair.

"Welcome! Please enjoy your stay," says a drag queen all dolled up and strutting towards me, smoking.

"Thank you," I reply. There is a chorus of laughter.

Why do I feel like I've just been dropped into a pit of snakes? I swear I can hear the hissing. I am not going to sleep well here.

"Come on, I'll show you where you'll be sleeping tonight," says Donna, indicating some stairs. I follow obediently.

"Sorry about them, they're not keen on outsiders knowing about us. They'd probably rather kill you themselves than have you stand trial. But don't worry, I won't let them. I need you to make sure that Adam goes to a MIU, not Kyle. Okay?"

I look around at the room and groan inwardly, it's another camp bed with a sleeping bag. My back already aches from last night. The room is grotty with peeling wallpaper and motheaten carpet. Donna pulls some metal earplugs out of her handbag.

"Here, if you sleep with these in then that lot won't be able to walk in. Of course, that also means you won't be meeting Adam or Kyle, so, the choice is yours."

"Thanks," I say, putting them in my pocket.

"Dinner will be a buffet downstairs at six if you want it, and there's a shower down the hall. I'll leave you to it now; can't imagine you want to spend time socialising with people who want to kill you." She closes the door.

Okay, so in a house filled with Dream-Walkers who will definitely be watching my dreams tonight, wouldn't now be the best time to fall asleep and get a message? If only Adam or Kyle think the same thing and try to reach me during the afternoon too… It has got to be worth a shot.

I kick my shoes off and lie on top of the sleeping bag. Resting my head back, I close my eyes and try to relax.

The beach.

I feel the warmth of the sun on my skin as I paddle in the shallow water. The sand is soft, and my feet keep sinking as

I walk. I watch out for crabs and broken shells. As I'm walking, I think I see a figure up ahead. I shout,

"Adam!" but he doesn't turn around. I'm sure it's him. I start to run towards him, splashing the wet sand up my legs. "Adam!" "Adam!" I reach the man and put my hand on his shoulder as I jump around to see his face.

It's not him.

This is the heavily made-up face of the drag queen downstairs, laughing, mocking me. Suddenly I feel snakes wrapping around my feet, up my legs, pulling me down into the sand.

"No! Stop it! Stop it!" I scream, trying to break free. "Let me go!" The sand is up to my knees now. "Help! Somebody, help me!"

I try to think of Adam, to picture him saving me. This is my dream after all. I can control it, but they can too. Kyle said a lot of what happened before was down to me, so I put this to the test. Under the ground is a massive turtle and it's going to lift me up, set me free, and bite this nasty piece of work. I will it to happen as I scream, sinking further into the sand. The drag queen continues to laugh at me, lighting a cigarette and sitting down on a picnic blanket. Then I feel it, a rumble from below. Cracks form in the sand. The drag queen stands back up. I can't help but laugh. I did it! I'm going to save myself!

The turtle rises with me on its shell, and I jump to the side and climb out of the way. He turns his head to the drag queen. He may not be fast, but that queen is too surprised to move. He bites him in half.

I wake up, sweating.

"Well, I did not expect that!" The drag queen says, sat next to me. "You are stronger than most."

"Er, thanks, I guess… Sorry to ruin your fun."

"Do you have any Dream-Walker blood in you? In your family?"

"No. I'd never heard about any of this until the other day."

"Interesting." He opens a compact mirror and reapplies some lip gloss before blowing himself a kiss. "I wonder…"

"What?"

"Never mind, I'm sure you're not. It's not possible. Would be far too coincidental, impossible. I'm being ridiculous. Ignore me. Welcome to the safe house, we'll not bother you now." He starts to leave and then decides to ask one more question, his long nails wrapping around the doorframe.

"How much do you know about your birth parents?"

"Nothing really."

"Hmm." He walks away, leaving the door slightly ajar.

There's still two hours until dinner. I consider what he said. Could my birth parents have been Dream-Walkers? One, or both? How would I ever know?

And if I am one of them, or partially one – of a particularly unevolved and almost skill-less variety – would that mean that Adam and Kyle would be let go? Could this be our solution?

*

Dinner is a buffet of cold meat, salad, quiche and savoury bits with the only warmth coming from the freshly baked rolls. The lovely bakery scent almost covers the stench of nicotine coming off the drag queen.

I load my plate up, suddenly ravenous, and start eating whilst trying to ignore the gaze of everyone around me. I seem to be the only one who's hungry.

"We've been talking, Ella, and we'd like to help you. I'm Paddy, by the way," says the drag queen. I keep eating. "The date for the trial has been set, but it's not for another two days, and we think we can get you out of this pickle. Or rather, you can get yourself out of it, with just a little bit of help from us."

I swallow a mouthful of sausage roll.

"Okay, what do you have in mind?"

"Training."

I look at all the faces in the room.

"Like…?"

"We want to test your skills. We think you're special. Either one of us, or some kind of opposite of us – you have some innate dream resistance, and we think if we can really flex that skill of yours then you will be able to prove to the Minister that Adam or Kyle couldn't have committed that crime. In fact, you could even say that they committed the crime, because you wouldn't know anything about Dream-Walkers if the HJD hadn't come looking for you. Clever, huh?"

"But what skills? All I did was change my dream a bit, to stop myself from dying."

"I was leading that dream, Ella, you shouldn't have been able to do that. Not as a regular human anyway."

"But nobody will believe I was in a relationship with Adam and didn't know what he was, what about Transference?"

"If your head is as firewalled as it seems to be, it is entirely plausible that Transference wouldn't happen to you." He raises his eyebrows at me suggestively.

"Also," a voice chips in, I look for the source. It's a girl with black hair and piercing red lips, "we'd like to test some of your blood, have it run through the database and see if there are any matches. If your biological parents were Dream-Walkers, they will most likely be on file."

"You know how to do that? Safely?"

"Sure, it's really easy. Don't worry, we're not going to slit your throat!" She laughs, but I'm unable to join in.

"You can trust us now, we think you're special," explains Paddy. I notice Donna smiling and nodding encouragingly. Great. One minute they want to kill me, now they want to 'train' me. Who wouldn't be a little sceptical about trusting them?

36.

The next morning, my training begins. After my blood is taken, of course. I'm not entirely convinced by Goth-Girl's technique, but it won't be the first time I've had a bruise after giving blood – even the trained nurses who do it repeatedly every day still get it wrong sometimes.

She assures me she knows somebody who works in one of the MIUs who is going to test my blood for us and let us know. It won't take too long, but they have to wait for a discreet opportunity to avoid raising questions before the trial.

So, after a chocolate biscuit or three (definitely more than required for the blood volume taken), it's time to begin. Donna decides to go first.

"You lie down and try to go to sleep, then I'm going to enter your dream and try to control it. Whatever I do, you have to resist. Okay? Then others will also have a go, and then if you're still winning, we'll try other things. Like multiple people, or trying to trick you, because that's what the Minister will say happened if he believes you have some inbuilt defence, but he still wants to prosecute. He'll try to say you went along with their ideas, were still influenced. So, you have to remain in control. Anything that happens, you change it, you make it light and fluffy. But if we make it sexual, you still have to change it, don't get sucked in just because it's a nice dream, you have to stay in control. Okay?"

"Okay."

"This is going to be a tough couple of days for you, but I think you've got this. Do you want some sleeping pills to get you there?"

"No, I think I'll manage. Just close the curtains."

"Okay, you get comfortable, and I'll wait over here."

What am I doing? Am I seriously opening myself up to be tortured in order to prove that I can't be? What if they're wrong? What if it was just a fluke yesterday and I spend the whole of today being murdered in my dreams?

It's for the best though, right? If I can convince the Minister that Adam and Kyle are both innocent, then Kyle can't release their dad. If what Donna said is true, that should be my main priority here. I'm doing this for the greater good. That man cannot be released. I close my eyes.

Slowly I feel myself drift into my slumber.

I'm sat on a park bench. It's Autumn, a little chilly, but not too bad with my scarf on. Leaves blow past my legs, and I realise I am not alone. A horrible looking bird, perhaps a magpie or crow, lands on the back of the bench. I've never been good with birds. I jump up and start to walk.

I hear footsteps behind me, getting closer, faster. I start to jog, and then I remember. I am in control; I don't need to be scared. I stop and turn like I'm ready to face whatever's coming and all of a sudden, I am knocked over by a motorbike. I stand back up slowly, concentrating.

I imagine the sky brightening up and all the slippery leaves blowing away. With the path clearer, I finally spot my opposition.

Donna is standing by a tree to the right of the path, not far from where I had originally been sitting. She swishes her long hair and smiles at me.

"Are you ready? That was just a warmup."

Ants start crawling towards me from all directions, climbing up my boots. I stamp. No, no, I focus. These are not ants, it's glitter. Magic glitter, it puffs away and disappears. Success.

I look back at Donna and she's with somebody else now, holding his hand. She puts his hand on her bum and turns slightly so I can see who it is. It's Adam; or Kyle. She's caressing him, pulling him in for a snog. I can't watch. Suddenly I'm the one kissing him, being held, I'm licking his tongue, feeling him close to me. The warmth of his lips on mine feels so good.

"Ella!" I'm shaken back awake. "How the fuck did you do that?"

"Do what?"

"You pushed me out of your dream! I couldn't get back in! You took my place, didn't you? You were kissing him." Donna accuses.

"I couldn't stand watching you two and then yeah, I was kissing him. I don't know how I did it though."

"That's different to changing the weather you know, or making stuff happen to me, actually pushing me out. That's a big deal, even if it was spurred on by jealousy." She pauses, "you do know that was Kyle, right? Not your darling Adam. You just can't seem to stop cheating on him with his brother, can you?" She laughs. "I'll send somebody else in to try and crack you. They probably won't give you any sex scenes though, sorry!"

211

I'm surprised to see the next person who enters, he hasn't spoken to me yet. He's okay looking, kind of average, nothing special, but he looks like he probably works out based on the size of his shoulders and biceps.

"Just so you know, I've been told to make this hard for you, so I'm sorry if this ends badly."

"It won't," I reply confidently, rolling over to go back to sleep.

Okay, okay, okay, what shall I dream about... Oh. Chosen for me, have you?

I'm strapped to an operating table. A man appears to my right wearing scrubs and a face mask, I don't like the look of the utensil in his gloved hands as he looms over my face.

"Open wide Ella, this might hurt a little."

Oh my God, he's going to pull out a tooth. I try to scream and break free but, I can't, I'm tightly restrained. Even my head seems to be locked into place. He looks at me as he heads in with the pliers, he looks so smug, confident, arrogant. I picture him like a high school jock from one of those American movies – I bet he'd play American Football and have all the cheerleaders falling for him. I see him running and hear them cheer, then I realise, I'm no longer tied down, I'm in the stands watching him, cheering along.

"Well, I wasn't expecting that. I didn't even get to hear you scream in pain. Maybe you are something after all," says the man, eyeing me with respect.

Next up is Goth-Girl.

I'm in a dark room and I can hear something crawling around. Rats? I go to sit up and whack my head. It's not a dark room, it's a coffin. A coffin with rats inside. One brushes up against my leg: cold, damp fur. It smells of sewage in here. I hear a door creak open nearby.

"Hello?"

"Not dead yet then?" A voice whispers.

212

*"Oh no, I'm quite comfortable in here with my friends."
I reply calmly. This is my dream; I am not scared.*

"Really?"

*I hear some shuffling and through a gap in a side panel
I hear something else enter my coffin like in an 'I'm a
Celebrity Get Me Out of Here' trial. Something that hisses.*

*No. It doesn't hiss, it's not a snake. It's a feather bower.
A pink one, with strands of silver tinsel in it like I had when
I was little, in my dress up box with those little plastic shoes
we all loved even though they looked ridiculous. I picture
myself in the mirror with the feather bower and the plastic
shoes, and an awful big-brimmed hat Mum gave me to
protect me from the sun. We go out to the garden and the
paddling pool has been inflated and filled.*

"Okay enough of that! I don't want to see you playing in
a paddling pool! How did you do that?" Goth-Girl asks.

"I don't know, I just go where my mind takes me." I
shrug.

"But you shouldn't be able to. If we say you're trapped,
you should be trapped. You're definitely not normal."

I laugh, "yeah, I'm beginning to realise that."

37.

Day two of 'training' follows pretty much the same pattern, a Dream-Walker I don't know tries to give me nightmares, and I flip them around to whatever the hell I think of in the moment. It's completely random, and completely frustrating for them. I don't think they're enjoying my ability to resist their powers.

I've also been thinking, and I can't remember the last time I had a nightmare. You know, the kind which make you sit up and put the light on and read or watch something before you go back to sleep for fear of the nightmare continuing the moment you close your eyes. I thought it was just something you grew out of, like having your parents tuck you in at night or read you a bedtime story, but now I'm wondering. I honestly can't remember the last time I had a bad dream. I don't think I ever have in adult life.

One of my favourite dreams with Kyle was when I fell asleep watching 'Shaun of the Dead' so of course my dream was set in a zombie apocalypse – proper nightmare territory. I was stuck in my bedroom, looking down at all the zombies as they dragged themselves towards my building. There was a bump at my front door which told me they'd managed to get inside. I barricaded the door, leaving the windows as my only escape route. But I wasn't afraid. I knew he'd come.

I stood by the window until Kyle rode in on a horse and the zombies backed away, forming a semi-circle around him. I jumped down from my window onto the horse and we rode away into the sunset. Upon finding a deserted farmhouse, we then spooned naked in front of a roaring fire. Warmth surrounded me on both sides.

Hold on, if I'm so good at controlling my dreams, then maybe Kyle was telling the truth about me taking the lead in our romantic scenarios. Maybe he didn't even want me to fall for Adam! He could have initially entered my dreams planning to scare me but been derailed by my rom com fantasies! This could all be my own fault!

At dinner, I can barely face eating I'm so nervous. Apparently, the boys are now ready for the trial, but whether that's really both of them, and who's playing who, is unclear.

"You'll be fine, they probably won't even get to you until the afternoon, if at all. It will start with the witness statements," says Donna, helping herself to some salad.

"The people who reported Adam?"

"Yeah, and anyone else from your area that they've got to corroborate the story."

"Oh, okay." I think about the graffiti in the carpark. One of my neighbours perhaps?

"And don't expect there to be a defence attorney either. It will be completely one-sided; they will say their lies and theories and it will just be accepted. Try not to let it wind you up too much. I know the first time I saw one of these

215

trials I couldn't believe how unfair it was. It's nothing like your human trials except in name."

"And appearance," Goth-Girl chips in, "it's quite like 'Suits' or 'The Good Wife' in the room." Donna glares at her. "What? I like courtroom dramas…"

"Will I be able to hear what's being said before I'm called up?"

"Yeah, you get to sit in a little 'victim room', sort of like a green room for TV shows. You can watch it all on a screen until it's your turn."

"Will there be an audience?"

An older woman straightens up and joins in the conversation,

"I should think it'll be full, deary, those brothers are Dream-Walker royalty, or criminal royalty at least, thanks to their father. Lots of people will be interested to see if they are going to join him in captivity."

I hadn't noticed her before. She's the only significantly older person here.

"What do you know about him?"

"I've heard a great deal over the years. When he was out, he was vicious and powerful. He manipulated everyone he came into contact with for personal gain, or pleasure, or revenge. He was not a man you wanted to cross. I do feel sorry for his wife though, finally at peace, I don't think she knew what he was until she was pregnant and apparently any time she thought about leaving him, he manipulated her into staying. She'd all but lost her mind until he was caught. God rest her soul."

"She warned me about her sons," I tell her.

"As she should! And you should have taken heed of that, though I daresay it was probably too late by then." She pauses to lick some crumbs off her lips and swallow. "You're not pregnant too, are you?"

I nearly choke on my drink.

216

"No! Definitely not!"

"Well, that's something then." She reaches for a breadstick. Donna chimes in,

"Most of their relationship occurred in Ella's head, and let's face it, we've all realised now that she was in full control. They were probably manipulated by her!"

Everyone laughs and I can't help blushing. It's not true that 'most' of our relationship was in my head, I only dream-dated Kyle for three months, I dated Adam for over double that. But, if I was in control, does that make me a dream-rapist? Did I dream-rape Kyle? There I was blaming him, and it might have been me all along.

PART 3

38.

Donna was right, I've been taken to a so-called 'victim room' to watch the start of the trial. There's a sofa which has definitely seen better days, a TV mounted on the wall, and a water dispenser in the corner with some plastic cups. The man who led me here has now taken a seat by the door as if guarding me. The air is stale, and I sense this room isn't used much. I sit down on the sofa, and it creaks as I feel springs beneath the thin sponge layer.

There is movement on the TV screen and the camera zooms in on a woman dressed in a smart green suit-dress with a black blazer. I suppose she's a lawyer.

"We are here this morning to hear witness statements for the crimes allegedly committed by Adam Clarke. The crimes are: dream-walking into a human's dreams outside of a MIU, of doing so to create love, and of telling a human about our kind. These are very serious crimes, and the punishment, if found guilty to the full extent of the law, will be life in a MIU. This man should not be allowed to walk freely if he is comfortable manipulating humans to satisfy his sexual needs and risking our society's exposure. First we will hear from Miss Jessica Carlisle."

The camera zooms back out so I can see the judge sat up at the front, a stocky woman dressed in the usual black robes, with a boxed area to her left presumably where each witness will go to speak, and where I will ultimately stand. To her right is Adam, or at least I think it's Adam, but his face has healed so I can't be sure. He's dressed in a suit and sat as still as a statue. I suppose they want the jury to be able to look at him as all of this 'evidence' is provided, to see if he looks guilty. Although, perhaps not, since Adam and Kyle and even Donna said these trials are more for show than anything else. If they will be found guilty anyway, why the farce? Perhaps they enjoy looking at people they're about to send down.

Also in the front section of the courtroom is a man who looks like a mad scientist, or that time travelling character from that 80's film, 'Back to the Future.' He looks like that guy, Doc. His hair is white and stuck out with a life of its own. He's also wearing glasses, and a lab coat as if he has just stepped away from his experiments for a moment but will soon be back in the lab. I wonder if he always sits in on these trials, or if he's here because this is a special case.

My new acquaintances from the safe house are also watching in the audience, but the camera isn't focusing on the crowds. I can only see those sitting closest behind the lawyer and the Minister.

Miss Jessica Carlisle takes the stand and I think I recognise her. I'm pretty sure she worked behind the bar that night we went on that double date with the meal and dancing. In fact, I'm sure it's her because I remember her eyeballing Kyle when he ordered us a round of drinks. I thought she just fancied him like everyone else, but maybe that was a warning he chose to ignore.

"Miss Carlisle, please tell the judge what you witnessed."

"I witnessed sexual dancing and snogging between the victim and the accused, Adam Clarke."

"And what kind of relationship did it appear to be, to you?"

"A sexual relationship. They appeared in love and like they would no doubt be rushing home to have sex."

I gasp.

"No further questions," says the smartly dressed woman. "Please bring out the next witness."

Well, I think I've found the culprit behind the graffiti in the car park. Walking in now is my neighbour from downstairs, the one Mum suggested I date, with the bald spot and poor fashion sense. He hasn't even dressed up for court. His hair is a mess, his shirt isn't the formal kind, it looks like a very creased t-shirt material with a collar, and it's untucked at the back. His jeans are torn, in a bad way, with mysterious stains down the thigh area as if he has wiped his hands on them, a lot. In fact, the only effort I can see he has made is to put trainers on instead of those green Crocs he likes to wear with socks down to the bin store. If dirty white trainers can ever be considered effort.

"Thomas Harvey, you are Ella's neighbour, what did you witness?"

"A drastic change in behaviour spurred on I can only imagine by dream manipulation. She was a single woman, very single, very quiet, not outgoing, and then all of a sudden, she was going out with this new man all the time. It was very unusual for her."

I snort. As if my going out more is proof of anything! Jealous much?

"And did you notice him staying overnight at all?"

"I believe so." Liar!

"And do you have any reason to believe they weren't sleeping together?"

"I can't comment, but they looked very loved up whenever I saw them. They're adults, I would expect they would be."

"Thank you; Next."

This woman is rushing through the witnesses, I wonder how many there are. She shuffles some papers around on the table by her side.

"Next we have a transcribed statement from Kristina Carmin. As a human she does not know of our existence, however she does know the victim. I will read it out." The judge nods her consent, and she begins.

"Ella was a great Team Leader, but she didn't have much of a social life. One night, when we were out celebrating our company's 10th anniversary, she met a guy at the bar. They then went on a date but apparently it was awful because he turned out to be a bit of a stalker. Then she quit her job. Not because of him, but well, maybe a little. But then, when we went out to celebrate her quitting, he saved her from being raped. I think after that they started dating properly. One of my friends went on a double date with them. As far as I know, things are still going well, but we haven't exactly stayed in touch. We were only ever colleagues really."

I hope she's home safe now. They've obviously acknowledged that she doesn't know anything about Dream-Walkers. Thank God she didn't mention the dreams I told her about!

The next witness does not appear to be so thrilled to be there. Being forcibly pushed to the stand is the owner of Adam's favourite café, Cherry B. It seems everyone knows Cherry; she gets no introduction.

"I understand you know the defendant?"

"Yes."

"And you have witnessed Ella and Adam together?"

"Yes."

"Did you know that Ella was just a regular human?"

"Yes."

"Did you point out to Adam that it was inappropriate to enter into a relationship with her?"

"No, I prefer to mind my own business, unlike some people." She scowls around the room.

"Did you ever see them kiss?"

"Only maybe a peck, nothing significant. Adam is a gentleman."

"You've known him a long time, has he had many relationships?"

"No."

"Why do you think that is?"

"Just hadn't met the right girl, I suppose."

"And you suppose Ella is the right girl?"

"Romantically perhaps. I don't think everything is so black and white as you people say. You know their mother was a human, right?"

"Yes. And that woman suffered. Do you want Ella to suffer?"

"No. Adam is not like his father."

"Did he not scare all of his classmates as a child?"

"That was not his fault, it wasn't deliberate. You know how it is when these skills develop."

"Ms Bakewell, do you or do you not believe that Adam and Ella are in love?"

"I do."

"And do you also believe that they are engaged in a sexual relationship?"

"I do not. He's a gentleman, and he's not stupid. He wouldn't do that unless he was absolutely one hundred percent sure that she was the one. He wouldn't let just anyone in on our secret. He is not the criminal you are painting him to be. He is innocent! Innocent! And, has anybody questioned his brother? I witnessed his arrival into town, when Adam and Ella were sat by the window and the look on that girl's face when she saw he has a twin... All I'm saying is if anybody did manipulate her, it was Kyle. Not Adam."

"Thank you, Ms Bakewell. We'll now take a short break."

The volume in the courtroom increases so much that I look around this room for a remote control.

I wonder if they have Kyle on standby for questioning. They must have known fingers would be pointed at the other twin too. But then, what if the person sat there is Kyle, pretending to be Adam?

39.

Apparently, they are questioning Kyle outside of the courtroom. In other words, they've decided which brother they wish to punish for this and are in agreement with Donna - Kyle can't go down. The question is, of course, can they tell them apart? The Adam I've been watching has barely moved, giving nothing away.

It's my turn next and I am shitting myself. I'd say literally, but I'm not literally. Although I have been to the toilet twice in this break already. I feel positively unwell thinking of the plan and what's going to happen, wondering whether they'll believe me or not. I might get Adam off the hook, but I'll also be throwing myself under the bus. I don't want to be an experiment any more than they do. Especially when I don't even know what I am, as I am apparently something.

I approach the wooden stand and confirm my name, preparing for questioning. Donna and the group from the safe house smile at me encouragingly. I try to catch Adam's eye, but he stares straight ahead. I still can't tell if it's him or not.

"Miss Thompson, do you know what a Dream-Walker is?" The woman begins.

"Sort of, vaguely."

"And how did you come to know that?"

"Kyle told me when he said people were coming for us and Adam."

"So you didn't know until Kyle, the twin brother of Adam, told you?" She asks, walking towards me.

"That's correct."

"How did you meet Adam?" She continues walking around the space.

"At a bar on a work do. As explained in Kristina's statement."

She spins around to face me again.

"In your own words, please, never mind what others have said. How did it go?" She's pacing.

"He invited me out for a coffee on the Sunday."

"Do you normally go out to meet strangers for coffee?" She stops right in front of me, making me doubt myself.

"Well not recently, and not without messaging them a bit first... I mean technically, doesn't everyone who dates online ultimately end up going out to meet a stranger? You never really know who you're talking to until you meet them. Even then, people lie. I'd given up on dating in general, but our meeting felt special; I wanted to get to know him."

"So, you fancied him?" Her hands are on her hips, mocking me.

"Yes."

"Would you have perhaps referred to him as 'the man of your dreams'?"

"Maybe. It's a popular turn of phrase."

She rolls her eyes for the benefit of the audience.

228

"Had you ever dreamt of him, before you met?"

I look away from her gaze and glance at the jury. Okay, here goes…

"Okay, I know what you're trying to get at here, but it's not quite that simple."

I see the Minister (mad scientist man) straighten up in his chair.

"I did meet someone of his appearance in my dreams, I recently found out it was his brother Kyle actually, but regardless, I was not manipulated. Nobody can manipulate my dreams."

The woman laughs in my face.

"That's impossible! Look, I understand that you care about them, but that is a ridiculous statement. You dreamt about your dream man, whichever one it was, and then you started a relationship because of those dreams, is that fair to say?"

"No. Not because of those dreams. Because of our relationship in real life."

"But you didn't like him at first, you said he was a stalker, isn't that right?"

"He just didn't come across well on a first date. He hasn't dated much."

"Well, I imagine it's hard on a first date, keeping all those secrets, but once he got to know you, let you in, things went better I assume?"

"He never told me anything, he never would have. I wouldn't even know about you people if you hadn't come for us, so Kyle felt it necessary to tell me."

"So, you never had sex?"

"No."

"People saw you kissing."

"So? We can kiss without having sex, it is possible. It's called self-control!"

"Okay, suppose I believe you. You're very defensive about it. I suppose he made you quite sexually frustrated. What about when you were dreaming before you met, how sexual did things get then?"

"In my dreams, I got carried away at times. But it was me getting carried away. I was in control. I control my dreams. No crime has been committed here. Maybe an attempt, but I only ever have the dreams I want to have. I can't help it. It's an instinct, an automatic reaction. If something bad starts happening, I flip it."

The Minister asks the smartly dressed woman if he may speak; she nods. He stands,

"Miss Thompson, when did you become aware of these abilities?"

"About two days ago, before I came here. I was taken to a safe house filled with Dream-Walkers and one of them tried to give me a nightmare or torture me or something, and I changed it. He was so shocked that he told the others, and then over the next two days they all tried it, but I always won. They're sat down there if you want to ask them." I point.

"Ignoring the blatant breaking of the rules about dream-walking outside of a Medical Investigation Unit, that's fascinating. But it is also quite impossible. I'd love to observe you do it, will you allow me that honour?"

"What, here?"

"No, overnight, I'd like to observe you before we proceed with this trial." He, the judge and the lawyer share a look of agreement.

"Just one night, right? Just to prove what I can do? Then I'm free to leave?"

"Of course, it's purely voluntary to help us with this trial and then you can be on your way, if you still want to leave. Although, you may wish to stay and learn more about yourself. I imagine this is quite a new and exciting development for you too. I'm sure you would also like to learn what you are capable of."

That doesn't sound like a one-night stay, but I don't think saying no is an option, so I agree.

Before I am led out, somebody opens the door at the other end of the courtroom. It's Goth-Girl and she's got a paper folder in her arms. The guards escorting me pause to watch. She walks straight up to the smartly dressed woman and whispers something to her before handing her the file. That woman then whispers something to the Minister who practically salivates. I swear, I can see the gob from my stand. It must be my test results, and clearly, they're interesting.

I wait eagerly to hear what they're going to say, if they are going to reveal the results because surely, they are relevant to the trial, but instead the lawyer wraps up.

"Thank you for your assistance today, Ella. We can see now that this is not such a cut and dry case. We therefore invite you to stay under observation tonight and will bring you back to continue the trial at a later date. Thank you so much for your co-operation. We look forward to getting to the bottom of this with you."

My escorts each grab hold of one of my arms and lead me away. I am no longer being treated like a victim. I look back at Donna and she winks at me. Is that supposed to be comforting?

I didn't like the sound of 'a later date' rather than 'tomorrow'. I think I may have made a terrible mistake. I struggle to look around at Adam one last time, but he has already been led through another exit.

They lead me to a lift that goes down to a basement level. It smells like a hospital. Behind very thick glass, I pass people sat in cells on their own looking depressed. That's going to be me soon.

231

We make a few turns down various corridors until I completely lose my bearings and then we arrive at the cell destined for me. The only furniture inside is a small bed with a white duvet cover and pillow. Oh, and there's a toilet. Yep, it really is like prison, only glassy.

"You'll stay here until you are called," says one of the men.

"Okay but you know I'm not one of them, right? So, I don't need all this thick glass? I can't dream-walk. I could stay in a hotel, report in for experiments... I'll co-operate, you don't need to treat me like a prisoner."

"The glass is not to protect us from you, it is to protect you from them," the other man explains, looking around at the other prisoners in glass cells nearby. His voice is soft with a slight Spanish accent. "I heard you say you can control your dreams, but maybe you will want some rest."

"Okay, thank you. Will it be long before I'm called?" I ask from inside the cell. They both shrug and walk off. Great.

I look across at the person opposite; he looks insane with crazy eyes, scratching his arms. If I didn't know any better, I'd guess maybe he's a drug addict. But surely they wouldn't lock up a drug addict. This is a MIU isn't it, these people are just used for experiments, they're not criminals and lowlifes... are they? Come to think of it, you do have to commit a crime to end up here, generally, so actually these could all be murderers and rapists and paedophiles. People like Adam and Kyle's dad.

What a place to stay.

Maybe I am glad for the glass.

40.

Nobody comes to see me for the rest of the day. It is me, myself, and I. And a toilet. Not that I need to go when I haven't had anything to eat or drink and did a higher-than-average number of 'deposits' before the trial started. It's quiet, but that's probably because the thick glass blocks out all sound; I feel like I'm in an air lock or, you know, like when your ears need to pop as you go through a tunnel on a train or take off on a plane. The glass is quite reflective so I catch my own eye, and I also catch the eyes of those around me. Like the creepy guy opposite.

Whoever he is, he's developed a keen interest in me. He keeps looking at me as he scratches his arms to pieces. I can see the redness from here, and it looks painful. I wonder why he's doing it. Is it drug withdrawal like I first thought, or is it because of something that has been done to him? One of the experiments?

The lights stay on overnight, so I have to guess when it's time to lie down and attempt sleep. When I do, the feeling is strange. With no external influence, nothing to fight off or flip, my dreams are dull. I feel like all my creativity has been zapped away by these glass walls. I feel like a water droplet, slowly running down a window. Perhaps a child watches me from inside a warm car on a long journey, but my mind is blank. I am a water droplet. I sit and then I run. I reflect and refract the city lights we pass by. Inside my cell, I have no personal thoughts, wants, desires, I am only an object, to be observed.

I'm not foolish enough to think that I am really alone. I might feel alone, and I might see that man across from me appear to be alone, but I have also noticed the tiny red light in each corner of the room. I know I am being watched and listened to. I also do not trust that if I were to dream of something personal that it would not be seen. The glass beside my bed is different. Whilst three walls are regular thick transparent glass, the fourth is opaque and shiny. I believe that sometimes a Dream-Walker sits behind there to watch or influence the dreams of the cell's unfortunate resident. I can't take anything I've been told without a pinch of salt. How do I even know if this is a MIU and not a prison? It definitely feels like a prison.

Food is delivered to me when I assume it is morning. Dry toast and orange juice. Couldn't they at least provide jam in an attempt to convince me that I'm going to be allowed to leave soon? I'm not feeling very encouraged by this situation, at all. Also, I want to know what was so interesting about my blood results.

It was a different man who delivered my food and then collected my tray afterwards, and he refused to say anything at all. I assume the trial is resuming today, but they will need to run tests on me before they make any final decisions. Surely, they won't just lock me away for testing and then prosecute Adam anyway, will they?

I try to do some yoga stretches to pass the time and keep myself nimble. The bed here wasn't any better than those camp beds I've been sleeping in, it has a thin springy mattress on top of a solid unmovable concrete base, so all I could feel were springs and then as soon as I moved my leg, I felt the cold chill of the concrete surrounding and quickly curled back up again.

It was pretty fresh in here overall actually, with no sign of a thermostat or anybody to ask for an extra blanket. At least moving around now warms me up a bit. I focus on the stretches and don't bother trying to practise any pranayama; the thought of clearing my mind for meditation sends shivers down my spine every time I look at that one opaque wall.

I know I'm being watched on the cameras, but I wonder if there is anyone on the other side of that wall, sitting patiently, ready and waiting for an opportunity. I know that I have beaten everyone who has tried to give me nightmares so far, but that doesn't mean I'll be able to beat everyone. And what if there are other things they can do, which they develop in these testing facilities? I don't want my head to be messed with. I just want to know what is going on and when I can leave.

When it is lunchtime (apparently) I am provided with a plain ham sandwich – no spread, just brown bread with a slice of cheap reformed ham between it. And a plastic cup of water. They don't even trust me with glass.

"Gee, thanks!" I say to the man who delivers it. Again, he chooses not to respond.

"What can I expect for dinner?" I ask when he returns to take my tray. He looks at me, smiles, and closes his eyes deliberately. I close my eyes too. I see in my mind a plate of plain rice, spat on and stirred, with some small chunks of plain processed chicken scattered on top.

"Lovely," I say as the door closes and locks behind him.

235

He's probably having me on, but I don't think the food will be up to much, spat on or otherwise. I need to get out of here. I didn't agree to come sit in a cell indefinitely, I agreed to be observed, tested, to prove my skills and Adam and Kyle's innocence. Me sitting here is proving nothing.

I decide to try to attract some attention. I stand up and walk towards one of the corners of the room, hands on my hips.

"Hello!" I wave.

"I'd like to speak to somebody about my voluntary stay!"

"I'd like to proceed with the testing and have an update on the trial!"

"Hello?"

"I didn't agree to this! Hello!"

I keep going like this for what feels like an hour but is more realistically twenty minutes. The only attention I seem to get is from the crazy man across from me. And I already had his attention. Now he's waving at me! I wave back.

He points to himself, then makes a heart shape with his hands and then points at me. I love you. Urgh! I turn my back to him.

I sit back down on my bed and try to avoid looking in his direction. It's quite hard because his movement keeps attracting the attention of my eye as it reflects in the glass.

The next movement is today's food man again, but this time he doesn't have a tray with him. He opens the door and says,

"You have a visitor. Come with me."

I follow him down and around the confusing corridors and into the lift. We exit on a different floor, and I'm led to another room which looks like a very clean lounge. My visitor is waiting on a sleek red leather sofa. Donna.

The door is closed, and we are left alone, except for the cameras of course.

"What's going on? Why haven't I been tested yet? Do they not believe me? Are they sending Adam down?" My questions tumble as softly as a tonne of bricks.

"Today they've been questioning Adam, or rather, they think they have. I'm still not convinced it's not Kyle, but I don't know where 'Kyle' is, so I haven't been able to check. Just in case, we can't let either of them go down, so you need to prove yourself to the Minister. They will probably come for you tomorrow, I'm sure you'll be fine. You handled everything we all threw at you."

"So, they do believe me then? Or that it is at least possible?"

"Some do, some don't. The Minister is very intrigued, the judge just wants to get it over with. Testing you means the trial will last longer. She normally takes a long holiday at Christmas, she's keen to fly out to Lapland with her grand-children."

"Right, of course. And do you know what my blood results were? I assume that's what was brought in before I was taken away?"

"I don't know, but I think that's what swung it for them to take testing you seriously. I think they found something unusual. Maybe your biological parent or something else. They test it for all sorts in this place, they could have found another anomaly or anything. Honestly, if I knew, I'd tell you."

"What like you told me I'd be thrown in prison if I tried to save Adam and Kyle with this stupid plan? Because that's where I am, isn't it? I'm kept in a cell with a toilet and a bed!" There's no way Goth-Girl hasn't told her what was on my blood report.

"Hey, you knew you'd be tested, and you agreed. You wanted to set the facts straight."

"But you're the one who didn't want Kyle to go down for it, I could have happily just blamed Kyle to set Adam free and been done with it."

"Then they would have messed with your head instead. Would you rather be insane or locked up?"

"Neither!"

"Well, we're a secret society Ella, and we kind of do what we want. The Minister is a little different, I'll admit – he's not one of us. But he is in charge of many of us and he has plenty of people on his side that will keep you here for as long as you interest him. Leading the Human Justice Department, he will reason that they need to test you to ensure you are safe and well enough to re-enter human society, but really, he will want to hold on to you until they know if your abilities are more widespread in the population, if there are others out there like you who can resist our wanderings. You might be the start of a whole new experimental area. Participant A, or whatever. I don't even think The Resistance would help you, and they love a fight with the HJD, but they help their own, and well, you're not one of us or them. So, you'll just have to do as is decided. It's probably best if you don't make a fuss."

She stands up.

"Maybe you'll get lucky. We'll just have to wait and see how your testing goes tomorrow. I'll let you know what happens to the boys if you remain out of the loop. I'll be your connection to the outside world; they like me here." She swishes her hair and nods to the man on the outside of the glass to open the door. She leaves and soon he re-enters to escort me back to my cell.

41.

It's been hours and I still can't sleep. I'm just lying here looking at the featureless ceiling. There are no passing thoughts to latch onto, nothing to help me sink into my slumber.

Maybe I'm a dream-leech. I can't sleep without sucking onto somebody else's idea or intrusion.

But I used to sleep, didn't I? I can't remember what I dreamt about before Kyle entered my dreams, but I'm sure I did.

Or was I always stealing ideas from others?

I close my eyes again, going for the traditional option of counting sheep. I can't even visualise sheep! I count anyway. 1, 2, 3, 4, 5, 6, 7, 8, 9, 10, 11, 12, 13, 14, 15, 16, 17, 18, 19, 20, 21, 22...

"Hello? Can you hear me?" Says a manly voice.

I knew someone was on the other side of this wall!

"Please, don't flip this dream, I have a message for you."

"Who are you? A message from whom?"

"Who I am doesn't matter, the message is from Adam," says the voice. I'm not sure if I'm awake or asleep. I must be asleep, how else could he be doing this? But I feel so awake.

"Is he okay? What's happening out there?"

"Let me just repeat the message."

"Okay."

It's like he presses play on a video, and suddenly I hear Adam's voice.

"Ella, I'm sorry. I had no idea what Kyle was planning. I should never have spoken to you that day our eyes locked at the bar. I should have known he was up to something. He was always scheming, even when we were younger. But I had no idea he would sink this low. He will pay for what he has done to us, but I'm sorry, I can't see you again. It's not right. It's... disgusting. I'm so sorry. I should have known."

Silence.

"Is that it?"

"Yes."

"He's never going to see me again? What, he's just going to leave me here to die? To be experimented on for all of eternity because of his brother? What the hell? No! You send him a message, okay? You tell him that I'm not accepting that. He owes me. Kyle doesn't get to win like that, to tear us apart. Tell him to come and save me or, or..." my voice trails off, what could I do?

"No, I'm not a messenger, I only agreed to deliver one message and that was it. You're alone now. Good luck."

"No! Come back here! I am not alone! Adam will save me, he will, he loves me."

"Are you sure about that? You betrayed him, as did his brother. I doubt you will ever see him again."

"Well then Kyle can save me! It's all his fault anyway!"

"Kyle is busy with his own plans."

240

"Please! Wait, don't leave me, tell me what else is going on out there, what is going to happen to me?"

"Goodbye Ella, sleep well."

I open my eyes. Was that real?

Was Adam really sending me a message that he's never going to see me again? What does that mean? Has he run away or is he being sent down for Kyle's crimes? It doesn't make sense! He would never leave me here, he loves me.

Maybe it was just a trick, somebody playing with me, because I wouldn't flip a dream that could be real... That must be it. It was a test, they're just messing with me, trying to make me feel like I'm all on my own; to make me feel vulnerable. Trying to wear me down before they test me so that I lose. Adam would never leave me here, no matter what. And what did he mean, 'it's disgusting'? What's disgusting? Me kissing Kyle, which I had no choice in, or the whole scenario (which I'll admit is quite messed up, but not technically disgusting since it wasn't even real)?

Or is there something else that I don't know? Something in my blood? Is he repulsed by whatever I apparently am?

No. I'm not playing this game. They are not getting in my head. If anybody wishes to talk to me, they will do so in person. Otherwise, I'm not believing it. The only person I am trusting now, is myself. I got myself into this mess by fancying Kyle when he strolled into my dream, so I can get myself out of it too. I am stronger than I look, even if I am starving and ironically sleep deprived. I can do this, whatever 'this' turns out to be. I am ready. I am strong. They won't know what's hit them.

Ha! If only I felt so confident as my pep-talk implies. I keep repeating it to myself in the hope I might start to believe it. I am strong, I will win. I will not spend my life here. This is only the beginning.

The door opens and the offering suggests it's breakfast time again. This time there's a hard-boiled egg to accompany my dry toast and orange juice.

"When I bite into it, is it going to be rotten, or is this actually a rare treat by this prison's standards?" I ask, sarcastically.

"Eat up, you need your strength today," says the food man.

"Oh really? Excellent."

So, today's the day then. Donna was right.

After my tray has been taken away, I do some more yoga stretches, a poorly remembered sun salutation, and continue my pep talk. You got this, girl!

They come for me sometime before lunch and lead me back through the maze of corridors. I must stink, I haven't had a shower since the 'safe' house and my hair feels as greasy as a used frying pan. I wonder if they'll let me wash and change first. I'm sure that's what happens in regular court, prisoners are made to look somewhat presentable before they're sent down for life, aren't they? And anyway, I was brought here as a victim, I should be being looked after, nurtured, cared for, not degraded like this.

But no, there are no toilet stops. I find myself back where I was previously, on the stand, but now looking entirely repulsive.

The smartly dressed lawyer is back again, wearing a purple suit dress this time, and she looks smug.

"Ella, welcome. Today we are going to test your theory, to see if you are right and if no dream manipulation was committed due to your ability to maintain control of your dreams. To your left you will see what looks like a jury. Today, they are not. Today they will be attempting to give you horrifying dreams, one by one, and then in unison. All you have to do, is rebuff them all."

"And then what?"

"And then Adam goes free."

"But what about Kyle and the other charges? What about me?"

"Please, bring out the bed." The lawyer instructs the security men on the door. They wheel around a hospital bed and place it at the front of the room.

I look at the audience. So many keen faces, I wouldn't put it past them all to have a go. But it's fine, I'm strong, I can do this. I have no reason to believe that I can't. So far, so good, eh? And if I'm stuck in experiments forever after this, I'll find a way out. This is not the end.

Just as I'm being forced to lie down and am having my arms and legs restrained like a psych patient, I swear I catch a glimpse of Kyle, or Adam, at the back of the courtroom.

But, he couldn't be here, right? Either of them. At least one must be in custody, the other would surely be miles away by now. Right? Why would he be here to witness this?

What am I even doing here? What has happened to me? How did I go from being a loner in a boring job to being tied up in front of people ready to fight in my dreams? In my dreams! When did I lose my mind? When did I have an accident and go into a coma? This can't be real, it can't be.

I laugh out loud.

"Are you comfortable?" The smartly dressed lawyer asks, frowning. I stop my mad patient laughter and answer.

"You couldn't afford memory foam?"

She purses her lips and clasps her hands together tightly as if wringing them out.

"Let's begin."

42.

The lights are dimmed, and I close my eyes and try to relax and steady my breathing. I can't stop thinking about Adam or Kyle watching me. Which one is it, and why? Did they come here to watch me suffer? Or to see for themselves what happens? Maybe it's Adam looking for proof that it was me making the romantic stuff happen in my dreams with Kyle, or maybe it's Kyle because it's been Kyle all along. Maybe he's always been there, hiding in the background. Maybe he never left my head at all. Maybe I can't do any of that stuff and I would epically fail if he wasn't here to pull the strings.

How would I know? I don't understand any of this and I feel so under-prepared. And what the hell was on my blood results? Why won't anybody tell me? Either I am one of them, or I'm not. Surely this whole test is pointless if they already know.

It must mean that I'm not one of them and they think I'm crazy, or that I'm something else. That has to be it, right? I can't quiet my mind. Do I want to be one of them?

I feel the first dream take over.

Thud. Thud. Thud. Water ripples in a puddle. I know where this is going. I'm in a forest and there is a Tyrannosaurus rex coming for me. I focus. It's not a dinosaur, it's a puppy! I picture a fluffy cockapoo puppy running towards me and jumping up, licking my face.

"Good boy!" I say, smiling.

The dream shifts.

It's dark and cold. I shiver as I realise I'm naked, my arms wrapped around myself, feet jogging on the spot to avoid standing on the cold pavement for too long. No. I find a long fur coat and put that on, immediately feeling warmer. I find some boots and put those on too. I look around. What is the point of this dream then? A twig snaps. I whip my head round and my eyes widen as I observe a naked man transform out of the body of a wolf. A werewolf. I watch as the last of his fur recedes. Well, I know exactly what to do with this dream, I chuckle to myself; have they not heard about me? I drop the fur coat to my feet and strut towards the bare-chested man. I stroke his chest.

"Well hello there," I say in what I hope is a sexy voice. "What would you like to do with me?"

The dream ends abruptly. Damn!

Now I see before me the ugliest man I have ever laid eyes on; pot belly, boils all over his face, food in his beard and wonky yellow teeth (around the gaps). Check mate. Except... In 'Scooby Doo' style I step towards him saying,

"And who's under the mask?" I reach for his jawline and begin pulling at his face. It stretches like plasticine and peels off to reveal one of the Dream-Walkers assigned to test me.

"You're going to have to try harder than that," I say.

245

For the next dream, I immediately feel my heart start racing.

I'm running, heart pumping, out of breath, don't look back. Something is following me. I keep running until I gain my awareness and stop. What is it? What's behind me? A lion, escaped from a zoo, chasing me, hungry. No, I don't think so. It's a lovely little pussy cat. I bend down to pick it up, and it nuzzles my face.

I'm winning. I wait for the next dream.

A man leers over me,

"'ere, bite on that luv," he shoves something in my mouth and then starts to unbutton his jeans. Oh no, I am not being raped. I spit out whatever it is and free myself from the ties restraining me. Then I really focus. It's not some horrible rapist, it's Adam, he's come to save me.

"Quick, come with me," he says, holding my hand and pulling me from the room. We run. But the dream isn't over.

"Let's go somewhere private," he says, his face now switching back to the rapist but jumping around like a damaged video tape.

"No, let's go somewhere public," I reply, pulling us into a shopping centre. It's busy with shoppers rushing around buying Christmas presents. Music is playing loudly, and people are in great spirits. I can smell gingerbread from a little stand which has been re-purposed for the season and usually sells doughnuts. The original doughnut sign can be seen beneath a peeling gingerbread sticker. "Shall we...?" I start to ask as the dream suddenly ends.

"We will now take a short break before resuming," announces the lawyer. "Well done so far Ella, I think you have surprised us all."

I am untied and taken to the 'victim room' from the first day, where I am offered water and use of a toilet. Still no luxuries.

246

The Minister comes to see me, clutching a steaming mug of coffee. The smell alone helps to revive me.

"I am astounded by your abilities; how do you do it?" He asks, his eyes twinkling like a caring granddad.

"I just think about nicer things."

"Fascinating."

He sips and I watch, wishing I could get that caffeine fix myself. Water doesn't quite cut it.

"Do you think you could teach others to do it?" He taps his fingers against the mug. I shrug.

"I don't know, I don't know why others can't do it already."

"Yes, I suppose it seems natural for you. Have you always known you were special?"

"Obviously not." I place my empty plastic cup on a nearby table. "Can I ask you something?"

"Certainly, so long as it's not 'can you have a coffee', as unfortunately that's against the rules. We find it sometimes increases abilities."

"No way!" I laugh. "No, I was wondering, what did my blood results show? Nobody will tell me."

"Ah. That." He strokes his warm mug and I imagine how nice it must feel. I miss that warmth when you sort of cuddle your hot drink, and it's still warm even after you've finished drinking it, so you keep hold of it a little longer. "I'm afraid can't reveal that at this stage. We need to, er, run some further tests to be sure."

"So, there was something unusual then?"

"I can't comment. I'm sorry. Anyway, I should let you rest before you head back out. There's not much left to do now, it'll soon be over."

Somehow, I doubt it'll soon be over. Even once this day in court is.

After a quick wee, I am returned to the bed in front of everyone. This time I don't spot Kyle/Adam. My pulse quickens. If it was Kyle doing it from afar and he's gone now, I'm really going to suffer. They're going to up their game and I'm going to crumble. I hope it was me. I hope the weird thing in my blood results wasn't that I appear normal but am convinced I'm special. That would not be good.

I wonder what has happened to him, was he escorted off, did somebody spot him? Or did he leave once he'd seen enough? If it was Adam, did he leave once he knew it was me lusting over Kyle all along? Did he walk away heartbroken and desolate?

I sense that everybody is waiting for me to relax and let them begin. But, I'm scared. I don't want to do this anymore.

Please.

I take a deep breath in and sigh it out like in yoga. Be calm, Ella, whatever is going to happen is going to happen. Just stay calm.

43.

I'm in a school building, it's generic, not the actual school I went to, but a school, nonetheless. I am told to report to the headmistress' office, and I feel myself panic; what have I done wrong?

They usher me in, and I take a seat. No parent is present so it can't be too serious, right? The headmistress stares at me.

"We know what you did, Ella." I wait for more. "Driving into a tree to avoid a lorry – how obvious can you be?"

"It was an accident! I panicked!"

"Don't lie to us," the headmistress glances at her colleagues as she leans on the desk she stands behind.

"I'm not lying!"

"So how come you're not paralysed too then? How come, only your sister's side of the car was crushed, but you were able to walk away?"

"It was an accident!"

"She was a dancer, wasn't she? Or a gymnast? She was going places. You were jealous."

"No!"

"Admit it Ella, you wanted revenge for all the attention she stole from you over the years; you wanted to make her suffer. You deliberately hit that tree with her side of the car. On impulse. A split-second decision to save your life and destroy hers. The ultimate opportunity. You knew it would look like an accident. You knew that the lorry driver would take the blame. Admit it, Ella-Rose Thompson!"

"It was an accident!"

"So, you're a liar then? Last chance to admit it." She walks to the side of the desk.

"It was an accident!" I repeat.

"Do you know what we do with girls who lie, Miss Thompson?"

I shake my head, hairs standing on end as she gets closer. Suddenly, I know what she's going to say before she says it.

"We lock them in the chokey!" She laughs the laugh of Miss Trunchbull from 'Matilda.'

"N-n-n-n-no, please," I beg as I'm pushed into a cupboard with nails pointing through. Just as the door closes and darkness surrounds me and the nails are so close to my skin that I daren't move an inch, I remember. This is a dream. I turn the nails into strawberry lances push open the door.

"How dare you!" The headmistress shouts at me. She grabs hold of my hair. "Shall we settle this another way then?"

I know what's happening, I recall the film. She grabs my pigtails and swings me around the room before throwing me out of the window. This Dream-Walker was not very original. I remember the film so well that I ensure I land safely and collect flowers as I skid along the neighbouring *field. My trousers are muddy but that's okay, my schoolmates cheer.*

A nice lady takes me aside and undoes my hair, she tells me she believes me that it was an accident, she can tell my heart is true.

"Quick, let's go," she whispers, and we run.

Various creatures follow us through the woods as we run but I pay them no attention.

"You can't run forever Ella, you must face us, you must face us all," says a voice from nowhere. The lady disappears. I am standing alone, panting for breath.

In front of me, moving slowly towards me, is a collection of hideously scary creatures. From left to right there's a zombie, a werewolf, a witch, a troll, an old guy who looks like a pervert and keeps touching inside his pants and licking his lips, a vampire (but not the good-looking kind), a giant snake, and... Adam? With his head hanging off. I know it's not real. It's a dream, it's a dream, it's a dream, I chant to myself. They want me to face them so I will face them, I will destroy them all. It's just a dream.

First, I imagine the ground shaking beneath me, I drop to my knees. A large crack forms between them and I, which stretches into a massive crater between us. It's now like we're on separate cliff edges. There's a fair distance, but it's not impossible to cross should they have the right equipment.

I remove all their possessions, even their clothes.

"Why is it always sexual with you?" Comes a voice from behind me. "Look at you, making them all naked!" Says the voice.

I know that voice, but is it?

I turn slowly. I can't see anyone, only darkness.

"Hello?" I stare into the emptiness. There's no one there. It must have just been wishful thinking that somebody else was going to get me out of this mess.

I'll have to do this myself. I need to concentrate, what can I do to stop them reaching me?

A hurricane might blow them over.

"A tsunami would work," says the mysterious voice.

The voice is right, a tsunami would work wonders.

I imagine a giant wave, headed for the other side of the gap. It will get us all, but it will get them first. I see it rising behind them, putting them under its shadow. Some start to run, screaming, falling down the gap as they take risky jumps to get across. Then it breaks.

As I wake up, I find most of the Dream-Walkers sat in the jury seats are coughing and spitting up water like they nearly drowned. Wow. Did I do that?

"Take her away," says the judge. They wheel me out on the bed initially before transferring my cuffs and marching me back to my cell.

This time I'm glad of the silence of the thick glass, the solitude, the blank mind. I rub my ear as I feel like I have trapped water in there.

Interesting.

KYLE

44.

It's hot. The air burns my nostrils and stings my eyes. I'm tied up, my wrists sore and unmovable. I'm in Izzy's bedroom; I recognise her bedside lamp and her furry rug on the floor. An old poster crinkles and rolls up at the edges as it feels the heat.

That's when I notice her feet, slightly poking out of the covers. She's in bed, oblivious. Like she was that night.

"Hey!" I shout. "Wake up!" "Izzy, wake up!" "FIRE!" I cough, the heat hurting my throat.

We're not alone. Her bedroom door opens, and in walks Philip. His greasy shoulder-length brown hair is loose, and the lenses of his glasses are cracked. He smiles at me, before walking over to the bed.

"No!" "Leave her alone!" I struggle in my restraints.

He pulls back the covers, revealing her body. Her nighty has ridden up, and her pert bum is exposed. He licks his lips.

"No!" I shout again.

He mounts the bed behind her and pulls her bum up towards him. She complies, sleepy and unaware. He pulls his trousers down.

I close my eyes. I can't watch. I feel sick. Vomit rises up my throat and I swallow it back down. It's not real; it's not real; it's a dream. Izzy is dead, and this is not what happened. Not in real life, at least. Wake up, Kyle. Wake up! Why can't I wake up?

I feel somebody's fingers on my face, forcing my eyes back open. The air stings them once more and tears escape down my cheeks. He's finished, and he's wiping his penis off on her bum cheek. He gets off the bed and pulls out a knife.

I have to fight back. Whoever is doing this to me can't be that powerful, I must be able to regain control. I can't just sit here and watch this.

I imagine that I have the knife and am charging at him. He lets me charge at him and then, before I can stop myself, he switches places with Izzy and I plunge the knife into her chest. Blood pours out and her eyes look at me in shock.

My knees give way and I fall to the ground.

"I'm so sorry Izzy, I'm so sorry." I cry big, inconsolable sobs. Ugly tears. Snot trudges its way towards my mouth. "I'm so sorry."

I'm still crying when I wake up and realise I'm still tied to this chair, with him.

He shoves a tissue at my face, smearing some of the snot. My arms are tied, I can't do it myself.

"Are you ready to reconsider yet? Or shall we go again?" He says with a smile. It's like looking in an evil magic mirror. He is me, after I sell my soul to the devil. He is the version of me which Adam sees me as, the 'bad' brother. But he is so much worse. He's been torturing me for hours. He knows too much.

How could I have been so wrong? So stupid?

I hope they will forgive me.

ADAM

45.

I watch as Ella is bundled into the minibus like a prisoner. I'm pretty sure I know where they're going, I just don't know why.

Ella isn't one of us. I know that, for sure. I stole her blood report. 100% average human being. Or rather, no biological ties to the Dream-Walkers. I couldn't see anything unusual. So how do they explain her inbuilt resistance? I suppose it makes sense that they want to test her further, but why there? With those people?

Ella isn't dangerous. She isn't a criminal. She's only mixed up in all this because I had a stupid crush on her which I would never have acted on if Kyle hadn't interfered.

I haven't seen him since I left them in London. I was about to make myself known when one of the security guys slipped me a note that basically told me Kyle was going to pretend to be me, and that I should stay away. I figured he was trying to do the right thing again, trying to make up for screwing up our lives, and it really looked like it was going to work. The witnesses and the fact that we were in a relationship were undeniable proof in the eyes of the HJD. Until Ella mysteriously developed these 'skills' anyway.

Did she really have control over those dreams with Kyle? Over those dreams with all of those people in court who tried to test her? I just can't see it. I don't believe it's possible. I would have known if she was different, wouldn't I? I would have felt it. She isn't one of us. I know she isn't. Something just doesn't add up. Or maybe I missed something on the report.

Because I don't want it to add up. If she was in control, then she definitely did fall for Kyle before me. There was no manipulation. She did things with him that we never did. She would never have gone out with me if not for him. Maybe that wasn't his first intention, but regardless, she fancied him first. I know we look the same, but no.

I wish I could wind back time and never pick up that shopping list she dropped. I would never have knowingly opened her up to that danger from Kyle. She could have gone on leading a normal life, and I would have continued caring for Mum and being sad and lonely, wishing for one day when I'd find love.

Now I've lost them both.

The minibus pulls away and I start the engine of my 'borrowed' car. I stole the keys from one of the audience members from the trial as they all pooled into the corridors. I prefer to pickpocket than dream-manipulate, it makes me feel more human and less like Dad. I will ensure the car is left with more fuel than when I took it, and I'll park it somewhere safe when I'm done. The owner may be a little inconvenienced now, but they'll get over it soon enough. Maybe I'll even give it a wash if I have time. It's a blue hatchback and it appears to reside somewhere with a high population of seagulls, if the roof and passenger side door are any indication.

After a session in the courtroom, most people go for lunch and drinks at the pub down the road so I'm hoping it won't be missed for at least a couple of hours. I should be far away before the car is reported stolen. If I'm lucky, they'll decide to have a few more drinks and come back for their car tomorrow, giving me even longer.

I start to crawl forwards but before I can accelerate and follow the minibus, another car pulls out in front of me.

A few miles on, it seems like the car in front is also following the minibus. Security? I doubt it. Even if Ella can do what they say, she's not a danger, she doesn't go walking into to other people's heads, she just defends her own. There is no need to provide back up.

Unless they don't know what she's capable of. Unless she did something truly shocking in that last part of the trial which they wouldn't let me watch. I was escorted away. All I heard was that she had beaten them all and the case was closed. The chatter in the corridor afterwards was loud enough to convince me something interesting happened though.

On a dual carriageway I try to pull up alongside the other car that's following, to get a view of the driver.

There are two men in the car, a fat man driver – surely it's not? It looks like... I think it's Nige', who drove us to London. Which means the passenger, sat with a dark hood over his head is Kyle. It has to be. What the hell is he up to now?

I follow them as discreetly as I can. They don't know this car so it's not an immediate tell but, given that we've been driving for a few hours now and all three vehicles have remained constant, I think it's pretty obvious I'm following, and it wouldn't take a genius to guess it's me in

261

here. Of course, they can't stop to confront me because then they might risk losing Ella. So, on we all go.

I'm starting to regret having that coffee this morning because now I really need a shit. Ella would find that funny.

I miss her.

I know we were fated to never work out, like Romeo and Juliet, but I was just starting to think that maybe we stood a chance, with her winning that trial for us, 'proving' her abilities. I know they're fake, they have to be, but it would have meant we could be together. Really together. The way we wanted. Sexually.

Maybe I should've just taken her when I wanted to, she might not have been scared off. She might have been willing to run away with me and live a life in secret. Nobody had to know. Except Kyle. He was always going to ruin it. But at least we could have had sex before he took off on whatever this crazy plan is.

Why is he doing this? That's what I can't get my head around. If he wanted to get me into trouble, he failed; if he wanted to get Ella locked up, he succeeded... but why? Why would some random girl interest him? What could he possibly gain? And if he is in her head even now, making people believe she has skills that she doesn't really have, then again, why? What could he possibly gain?

Some people believe that twins have a special connection, we can read each-other's minds. Not us, not at all. We could have been separated at birth for how 'connected' we are. Even being raised in the same house we had entirely different upbringings.

I was always a mummy's boy, but he worshipped our dad. He was always asking him questions about what he could do and had done, it fascinated him. I just wished I was normal, especially after the sleepover. I had no friends, but he had loads. As we got older, the only girls interested in me were ones that he had already turned down.

I was relieved when my dad disappeared, figured now we could start to live a more 'normal' life. Mum was human so it made sense that we would distance ourselves from the Dream-Walker community. Nobody even knew if we would develop the proper skills or not, at that point all I could do was share dreams involuntarily with those around me. There was no deliberate starring in or twisting of dreams; not by me anyway.

As soon as Kyle could do it, he did it to me. Repeatedly. Before I realised what was going on. Before Mum realised what was going on. He tortured me, he ruined my life, made me crawl even deeper into my shell. And then he left. Ran away as soon as he could, leaving just a note which said he had gone to find and join The Resistance.

Frankie-Lou was his girlfriend at the time, and she was devastated. He left right before prom night, and she'd been hoping they'd be crowned King and Queen. I quietly offered to pretend to be him for her, so she could still win, but she spat in my face. The bitch. I can't believe he's still messing her around all these years later. Some women are glutton for punishment, but I think she might deserve it.

We take a turn off the main road and the jellybean shaped air freshener hanging off the rear-view mirror swings wildly as we head down a bumpy country road. Our convoy is even more obvious now there are fewer cars around. From what I can see, I think Kyle still has the hood over his head. I can only imagine he is using the darkness to help him focus. But why would he need to? Is he in her head now? Is he always in her head? Why?

Eventually we pull up in front of a tall grey building, there's a security gate so I pull off to the side and jump out. Nige' does the same, then he goes around and helps Kyle out of the passenger side.

He looks like a prisoner being led around with a hoodie over his head like that. Or like somebody who's been

263

abducted by terrorists. I wonder if he'll be on the news later, 'send ten million to this account by midnight or he dies.'

I should call Jack Bauer over at CTU and get him on the case. Ah, I miss 24. Now that was a good series. I imagine the beep of the clock in my mind. What would Jack do?

I don't know whether to follow them or Ella, as I can see Ella's minibus being let through the main gate and turning into what I can only assume is underground parking. Kyle is being led to the front right of the building, towards some thick bushes.

I follow him, staying back, ducking behind every object we pass. Nige' bends down and pulls up a drain cover. With one final look around, they descend. It must be another way in!

I'm not going to follow in case they get caught, and because if it's just a ladder or staircase or something with thin crawlspaces (but big enough to fit Nige') then they will see me even if others don't. I will handle this my way. I am going to ask to visit her.

I walk up to the main door and press the bell.

ELLA

46.

This new place is different. More technical. It's all sliding doors and security patches and even iris reading sensors (or that's what it looks like anyway, they go and put their eyes up to a scanner thing). It's very 'James Bond.'

I've repeatedly asked my transporters why I've been moved and what's so special about this place and why they couldn't test me where I was, but nobody will tell me anything. I've asked to see the Minister about my rights, and they said I'll see him in good time. When I asked about dinner, the man actually smiled and said, "if you thought it was bad before, just you wait." So now I'm really happy about my new accommodation. Not.

The cell itself seems pretty much the same as before, except the walls are all that funny reflective opaqueness so I can't see out at all, but others can probably see and listen in. I don't feel very safe here, but I guess other people would feel safe from me, on account of the number of security measures it takes just to get inside. This is not the kind of place one could break out of, Dream-Walker or not. There are just too many security measures, it would take years to plan.

I sit down on my latest uncomfortable bed and wonder if I will ever feel memory foam again. I think back to that dream which caused me to be sent here. Whose was that mysterious voice I heard? Has somebody been in my dreams this whole time, making it look like I can do more than I really can? Why would they do that? It better not have been Donna, sending me down so her precious boys stay out. She seems like someone who doesn't care who she tramples to get her way.

The floor is cold as I decide to drop down and do some more yoga stretches. Sitting in that minibus for hours has given me an achy back again. I try to remember things that are good for it.

As I'm lying with my feet up the wall and a pillow under my lower back, feeling surprisingly calm, there's a beep and my door slides open and in walks... Adam?

"Adam? Is it really you?" I roll to one side and stand up to hug him. He smells different, but who am I to talk? I probably reek. "How did you know where to find me?"

"I followed you here of course! I'm going to get you out."

"Really? Oh my God I'm so glad to hear you say that!" I hug him tight again. "But how? This place is ridiculously secure!"

"I have a plan."

I jump up and down with excitement.

"Thank you, thank you, thank you!" I kiss him but he pulls away too soon. "So, what's the plan then?"

"Well, I can't really say," he eyes the corners of the room, "just do as you're told and trust me that it won't be for long. No one is going to hurt you." He smiles. "I'd better go, I'm not meant to be in here."

"Why can't I come with you now?" I refuse to let go of his hand as he backs away.

"We'd get caught. Trust me, I have a plan."

"Okay, and you're sure this will work? This place is kind of high tech."

"Oh, it will definitely work," he says confidently with a slightly smug smile that triggers a thought at the back of my mind which goes just before I can grasp it. "I love you, Ella. See you soon."

He blows me a kiss and then disappears back out the sliding door.

ADAM

47.

"I'm here to see Ella-Rose Thompson," I state to the man at the reception desk. His face pales as he looks at me.

"What?" I ask. He clicks and types a few things on his computer before looking from me to his computer and back again. "What?" I ask again.

"She's, er, she's not allowed visitors. You have to leave." He stumbles over his words, adjusting his tie nervously.

"Why? She's only here for observation, isn't she?" He looks at the man at the door before answering.

"She's being charged. She's not allowed any visitors. You have to leave." The door man makes his way over as if I'm a disgruntled customer about to cause a scene.

"Is there a problem here?" He asks.

"I just want to see my girlfriend."

"Well, unfortunately, you can't. Please come with me."

I sigh and follow him towards the exit.

"Look, man, level with me. What's really going on here?" I ask him, thinking I might get more out of him than the nervous reception guy. He scrunches up his face and then moves so that nobody other than me can see his face.

"Honestly, it's personal. It's not about who you want to see, it's about who you are. You can't be here."

"It's about my dad, isn't it?" He gives a slight nod. "He's here?" He nods again.

I leave.

So that's it then, Kyle's big plan. It's not about Ella anymore, he's here for our dad. Our awful dad. He's going to try to break him out.

I cannot let that happen.

48.

Call me Clarke, Adam Clarke. I have just gained access to the security cameras inside the facility.

There are a lot, but so far, I have managed to find where Ella is being kept. She looks okay, alive anyway. I'm still searching for where Kyle is hiding. Knowing him, he's in a blind spot, but bearing in mind that he went in with Nige', there's bound to be a clue. That's a big man to hide. I'm scanning each image for anything unusual, anything they could hide behind, any quiet corridors. I click from camera to camera.

There are a lot of staff inside, more than I expected; lots of lab coat wearing scientist types as well as tougher looking security guards. In one of the labs, I can see two people lying on beds, restrained, with wires attached to their heads. The scientists are watching a monitor and making notes. At least nobody looks distressed.

I wonder if I will recognise my dad if I find his cell. It has been a long time since I last saw him. I keep clicking through the cameras. A male lab technician/scientist type pushes a trolley down a narrow corridor, swipes an ID card, enters a code, and scans his thumb print. I can only see the back of his head, but he looks familiar. Alarm bells ring in the back of my mind. Who is this guy?

I follow him through the door onto the next camera view and wait to see where he is going and if he'll turn around. He enters another door, this time scanning his eye. This must be an especially secure part of the facility. He comes to yet another door and it looks like he is saying something out loud – voice recognition? Blimey.

He parks his trolley up outside another door but does not immediately move to enter. Instead, he turns around.

I know that face.

It's my face.

It's Kyle's face.

But, how?

I know Kyle knows a lot of people, but to have them set him up on the system with the thumb print and the iris scan and the voice recognition and to not have people question his sudden appearance at a facility he has fought hard against, and which holds his dad? Surely nobody is so stupid as to have let him past the front door. He could get through the computer stuff, but people would see him, they would ask questions; it is an obvious risk that they would not take. The Minister is not stupid. He would not take that chance. He would not believe any lies about Kyle 'changing' and wanting to help, no way. He just wouldn't.

But me? Would he believe that I wanted to help? Maybe.

Could Kyle be impersonating me? Could that be why I was refused entry to see Ella? Because they thought I was Kyle? Has he told them I'm a risk, but he isn't?

Whilst he hunches over the trolley searching for something, I click on to the next camera. Oh, it's him alright.

My dad.

I feel a shiver run down my spine. The cell is dark, with just a single bulb above his head. He isn't lying down like the others, but he isn't free to walk around either. He is locked into an 'x' shaped something and it looks as if it gently moves from horizontal to vertical constantly. At the moment, he is almost completely vertical, and I imagine I can see into his dark eyes. The quality is a little blurred in the poor light, but I can see those eyes I remember. The darkness, the fear they generate.

I'm not embarrassed to say I was afraid of my dad once I learned what he was capable of. I wasn't before, back when he was just Dad. But once Kyle started asking questions about the things he had done, re-awakening his desires to do those horrible things, for every step Kyle took up the ladder of adoration, I took one down towards fear and disgust.

How can you be proud of somebody who inflicts mental harm on people, for fun? Sometimes they deserved it, but more often they didn't. Just because he wasn't committing physical crimes, and there was no evidence, doesn't make it okay. He doesn't deserve to be free. He'd only do it again.

I click back to the other camera to see what Kyle is up to, and my confusion spirals. Ducked down in the corner, he is speaking to someone. Someone who also looks like me.

How?

I keep watching, trying to get a better look at this other person. He's dressed in black, but I can't make out much else. It's my face though, again.

ELLA

49.

They're taking me somewhere. I guess to begin testing or whatever they are going to do with me.

There are two security guards and a lab man in front, leading the way. Nobody has said a word.

My shoes squeak on the floor and I look around everywhere for clues. Adam said to do as I'm told, so, is this it? Is he going to save me now?

The lab man stands in front of an eye scanner whilst putting his thumb on another scanner before holding a door open and guiding me into an examination room.

Everything in here is white and smells strongly of bleach. Don't people use bleach when they're cleaning up blood? I hope I'm not going to bleed in here! I try to push the thought to the back of my mind.

"Will the Minister be joining us?"

"No." The lab man replies, with his back to me.

We are alone now, the guards left once they had secured me to a reclining chair like you might find in a dentist's surgery. I think of my unbrushed teeth. I've been scraping off plaque with my nails.

"But he will be watching."

I look up at the cameras in each corner of the room. Of course.

"So, what's the plan then? More of the same, or do you have something a little different to try this time?"

He turns around.

"Oh, yes, something a little different." He's holding a needle. "We're going to create a distraction."

I am too stunned to even attempt to move away from the needle, restrained or not. I'm frozen, my brain shooting questions around my head too fast to comprehend. I'm frowning, mouth open.

"Kyle?"

"No."

"Adam?"

"No."

"Who are you and what are you doing? What did you just inject me with? What's going on here?" I finally begin to attempt to wriggle out of my restraints.

"I told you, we're going to create a distraction. That was just a sedative, to make sure you don't wake up too soon. The Minister is going to *love* this." He smiles. I can already feel the drowsiness, it's strong stuff.

"Bu- who are you?"

"I'm Damian. It's a pleasure to meet you." He shakes my hand as I feel myself slipping… down, down, deep, deep, sleep.

I'm on a rollercoaster, going up towards the sky. It's the big build up, I'm forced to squint into the sun as my head hits the head restraint. It judders up, up, higher and higher and then it stops. Hovering on the precipice, I can see the ground, but there is no track. My heart races, I tighten my grip on the chair. I'm going to die, I'm going to die; I scream as the power kicks in, and I'm thrown into the unknown at a million miles an hour; I scream like I've never screamed before; I scream like I'll never scream again.

Tears run off past my ears as I'm hurtled around screaming. It's not real, but I can't stop it. I imagine a calmer ride, the Toddler Teacups, but nothing happens. I'm doing corkscrews, vertical loops and horizontal loops, and there doesn't seem to be an end in sight. There's no track to foreshadow what happens next. This is the most terrifying ride I've ever been on.

I try to change it again. I think of a bouncy castle, the soft manageable bounces, as my head judders from side to side whacking the head restraint. Come on, Ella, change it, change it.

AHHH! I'm free-falling, the seat has opened and sent me falling towards the ground below.

It's a dream, Ella, it's a dream. Maybe you can fly? Do you have a parachute? Is that a massive bouncy castle below you?

I keep falling, it's a never-endingly long way down and I'm screaming and flapping my arms. My throat is raw.

"Kyle," I think, "if you're in here, please help me."

I can see the ground I'm headed for now, mostly cement. But there is a lake of some kind, please let me land in the lake.

I'm going to make it, I think... Wait, is it frozen? Oh my God no! No, no, no, no!

I hit the ice with a thud which causes it to crack and plunge me into icy water, stinging and cleaning my fresh cuts. I can't move, I'm in so much pain. I think I've broken bones. I'm going to drown. I can't get back to the surface. It hurts too much to kick and my arms aren't strong enough.

I have gills like a fish, I tell myself. I'm not going to die. But nothing happens so the panic returns. I can't breathe. I'm losing focus, my eyes are blurring, I can't even remember which way is up. I'm sinking, being pulled, down, down.

Then I'm alive, I'm on an operating table, there's a curtain hiding my lower half. Am I having a caesarean?

"Doctor! Doctor!" I shout.

"Please calm down, you'll upset the baby," says a voice to my right. It's no normal doctor though, he has a frog head and scaly green arms. He moves behind the curtain.

I feel a knife slicing me in half – shouldn't I be numb down there? I scream again, picturing blood pouring out of me. I'm going to die; I'm really going to die now.

"Stop!" "Help me!" "Please!" I scream.

"Shh Mummy, don't you want to meet your baby?" Asks the frog faced man.

Wrapped in a blue knitted blanket held in his scaly green arms, is a baby boy, my baby boy. He presents him to me, places him against my chest. I use all my strength to move my arms to cradle him and look.

I scream again,

"Stop it! Stop fucking with me! Stop it now!"

The baby in my arms, his face, it's not the adorable squished up face of a new-born. It's not a bit pink, it's not slimy, there are no cute little hairs atop his head. This is the face I know so well, the face that fits three adult males I know of so far. The face of my dream man. The adult face. Stubble and all.

"Isn't he cute?" Says the frog faced man. "You're so lucky he's not one of those ugly babies, like me. Would you like to meet the rest?"

"Wha-?" I start to say as he presents me with another, and another, and another, until there are six babies with dream man faces looking up at me.

"Well done Mummy, six healthy baby boys."

"Take them away!" I scream, "take them away! This isn't real and I'm not playing anymore! You stop it and take them away, let me wake up!"

"Oh Ella, why don't you just keep two, eh? Like Dorothy did. Two's a nice manageable number. We'll take care of the rest." He has a twinkle in his eye like he's in on this dream and he's enjoying it.

"Stop it! I know it's you... Damian! Wake me up!"

"But we're just getting started," he replies. "Besides, I've not sown you back up yet, you can't leave like that." He pulls down the curtain and I see my stomach gaping open like a massive hole.

"It's not real," I say. "I'm not scared anymore."

My heartrate and breathing says otherwise.

"What are you going to do about it then Ella? Go on, that's why we're here after all."

"I can't!"

"Try."

"I have!"

"Try harder."

"I can't! I'm tired and in pain and injured and I can't take anymore. You're going to kill me!"

"Don't be silly Ella, you never really die in your dreams."

The image fades out. Where am I going now? I can't see anything. But I think I can hear voices somewhere in the distance, echoing.

"It's nearly time," someone says.

"When the alarm bell rings, that's when you take him. The Minister will be distracted and he'll ask for help, everyone will rush around. They won't even think about him. Are you ready?"

"I'm ready."

A new dawn arrives in my dream state, the lights go on and I realise I'm standing on top of a tall building looking out across a city. There's a big wave coming, a tsunami, like last time. Except this time, it's coming for me.

"Ella, do you know what brought you here?" says a voice beside me, "what the final straw was?" *It's Damian, back to normal in his lab coat. Maybe the sleeping drug is wearing off if I can see him how he truly is.* "It was the tsunami. When you washed away all those Dream-Walkers, they actually spat out water. The Minister couldn't believe it, nobody could. That's beyond our normal abilities. They had no choice but to bring you here. Like I said, nobody dies in their dreams. But you nearly killed them. Some of them nearly drowned."

"But it wasn't me, I didn't do it."

"Oh I know that, I did it! I'm much stronger than any of them realise. But now we're going to really test it, we're going to see if you die when I drown you the same way."

"Please, don't! Let me go!"

"Sorry. You need to be dying for this to work. We're creating a distraction, remember?"

"A distraction for what? You're in my head!"

"I am, but Kyle isn't. Not anymore anyway. He's ready and waiting for my cue."

I see the wave getting closer, the houses and tower blocks disappearing.

"Please! Don't kill me!"

"I'm sorry, but this has to work. It has to be believable. Your death will serve a much greater purpose than your life."

I spit at him.

"How dare you determine what my life is worth!"

"I know everything about you, Ella. You're a disaster; what have you achieved in your life besides the ability to quote 'Bridget Jones' Diary' verbatim, and nearly killing *your sister? I'm doing the world a favour. Just lie down and take it. Go on, lie down and let it all just wash away."*

"No!"

I look around for somewhere higher to climb to. I imagine a helicopter with a rope ladder coming to rescue me. Come on, come on, I can do this. I must be able to save myself, it's not real!

The wave is getting closer, Damian is sitting calmly, watching me, smiling.

"You're sick!"

He laughs, not even bothering to retaliate.

I squeeze my fingers into fists, my nails cutting the inside of my palms. Please, somebody, get me out of this.

The wave is impossibly close now, I only have seconds left to do something.

Please, please, don't let me die in my dreams. Please!

Just as the wave is about to crush me, I feel a tug on my right arm and I find myself flying up. The water barely touches my feet as I'm pulled towards the clouds. Somebody has saved me! We keep flying for a while, I presume searching for somewhere safe and dry to land.

"Are you okay?"

"Adam?"

It's him, it's really him. I hold onto him like I'll never let go.

"I can't wake up."

"You've been drugged, you won't be able to until it's all gone from your system. But you're safe now, I've had that guy locked up, I'm getting you out of here."

"But what about your dad? And Kyle?"

"I had to choose, Ella. I chose you."

"Then you have to go now, chase after them! He can't be free! He's dangerous!"

"They caught him before, they'll catch him again," he says calmly, rubbing my back.

"No! You have to stop them!"

"I need to make sure you're okay."

"I am, see, you saved me, I didn't drown. Please, go and stop them!"

"Are you sure? Stay here until you wake up, nothing should happen now."

He kisses me and squeezes me tight again.

"I love you, Ella."

"I love you too." A happy tear runs down my cheek. "Go!"

ADAM

50.

With Damian now secured in a cell, and Ella waiting for the sedative to wear off, I am free to chase my idiot brother and dangerous father to the ends of the earth. Or more likely, home, because Dad always was a confident prick. He thinks he's invincible, too powerful to be caught. But he's not. He was caught before, and he will be caught again. I'll make sure of that.

I just can't believe Kyle could be so stupid to go along with that plan, even if he does love and admire Dad. To put Ella's life at risk? I know he cares about her too, despite what he says. This can't have been his plan. Whatever his plan was, it was hijacked. He would never have taken it this far… would he?

And since when did we have another brother? Is he some lab experiment? A clone?

I slam the car door and start the engine. If only I could fly like in dreams!

*

It's dark by the time I get back, parking the borrowed car in a secure and well-lit car park, with the key carefully balanced on the driver's side rear tyre. Hopefully nobody will look there, and the car will be ready and waiting to be found by its owner. No harm done. I step away and follow the pedestrianised cobblestone towards home.

There's a light on inside. I put my key into the lock quietly and turn it slowly, pushing the door open and stepping inside. I can't hear any talking. I close the door behind me and head through to the lounge.

In the middle of the room tied to a dining chair is Kyle, gagged and blindfolded. I remove the blindfold first. He looks relieved to see me. I remove the gag.

"You okay?" I ask.

"No, help untie me. Dad fucking lied to me, he's everything they said and more, Ad', he's a monster. Is Ella okay?"

I untie his wrists, but his legs I let him do himself.

"She will be. No thanks to you."

"I'm sorry, this wasn't the plan, I didn't know... I didn't know..." His voice trails off and his shoulders bounce as he starts to cry.

I can't remember ever seeing my brother cry, not even at Mum's funeral. He doesn't show emotions, he's the tough one; the protector; the fighter. It's uncomfortable to see.

"I really was just trying to get you two together, and then when I had the idea of making her seem to be a Dream-Walker too, I thought that would get you both off the hook. You'd be able to be together without hiding.

Honestly, I really did have good intentions." He sniffs and wipes his nose on his forearm.

"What happened? What went wrong?"

"They were watching us, and I played right into their hands. Damian, whoever the fuck he is, he was working with Dad. He got to me right before her big test day in court, tortured me until I agreed to go along with their plan. He's powerful, scary powerful. Like Dad, I guess. Freaked out those Dream-Walkers on the panel and of course the Minister wanted her examined, transported her just where they wanted."

"But I saw you go there and sneak inside, what were you up to?"

"Damian forced me to help him and to keep an eye on Ella's dreams until he was ready for his big moment. He even had me pretend to be you again so that she'd remain hopeful of escape. Nige' was working for him too, fucking sell-out. He delivered me on a plate, wasn't interested in deviating from the plan for any price. They must have paid him a fortune."

"So where is he now then? Where did he go?"

"Who, Dad? I have no idea. Nige' stood guard whilst I opened the cell as Damian was busy causing havoc in Ella's dreams, and he never even stopped to say thank you. I feel like such an idiot. All those years idolising the man and he couldn't even give me a second's glance."

"We need to get him. No one is safe whilst he's out there, especially people like Ella, whom he sees as dispensable, people to be used as objects to get what he wants. What does he want?"

"I don't know! All I know is that 'Damian' our mystery sibling was working with him, and this wasn't some spur of the moment plan. He knew all about us. Did he get away too?"

"No, I put him in a cell when I got to Ella. The guards are keeping an eye on him, the Minister was watching and falling for the distraction as planned, so they know what happened. Ella will be free to go once she wakes up and feels up to it."

"Okay, so we need to go back then, we need to question Damian." He says, standing and stretching his legs.

"No, I think we should focus on Dad. Besides, that's a long journey; we can't afford to go backwards, we can't waste any time. What else have you heard about him over the years?"

"Same as you, I guess, but I didn't listen to it. All those stories about the horrible things he did to people and kids; I just thought it was discrimination because he was so powerful. Propaganda, or whatever. I didn't believe he could really be that bad; I thought people were just scared of his power."

"Okay, but what about Damian? Are there others?"

"I don't know!"

"Fuck! Okay. Well, what about where he was caught last time, where was that?"

"Some creepy dugout hidey-hole a couple of hours away I think."

"Do you reckon he'd go back there?"

"No. He's clever and powerful and I just let him out. He could be anywhere!" He kicks the chair. "I feel like I've just released Lord Voldemort!"

"Wait. He would have planned where he was going, but he'll also be checking up on us, don't you think? He'll be ready and waiting to jump into our dreams to check if we're on to him and to try to find out what happened to Damian once he realises that he can't reach him. So, is there any way we can reverse it, so that when he gets into our head, we can get into his? Is there anything the MIUs have been working on or discovered?"

"I doubt it; they don't exactly have the most forthcoming participants. Dream-Walkers there tend to hide anything extra they can do rather than revealing it and bringing further tests upon themselves."

"True. So, Damian really is our best bet then. Fine, let's go back, talk to him, pick up Ella and hopefully then we'll know where to go next. Yeah?" He nods. "Want a tissue?" He nods again.

Just as we're ready to leave and Kyle has freshened up to look a bit more like himself rather than a snotty nosed three-year-old, we're interrupted.

"I think you'll be needing these," my car keys dangle before my face.

Kyle and I stand still, stunned, staring at Dad. I don't know what to say. Kyle launches himself at him,

"You bastard!"

He is swatted away like a fly.

"Now, now, that's no way to greet your father. Come here and give me a hug the both of you, I've missed you."

"What, so you can stab us in the back again? I don't think so," snaps Kyle.

"I had to do what I had to do to get out, you understand that, right?" His smile doesn't quite reach his eyes. "I thought you of all people would understand Kyle, you wanted me to get out, didn't you? At least that's what you used to say in your cards."

"Before I knew what you were," he snarls.

"And what might that be? The Bogeyman? The Devil?" He laughs.

Neither of us respond, we just glare. Maybe that's the only twin thing we do – we're really good at stare downs.

"If you're upset about that human girl, don't worry, we'll find you someone much more suitable, Adam. You really shouldn't lower yourself to dating humans."

"Why not? You did." I reply.

291

"Your mother was a mistake. Look how that turned out!"

I clench my fists, anger starting to boil over.

"Our mother deserved better than you!"

He laughs again.

"Honestly boys, what have they told you about me?"

Just as I'm about to speak, I blink to clear my vision. That's all it takes.

I feel small, my feet dangle off the couch, way off the floor. Mum is screaming at Dad to be more careful, whipping him with a tea towel as Kyle nearly touched the hot oven and is now sat on the floor crying because she told him off.

"Stop it! Don't do that to me, I know you're only showing me what you want me to see. I won't believe any of it. I don't trust you. I hate you!"

"Alright, alright. Kyle, how about you? How are you feeling now that you've calmed down a bit?"

"I hate you too," he responds.

"This is about that girl, isn't it? How did I end up with two pussy boys who've fallen in love with a human? A weak pathetic human? If it wasn't for her, you'd trust me, wouldn't you? You'd come with me? Help me?"

"Help you do what? Destroy the world?" Shouts Kyle.

"Quiet, you have neighbours!" Dad orders. "You do still have neighbours, don't you?"

"Why? What do you have planned for them?" I ask.

"Nothing. What if we make a deal, eh?"

"We're not making any deals with you." We stand together side by side, arms crossed.

"You realise I can make you do whatever I want, right? I'm only asking because I respect you, you're my boys." We roll our eyes and sigh.

"Please boys, do this for me. Do this for me and you'll never hear from me again. You can go on to live happily ever after with humans or whatever you want. I just need your help, just this once, and then I'm gone. I promise." I look at Kyle, hesitating.

"What do you want us to do?"

ELLA

51.

As I start to wake up, feeling like I'm dragging myself up from a deadly deep sleep, I squint around the room and rub my eyes.

I'm no longer secured to the chair and that scientist man is gone. Ah, that's right, the one who looked like Adam and Kyle. Their brother. What did Adam say about him?

I feel lethargic and like my brain can't quite kick in. So many images flash through my mind that I can't quite focus on any of them enough to remember what happened. I was falling, no, drowning? No, flying? Ugh. I'm not sure.

But I'm awake now, that's what matters. I'm awake and I'm alive.

"Here, have a drink Ella, it'll make you feel better."

The Minister enters the room holding a glass of water. He looks apprehensive.

"I'd like to speak to you about what happened here, to issue my sincerest apologies, and ask you if we can come to some agreement so that you will not press charges. What happened here was a one off, it's never happened before and it will never happen again, I can assure you. But I cannot afford for it to become public knowledge. You must keep the Dream-Walker secret." He takes a seat opposite me.

I take a big gulp of water and nod at him in agreement.

"I can't really remember right now, but of course I won't tell anyone about the Dream-Walkers; I love Adam, I would always have kept his secret."

"Thank you. But you must understand, we need some reassurance that you won't get angry about what happened and choose to sell your story down the line."

"Okay, like what?"

"Would you let me, us, harvest your eggs?" He leans forwards in his chair, his hands together as if he is begging me.

"Excuse me?"

"Just as a precaution. If you ever tell anyone about what you've learnt here, or what happened here, we will release a counter-story which paints you in a much darker light. Babies you've given up for adoption, sacrificed for testing, that sort of thing. What do you say?"

"I say, why do you want my babies?"

"No, no, it's nothing personal, it's just an insurance policy – you take us down, we take you down too." He's so calm, as if what he's saying isn't completely outrageous.

"I don't believe you. What was on my blood report? Why won't anybody tell me?"

"You're not a Dream-Walker Ella, and you don't have any natural resistance, that was always Kyle or Damian messing with you. You're just a human. Ella, this is just to help convince the rest of the Dream-Walkers to trust you. There's nothing sinister going on."

I can't help but snigger a little.

"Nothing sinister? You have got to be kidding, right? And what about Adam and Kyle's dad then? Him being out in the world, no danger there, eh? Actually, I think the humans do need to be told about what's going on here, they're in danger now that you let a criminal like him escape!"

"That would be a very bad decision Ella, I want to be able to let you go, but I can't if you're going to tell people." He stands and begins pacing in the small space beside my reclined chair. "We will have to take extra precautions. Medical precautions. The old-fashioned kind. Have you heard of a frontal lobotomy?"

Shit. I should've just let him take my unfertilised babies and run. But Adam's going to come back for me soon... Everything will be okay... won't it?

*

They've put me back in my cell. The Minister said he would give me some time to think about my decision, and if I don't agree, they will keep me here for as long as I'm useful, then most likely deposit me to an insane asylum once I lose my mind.

It's been hours, feels like days, since Adam told me in my dream that I would be freed. I'm starting to wonder if that was even real, if it was really him reaching out to me, or just something I made up, or someone else made up, to give me hope. How would I know? I don't know anything anymore.

But Adam loves me, he always did; he won't leave me here to suffer. He'd rather die than have me suffer.

Unless he *is* dead. If he went after his dad, what if something happened to him? What if his dad hurt him, or trapped him?

Or maybe he thinks I'm okay, that they have let me go, so he's chasing his dad whilst thinking I'm safe and well... but I'm not. I feel repulsively dirty with my unwashed hair and unbrushed teeth and overworn clothes and knickers, and I'm facing insanity, testing, or egg harvesting – none of which make me feel safe.

What am I going to do if he doesn't come back? This can't be my life; it just can't be.

Somebody delivers me some mushy baby food and then disappears.

I can't live the rest of my life on baby food, nutritious or not! I need to get out and have real food, like bacon and eggs. Ooh that'd be good right now. Or spaghetti carbonara. A roast dinner. Apple crumble! Yes, please! I can't die or lose my mind without having another apple crumble! With custard, of course.

I smile as I realise that possibly my only happy memories from my childhood were Sunday afternoons sat around the kitchen table with Mum, Dad and Viva. There were no classes or training sessions on a Sunday afternoon – unless they were working towards a particularly special showcase. Otherwise, by 12pm we were all free of her commitments and able to have a real family-time Sunday. Mum always cooked a roast, and always prepared a homemade dessert – never just a shop bought cheesecake. We had apple crumble or pie, rhubarb crumble, banoffee pie, Eton mess, fruit salad if she was being really lazy, or homemade ice cream. Somehow she managed to do everything – get Viva everywhere she needed to be, keep the house clean and tidy, cook from scratch and complete crossword puzzles; she did everything except worry about me.

Perhaps in my position as 'big sister' she assumed I didn't want to be checked up on. Perhaps it's my own fault for being so independent. But, aside from those Sunday afternoons, my family had very little role in my upbringing. I spent most of my childhood between the pages of the books I loaned from the library. I don't think they even knew how well I did in school, or if I had any friends. Their focus shifted to Viva, and from then on, I was on my own.

But on a Sunday afternoon, we were a proper family. We laughed and joked and played – Viva even slouched, shock horror, allowing herself a break from being perfect.

It's funny how thinking about food can bring up such powerful memories, isn't it? I can almost taste those perfectly fluffy and crispy roast potatoes now, covered in Bisto gravy, mmm.

ADAM

52.

I can't believe we're doing this.

This is what my life has come to. Making a deal with the devil.

As Damian has high security access to all areas of every MIU or location under the control of the Minister, our darling dad cannot do the next part of his plan without us, because we look like Damian.

It turns out he really is our brother too, we were triplets, identical triplets which is extremely rare, but he was taken away at birth and kept in one of those cages Dad grew up in. Apparently, it was a deal, they wouldn't hassle us for regular check-ups so long as they had our brother with them, to monitor and mould into whatever they wanted. Mum didn't even know about him because we were all born by emergency c-section; she believed them when they handed her two baby boys. How was she to know there should have been a third? Even the scans were doctored. It was decided right from the beginning. Just another of Dad's schemes.

Damian always wanted to meet his dad though, like any child in care without a parent would. So, as he grew older, he made sure he followed the rules to the T, gaining trust and responsibility. He was allowed to become a scientist and conduct tests and experiments, which also enabled him to disguise some of his own capabilities, because he learnt how they were monitored. Like Dad, he didn't want anyone to know the full extent of his power.

When he heard the rumours about Dad being moved to the most secure MIU, he started to dig deeper into his history. He read and re-read Dad's file and came to the conclusion that this man was most likely his father. He started applying for transfers every time a vacancy came up, which was rare, but eventually he got there.

Once he was in, he quickly made contact with Dad and verified his suspicions. From then on, dearest Damian was the best son our dad could ever have wished for – not a disappointment like me, or Kyle (to a lesser extent).

Damian became Dad's eyes and ears for all things security, and together they began plotting his escape. Not just his, Damian's too, because Damian was still under the control of the place he was raised, he was not a free Dream-Walker, he could only work because he had gained trust, not because he was free.

There are living quarters for people like him, close to each MIU. They are monitored almost as much as the participants. Dad and he planned to escape together, to be a 'family'. Ha.

I don't believe my dad ever intended to have a 'happily ever after' with Damian, even in the sense of happy comradery as they go around destroying lives and manipulating people, he's just not that kind of man. He's a user, and Damian was just a helpful means of escape.

I bet Dad couldn't believe his luck when Damian turned up like 'Daddy, Daddy!' I bet he was so needy and pathetic, like I was as a child; back when I had no idea how much of a 'bad man' he was, before stories of his worst crimes became fearful gossip.

And now here I am, teaming up with a man who I know dream-rapes for fun. A man who enjoys making people hurt in their sleep, thinking they have been stabbed or chopped to pieces. A man who cuts their fingers and toes off, one by one. A man who squashes eyeballs and testicles like grapes. I believe every story I've ever heard about him.

In her final years, Mum told me about the domestic abuse she experienced. He didn't have to aim for places she could hide bruises because there were no bruises. Not on the outside anyway.

He doesn't deserve to be free. It sickens me to do this. But I have to, for Ella.

I look at Kyle, he looks as nervous as I feel. I thought he'd be a bit more blasé about this, given some of the things he's done in the past, for The Resistance.

I suppose neither of us are up for hurting women.

Dad is sitting in the driver's seat of my car, looking like the cat that got the cream. He has us right under his thumb and he'll have no qualms about squashing us if we try to back out. I considered reporting my car as stolen as he drove us here, but even that he'd get out of in a blink. He's invincible and he knows it. I would need a whole team of people to take him down. We have no option but to do as he has asked, and hope he keeps up his side of the deal.

We look up at the high-rise building: lovely modern flats. It's no surprise the Minister lives here, and I bet his wife feels safe as anything up there looking out over the city. But today she will unfortunately pay for what the Minister did to Dad over the years, she will suffer for his unrestrained enthusiasm for medical discovery.

Apparently, she has met Damian before, so when we pass through the scanner and show up at her door, she won't be afraid. She should come with us willingly. But if not, that's where the other one comes in. It'll take two of us to sneak her out of the building if she tries to fight us.

Dad's going to take her away, use her to get ransom money, supposedly. But it doesn't sit well with me. He could get money any number of ways, he doesn't need us to do this for him to get money. He could even just Dream-walk into the Minister's head and make him think he has his wife.

Something just doesn't add up here, and Kyle knows it too.

Dad gives his cue.

53.

We're in, but nothing about this feels right. I can tell Kyle is on the same page as me. This feels like a set-up, there is something Dad's not telling us; but what?

Having passed through all the security and made it up the lift, Kyle is now attempting to hide behind a tall plant as I knock on the door, playing the role of Damian, as it has been so caringly thrust upon me.

"Who is it?" She calls from inside.

"It's Damian, I need you to come with me." I reply.

A few minutes pass and I roll my eyes at Kyle, and he shrugs back, then I hear the chain undo and she opens the door.

Standing there in all her glory (lacy underwear) with a thin satin robe draped across her shoulders, is the fifty-something partner of the Minister – Mrs Charmaine Krunk. I try to not let my shock show, but my eyes basically pop out of my head. Damn, for an older woman, she sure does look fine, and confident. I have no idea why the Minister spends so much time working when he has this woman waiting for him at home.

"Damian, darling, why don't you come in for a moment first?" She pulls me inside by my t-shirt. "I've missed you," she says, walking over to a chaise longue and lying down, stretching one leg up to the sky. "Come here."

I shuffle towards her. Fuck, I can't do this. Why couldn't Kyle pretend to be Damian? He could do this. But I can't, I just can't.

"We really have to be going," I say.

"Oh, don't be such a party pooper, come here," she pats a space next to her.

"There isn't time. The Minister, your husband, is expecting us."

"Since when did that ever bother you before? Come now, stop playing hard to get. Take me, right here, right now." She stares right into my eyes and I gulp as she undoes her bra. Well, I wasn't expecting those.

Despite my feelings for Ella, I can't stop myself from getting turned on. I hesitate and before I know it, she's jumped up and thrown herself at me. I'm holding her with her legs wrapped around me as she snogs my face with such longing, I can't believe it. Was Damian really having an affair with the Minister's wife?

I snap out of it and once again try to push her away, push her down off me, but the only way seems to be to collapse onto the bed. She squeals with delight.

"Take me Damian, take me!" She grabs my hand and pushes it into her lace knickers. She's wet. Fuck. How am I supposed to get out of this? She starts undoing my jeans, reaching inside my boxers. I should not be turned on; I should not be turned on.

I think of Ella and smack her arm away, perhaps a little too hard. She looks up at me in shock.

"What's wrong?"

"We have to go, now! Put some clothes on!" I order, rebuttoning my jeans.

"Why?"

"Because we have to! Your husband is waiting!"

"Why are you lying to me Damian? My husband knows I have needs, and you are here to fulfil them, are you not?"

"No! I am here to collect you."

"But what's the hurry? We can have some fun first, can't we? He'll wait, he always does. And you know he'll pay you well." She reaches towards my crotch again.

"No! Stop it! Get changed, we're going!" I shout.

"Did you meet someone, is that it? One of your Dream-Walker friends? Did you fall in love so now you can't fuck the boss's wife?"

"Get. Changed."

"One more time, for old time's sake?"

"No." I walk back through the lounge and open the front door. Kyle is ready and waiting. "You get her, she's a fucking nympho."

Kyle strides in and walks up to her.

"Get your fucking clothes on right now and come with us."

"Us?" Then it dawns on her. "Ooh, there are two of you? Oh, I'll certainly 'come' with you, excuse the pun!" She winks at him and laughs. He slaps her around the face.

"Any more of that, and we'll have to take tougher measures."

"Ooh, are you going to tie me up? I'm up for that if you are!"

He slaps her again. Harder. Her eyes water.

"Get your clothes on and come with us. I won't ask again."

He comes to stand with me by the door.

"Okay, okay, I'm getting dressed," she says, opening her wardrobe. "Honestly, I just wanted a bit of fun…"

As we take her down in the lift, she continues to inform us that we smell 'divine' and she's never had two men at once, but she'd like to try. I think now I understand why the Minister leaves her at home. He's probably had enough, especially as an older man. This woman sounds insatiable.

We walk her outside and head to where Dad should be waiting for us in my car. Except he's not. He's gone. What the fuck?

We look around in case he's just moved along a bit, but he's definitely gone. I leave Kyle with the madam and go ask the man at the door,

"My, er, friend was waiting for me over there. Did you see where he went?"

"Your dad? I don't know where he went, but he said to give you this," he reaches into his pocket and pulls out a receipt which he scrunches back up, and a shopping list which he passes to me.

Not just any shopping list, *the* shopping list. The one that connected us to Ella. How did he even…?

The man clears his throat and approaches Mrs Krunk, "are you okay ma'am? These blokes not bothering you?" Her face is still red from where Kyle slapped her.

"I'm fine, these two gents are just taking me to see my husband, aren't you dears?" Oh, now she wants to go see her husband, eh?

"Actually Mrs Krunk, I think you should go back inside, you look flushed, I think maybe you're unwell. We'll tell Mr Krunk he'll have to reschedule your dinner for when you're feeling better," says Kyle.

"Oh, I see, well I am feeling quite warm. Perhaps one, or both, of you would like to escort me back upstairs?"

"Unfortunately, we have to go, but I'm sure you'll be okay, this man will make sure you make it back upstairs safely, won't you?" I smile at him.

"Of course. Ma'am would you like me to get someone from Reception to go up with you?"

"No. I'll be fine." She snaps and heads back inside.

We move away from the door man, and I read out what's scribbled on the back of Ella's list.

"Sorry boys, I couldn't resist. Hope you enjoyed yourselves tonight, I heard she's a lot of fun. A lot more fun than that girl you've been messing around with. Maybe now you'll move on. But if you still want her, you're going to have to hurry, the Minister's not in the best of moods. I can't imagine why, can you? Loves ya! XOXO Dad."

ELLA

54.

I don't know what's upset him, but something has. It's late and the 'reasonable' Minister from his earlier visit has gone and what stands before me now is a very angry and bitter old man. I felt it as soon as he entered my cell. There was no fake politeness, no offer of a drink, oh no. He is in a mood, the kind of mood that would rival a teenage girl on the cusp of her first period. He's about to wake up with bloody knickers. That's how mad he is.

"In light of recent revelations, I will no longer be offering you the egg harvest and leave option. So, it's the lobotomy or staying here until you're insane options left on the table. Which would you rather? Quick or slow?"

"Uh, slow, I guess." I reply. Slow at least leaves the chance of an escape before I go insane. It leaves some hope.

"I thought as much."

He removes his glasses and rubs his eyes. The mood dissipates and is replaced with sadness and regret,

"I always knew my wife was a whore, but I never thought she'd try to blackmail me." He sighs. "I guess you never really know someone, do you?"

He stretches his arms and clicks his back as he makes his way back to the door.

"If I can give you one piece of advice for your stay: give up. Let go. It's not worth it. He's really not worth it." I hear the door lock behind him.

What?

What was that supposed to mean?

His wife is blackmailing him, about what? I didn't even know he had a wife! And what does he mean 'he's not worth it'? Why? What's happened out there? Why does everyone talk in bloody riddles around this place?

ADAM

55.

We need to find a car, fast.

"You up for flexing our skills a bit Ad'?" Asks Kyle. As much as I don't want to steal another car, I have to agree, for Ella.

"I guess so. We need to get to Ella, now. What are you thinking?"

"I'm thinking we walk to the petrol station, wait for a nice ride to turn up, or any ride really. Let them fill up, then once they've paid, you make them blink and I'll make them think they just sold us their car. And then we'll go. Sound good?"

My good deed of giving the other car owner extra fuel will be counterbalanced by stealing someone else's, but how can I say no? Ella needs us.

"Yeah, alright. Let's do it."

*

Half an hour later, we're speeding up the motorway in a silver Mercedes. Not bad. We waited for the second car to come along, as the first was a yellow Fiat Cinquecento and we just didn't want it. Plus, it was an old lady's car, and we didn't want to leave her stranded in the dark. But a businessman in a Merc? He'd be fine.

"What do you reckon, an hour? Two?" I ask Kyle.

"Should be three, but at this speed I'm hoping it'll be closer to two. We'll get her Ad', she'll be okay."

"I hope so, but what if the Minister inflicts some cruel punishment because Dad's made him think we've been sleeping with his wife? She might be brain damaged by the time we get there!"

"Positive thinking, she'll be fine. He's a scientist, he'd rather use her for tests no matter what."

"That still doesn't mean she won't be brain damaged!"

"I know, but she's going to be okay. She has to be okay." I see his jaw tighten.

"You care about her too, don't you?"

"No. Well, yeah. I mean, kind of. But I'd never get in the way, she's yours Adam. She loves you."

"She loves me because of the connection the two of you had in her dreams. She loves you." Much as it pains me to say it, I still believe that's true. Kyle was the man of her dreams, not me. I was just an unaware impersonator. A poor replication of her true dream man. I know I lack the spark and charisma which Kyle carries with ease.

"What we had wasn't real, Ad'. It was just foolish dreaming. What you had was real. She loves you."

"I don't know," I say quietly.

"And regardless, whoever she loves, she doesn't deserve to be locked up and have tests carried out on her for the rest of her life. Or worse! So, let's just focus on that. Let's save her first and then see what she has to say."

"Okay."

We continue the rest of the drive in silence.

ELLA

56.

They haven't done any tests on me, yet. I guess the Minister has other things on his mind, or maybe they've decided to let me rest now until tomorrow. It's been a long and stressful day.

I wonder what's happened to Damian, the 'other brother.' I would love to ask him a few questions. Maybe he's the one being tested and pulled apart now, for being a double agent, as it were.

I bet the Minister is furious his own employee helped the biggest most powerful Dream-Walker escape. And with his wife apparently blackmailing him, he must be really distracted.

In fact, this might be the best time to escape. There's no way he's watching me personally, and other people take breaks. There must be a small sliver of opportunity. More than there's been at any other time since I've been here. If only I could figure out a way to open the door.

Even the food man comes with a helper in this facility, so I couldn't attack him even if I was capable.

But maybe they can be reasoned with? They may or may not be human, but I know we all have feelings. And I'm innocent. I've been proven innocent. Perhaps they can be persuaded.

It's got to be worth a try.

Yes, that's what I'll do. When my next meal arrives, I'll try, once again, to get them talking. Donna said everyone was talking about us, about the trial, so they must know all about it. Surely, they'll want to help; wouldn't anyone?

Actually, maybe Donna could help. If only she'd come to visit me at this new place. She could make my case or pal up with some of the workers so they can sneak me out.

I can't rely on Adam and Kyle, they might never come back.

And do I want them to? Really? My life was a lot simpler before they turned up. More boring, certainly, but safer. But how could I ever turn my back on them now? I love them both.

Adam because he is my boyfriend, if he'll still have me, we dated and fell in love. I know everything about him now, and he makes me happy.

But that only happened because I fell for Kyle in my dreams – I thought Adam was the physical embodiment of the man of my dreams. I also thought he saved me from being raped, and that was Kyle too.

When Adam kisses me, it's nice, it's loving and warm, like hot chocolate, it fills me with joy. But when Kyle kissed me in London, my heart leapt.

But I don't know Kyle, not properly. All I know is he's charismatic, sexy, and he works with The Resistance which sounds immensely dangerous and exciting. In my dreams he was my perfect man, but they were only dreams, and I don't know how much of that was him and how much of that was my obsession with rom coms. I think he's a bit of a bad boy, with a soft centre. But who knows?

My love for Kyle was built on fantasy; my love for Adam is what's real. I can't walk away from either of them now. They have turned my life around and upside down, but I still wouldn't change it for anything.

When was the last time I had this much excitement in my life? When it wasn't just work and rom coms and wine, day in, day out? Before them, my life was dull, I was living in greyscale. With them, it's technicolour. It's scary but exciting and dangerous but exhilarating. But which one of them do I really love, do I really want to be with?

Adam, of course. You don't build forever with dreams, you build it with bricks. Or, mud and cowpats in our case. I smile.

I don't know why I even questioned it. Dreams don't come true. True love isn't written in the stars, it's built. It's built on muddy walks and cinema dates; it's built on kisses in the rain and snow; it's built on all the little things we learnt about each other over hot chocolate at Cherry B's.

My dreams weren't real, I wasn't even myself in those dreams. I played the role I saw played out in all my favourite rom coms. But life, the ups and downs that Adam and I have been through, that's real.

I love him.

I don't know who I'm trying to convince here, sat in my cell alone, but I do. I love Adam and I bloody hope he's going to save me.

Hours later, there's a beep and my cell door slides open, making me jump.

"Adam!"

I jump into his arms and he spins me around, both of us grinning from ear to ear. It's him, not one of his brothers impersonating him, it's really him. The living, breathing, love of my life. He slows down our spin and I close my eyes and kiss him. Yes, that's true love's kiss. I have everything I need right here.

I open my eyes and realise that Kyle is also here, waiting in the corridor. He gives me a small smile. I know he cares. But, he has his own stuff going on. He doesn't want me, not really. He'll understand. And I'm sure he'll disappear off with The Resistance again soon enough. I don't need to worry about him.

"We'd better get going," says Adam, "we don't have long."

We hurry down the corridor. Miraculously, a fire exit is open and we're able to get out, just like that. It's not the amazing escape I'd been anticipating, but I'll take it. I run out to the carpark and don't look back. I never want to go back there again.

"Oi, prisoner," says Kyle as we open the doors of a silver Mercedes. He rummages in the side pocket of the door. "I've got something for you."

I get in the back of the car and wait for him to locate the mystery gift.

"Here." He passes a men's bathroom bag between the front seats to me. "It's got mouthwash and toothpaste in there, a toothbrush too if you don't mind a stranger's germs. I thought you might want to freshen up before anymore tonsil tennis with Adam."

"Wow, that's…" thoughtful? Kind? Weird?

"When did you find that?" Asks Adam, that jealous streak shining through again.

"Chill bro, it's a businessman's car, of course he has an overnight bag." Kyle smiles at him. "It's no big deal."

"Hmm."

It's good to be back with them, but I haven't missed that sibling rivalry one bit. Adam closes the passenger door and comes to join me in the back. The sooner Kyle disappears again, the better. For all of us, Adam, me, and my butterflies. I open the mouthwash, wipe the rim, and take a swig, quickly re-opening the car door to spit before Kyle drives away. Much better.

THREE DAYS LATER

"It's Christmas!" I give Adam a little shake to wake him up. He rubs his eyes and smiles,

"What are you, five?"

"No, I'm just happy we get to spend Christmas together. I wasn't sure we were going to get to, you know, when I was locked up. Do you want to open your presents?"

I bounce off the bed before he can answer and start moving the pile of presents from under the tree to on top of the duvet.

He sits up,

"Okay, let's get this over with." He teases.

"Don't pretend you're not excited too! I know you want to know what I got you!"

It's a remote-control airplane; he told me he had one as a child and I thought it'd be a brilliant surprise. Other than that, it's the usual, some aftershave that's a total aphrodisiac, a toothbrush to keep at my place, Christmas socks, Santa boxers, and a gift-card for Cherry B's. I make him open them all before I open mine.

"I'm sorry I didn't get you so many, I didn't realise you would get me so much. We can go shopping for more."

"Don't be silly, I got the best present of all, I got you!" I say, grinning, "and this, of course," I shake the mysterious gift box. It is wrapped in silver and gold shiny paper, and is a small box, so I'm expecting jewellery. I tear the paper off slowly, and then hold my breath as I remove the lid.

I laugh.

"I'm sorry, it's not funny. It's just… is this…?"

"Yes, it's a necklace that represents our relationship."

"It's beautiful…" I pull a face to stop myself laughing.

There's a pendant to represent each of our various dates and parts of our relationship. It's very cluttered and chunky. Who else has a shopping list (scroll) pendant between a cow and a pair of square glasses?

"Thank you," I say, and kiss him.

"You can say if you don't like it, we can take it back and exchange it."

"Don't be silly, it's perfect!"

"I just thought it would be unique, like our relationship."

"It's definitely that," I say, kissing him again. "What time do we need to leave?"

"About 10."

"So we have time then…" I raise my eyebrows at him and stroke his bare leg under the covers, reaching towards his penis. He stops my hand.

"No, not now. Um, Ella, actually, we need to talk." He sits up straighter in bed.

"What's wrong?"

"Ella, I don't know how to explain this to you, but when we have sex, um, so far each time we've had sex, I see you with Kyle."

"What do you mean?"

324

"Well, remember what I said about Transference? How you would see everything I've ever done and all that? I imagine it's like that but instead, I'm seeing you and Kyle together. I'm seeing you making pottery together like in that old film with the ghost; I'm seeing you walking a puppy; I'm seeing you get married."

I'm in shock.

"But I didn't experience Transference. I was fine. How is that possible? And none of that stuff, none of that is real. I mean, not even dream-real. We didn't do that."

"You don't need to lie to me Ella, I know you had a relationship with Kyle in your dreams. I just didn't expect to be confronted with it every time we... you know." He raises his eyebrows.

"But we never made pottery, we never had a puppy, and we definitely never got married." I shake my head at him violently.

"I've been trying to think of a sensible explanation and all I can think is..." he pauses. "I think you might be pregnant."

"WHAT?"

"Well, if you were carrying a Dream-Walker, then maybe they could do the Transference and show me all of yours and Kyle's dreams together."

"But that stuff didn't happen! It's all in your head! You're just being jealous." He looks at me and says nothing. "And how could I be pregnant? This year, aside from the past few days, I've only had sex in my dreams! And that was so long ago, I would have given birth by now! There must be another explanation."

"Perhaps you're carrying a dream baby." He suggests, stone-faced.

"Oh come on, Adam. Just admit you're still worked up about what happened between me and Kyle. This is just your mind playing tricks on you. Do you want to take a break? Stop having sex?"

"I'm serious."

"You're being ridiculous! I'm going to go have a shower and start getting ready. You'd better not bring this up over Christmas Dinner!"

I storm off to the shower.

I can't believe he thinks I'm carrying a dream baby. What the hell? I knew he was still bothered about what happened between Kyle and I, but I thought he was getting over it. I chose him, after all. Maybe we rushed into this too quickly. We should have taken a breather to cool off and reassess our feelings.

But it was so close to Christmas, I didn't want to go off on my own with the HJD likely still after me. And he seemed fine. He seemed ecstatic, actually. He was super keen to have sex, like he always should have been. We did it three times that first night. Although, now I think about it, he did seem to lose a bit of enthusiasm between each go, and he did spend longer in the bathroom in between. Well, at least now I know it wasn't because I'm bad at sex. It's because he's haunted by imaginary scenes of me and his brother.

He's lucky he's only seeing things he's making up. I mean, if he saw some of our real steamy moments, he'd probably leave and never look back.

I hope he doesn't let this spoil Christmas. I really want to have a good Christmas this year. It's been a while since I've had this family vibe on the day, and I've been looking forward to it. Cherry will dilute the awkwardness, I'm sure.

*

We hold hands as we walk up the path to Cherry B's house. She invited us and Kyle over for Christmas dinner with her

326

because she doesn't have any family around anymore and she said she felt like she owed it to their mum to make sure that the boys still have a proper Christmas.

She has ornaments on and lights around her bay window, it's like an extension of her café. When we press the doorbell, it plays 'We Wish You a Merry Christmas.' I squeeze Adam's hand.

"Please, at least wait until after dessert before you confront Kyle. Don't ruin this for Cherry." I ask, he nods in response.

Cherry opens the door wearing a red crushed velvet dress topped with a reindeer apron.

"If it isn't my favourite couple! Come in, come in, Kyle's already here. He's taken over the kitchen, so we can talk about how you've been since the trial." She ushers us in to the lounge.

On a coffee table, there's an assortment of savoury snacks and dip, and there's a cat sat on the back of the sofa, moving its tail slowly, observing us.

"Help yourselves and don't mind Tilly, she's as friendly as anything, just don't let her have the dip!" She laughs to herself. We sit down and Kyle appears holding a glass of wine.

"White wine for Ella, and what will you have Adam?" He asks.

"Whiskey," says Adam.

"It's a bit early for that isn't it?" I nudge him.

"If it's not too early for wine, it's not too early for whiskey. I'll have it on the rocks, and don't be stingy either. I need it." He tells Kyle. Kyle looks confused but obeys politely. Poor guy doesn't know what's about to hit him. Adam is really going to kick off later.

We start with melon balls, and I am instantly transported back to those Sunday afternoons around the kitchen table again. Mum was always a fan of melon as a starter, she loved using the melon baller, said melon tasted better when it was spherical. And she was right. My dad used to tease her about it because he preferred to have it cut up and served as boats, but she always did balls. Viva and I used to use our spoons to flick the balls at each other like cannons if we were left unattended. Sometimes Mum did three types of melon, a 'melon medley' she'd call it. Today there's just the one type, Galia, if I'm not mistaken.

Next, we have turkey and gammon with all the trimmings. Pigs in blankets that I can't remember having in years, and brussels sprouts, all covered in delicious thick gravy. We talk about safe topics like happy Christmas memories, old pets, and snow days.

Adam has another whiskey and I ask for water, at least one of us should keep a clear head.

For dessert we have Christmas pudding, and Cherry asks Adam to light it. I see a flicker of pride when he succeeds. It's homemade and it's delicious. Cherry tells us how she made it as we all smother it in cream or brandy butter and tuck in. I've missed home-made desserts. Once again, I think of Mum.

I wish we hadn't left things the way we did, with her blaming and hating me, and me too sick of arguing about it. Maybe now, with the distance of time, we could finally make amends. Then again, it's probably safer not to invite more humans into this new world I've found myself in. It's rather unpredictable. And besides, just because Viva has apologised to me, doesn't mean Mum has accepted it was an accident. She'd probably slam the door in my face.

I look up as I finish scraping my bowl and realise I'm the last to finish. I quickly squeeze Adam's hand under the table and shake my head with meaning. Please not now.

"Are we having cheese and biscuits?" I ask.

"Does anyone have room for them?" Asks Kyle.

328

"No, but it just feels right. We should have a little," I say. "Let me help clear up and bring them through," I offer. I am only trying to delay the inevitable.

Cherry and I clear the table and Adam and Kyle remain. That was not the plan. I rush around the kitchen, loading the dishwasher and grabbing the bumper pack of biscuits for cheese, pouring them onto a plate. I find the chopping board and place a couple of types of cheese on there with knives and carry it through. I'm too late.

Cherry follows me through carrying the plate of biscuits. We stop in our tracks.

"What do you mean, she's pregnant?" Says Kyle. "You can't get pregnant in your dreams!"

"When we had sex, I saw it all, Kyle. I saw everything you did together, and it made me sick. But I've been thinking, and it makes sense, doesn't it? If she's carrying a baby Dream-Walker then of course I would see what made them come to exist, and what they want me to see. Baby Kyle Junior is in there trying to make me back off!"

"There's no baby, Adam, this is just in your head." I say calmly.

"I have to agree with her, Ad'. Dream sex doesn't make dream babies. End of."

"Well then, did you make her think she was dreaming, and then rape her?" Demands Adam, accusingly.

"Of course not! Jesus!"

"Okay, can we refrain from blaspheming on Christmas Day?" Asks Cherry. "Why don't we all calm down and discuss this like sensible adults?"

I look at Adam, he's finishing his drink again.

"Okay Kyle, if Ella isn't pregnant, then how do you explain me being able to see what happened between the two of you? She's not a Dream-Walker, I saw her blood report. Go on, you tell me how that's possible." He slams his glass down.

329

"You didn't see anything, Adam! Nothing you told me you saw actually happened in my dreams with Kyle, you made it up!" I shout. "Kyle, tell him, we never did that ridiculous pottery scene from 'Ghost'!"

"That what now?" He says, confused.

"We never made pottery, did we?"

"Erm, no…" He raises one eyebrow.

"That doesn't prove anything!" Says Adam. "Maybe that was a snippet of what's to come!"

"Alright, alright, everyone. Let's just take a breath," says Cherry. We all quieten like naughty school children. "Now then, what are we going to do about Adam's nightmares?"

Before Adam can respond, most likely with *they're not nightmares*, 'We Wish You a Merry Christmas' interrupts our conversation. The doorbell. Cherry rushes to the window, followed by Kyle.

A blonde-haired man peers through the window back at them, wearing a long coat and a thin red scarf. His bright blue eyes search the room. Jeremy. What is he doing here?

"It's the Minister's son," says Kyle. "You'd better go." Jeremy is the Minister's son?

Adam reaches for my hand and all the harsh words are forgotten. It doesn't matter what he's going through, he loves me, and he's going to keep me safe. I look back at Cherry and Kyle as he pulls me towards the back door.

We leave them and run.

THE END

(UNTIL BOOK 2...)

Acknowledgements

First, I would like to thank Mum and Daisy. You were the first people I trusted to read my manuscript and without your honest feedback, it would never have evolved into the book it is today. I hope you enjoyed the changes.

Next, I would like to thank Dad, the keenest reader I'll ever have. I'm sorry this one isn't your cup of tea, but I couldn't have done it without your endless enthusiasm and encouragement. Thank you for believing in me.

Dean, thank you for putting up with my writing obsession, for letting me get on with it, listening to my nonsensical rants, and providing snacks.

Andrew, you've been chasing your dreams for a while now. Thank you for inspiring me to finally jump in with both feet and chase my own. You never know unless you try, eh?

Finally, and most importantly, I thank you, my reader. Thank you for taking the time to read my first self-published novel, and for taking a chance on an unknown author. If you enjoyed it, please leave a review to help others discover it too.

I'll see you in Book 2!

Chloë x

About the Author

Chloë is one of us.

She's that girl who reads on her lunchbreak, on the train, at the hairdressers; that girl who has bags under her eyes because 'one more chapter' rolled on and on until the book was finished at 3am, on a work night.

Chloë is also a writer and, until recently, she kept that pretty quiet. She hid her 'true' passion beneath her love of other people's books, by studying English and American Literature at University, and only ever talking about what she was reading, not what she was writing.

Many of her acquaintances will be surprised to hear that she has written a novel, but not those who truly know her. From a very young age Chloë filled notebooks with stories and even convinced her younger brother that she was sneaking out at night, through a secret passage in the airing cupboard.

'Duplicity (The Dangers of Dreaming: Book 1)' is her debut novel.

FOLLOW ON

Instagram and Facebook
@chloeblythauthor

WEBSITE

https://chloeblythauthor.com

If you enjoyed this book, please post a review online to help other readers discover this new series. Even a few kind words will make a difference.

Thank you!

Printed in Great Britain
by Amazon

78900366R10193